DEATH TO [illegible]

Ellis Peters has ga[illegible] recognition for he[illegible] monastic life in the t[illegible] Cadfael series of novels. *Death in the Landlords!*, set against the colourful background of contemporary India, is further proof of her extraordinary story-telling talent.

Also by Ellis Peters
A Rare Benedictine

The Brother Cadfael Chronicles:
Brother Cadfael's Penance
The Holy Thief
The Hermit of Eyton Forest
The Confession of Brother Haluin
The Heretic's Apprentice
The Potter's Field
The Summer of the Danes

Death Mask
The Will and the Deed
Funeral of Figaro
Flight of a Witch
City of Gold and Shadows
The Piper on the Mountain
Mourning Raga
The Horn of Roland
Never Pick up Hitch-Hikers!
Holiday with Violence
The Assize of the Dying

Writing as Edith Pargeter

The Lily Hand and Other Stories
By Firelight
A Means of Grace
The Soldier at the Door
A Bloody Field by Shrewsbury
She Goes to War
The Eighth Champion of Christendom
Reluctant Odyssey
Warfare Accomplished

Sunrise in the West
The Dragon at Noonday
The Hounds of Sunset
Afterglow and Nightfall
being the Brothers of Gwynedd quartet

Death to the Landlords!

Ellis Peters

First published in 1972
by Macmillan London Ltd

First published in paperback in 1988
by HEADLINE BOOK PUBLISHING PLC

10 9 8 7 6 5

ISBN 0 7472 3122 2

Printed and bound in Great Britain by
Clays Ltd, St Ives plc

HEADLINE BOOK PUBLISHING
A division of Hodder Headline PLC
338 Euston Road
London NW1 3BH

Prologue

On the Road to Thekady: Saturday Evening

The sadhu sat just within the shadow of the trees at the left-hand bend of the road, not fifty yards from the mottled and overgrown wall of the forestry bungalow's green enclosure. The road from the plains up to the lake coiled through the belt of forest towards the crest of the hills in great, smooth serpentines, a polished steel-blue ribbon shading off to ash-grey at the edges, then to ochre, before it faded into the bleached grass on either side. At each sweeping curve the trees withdrew to leave ample space for the turns, and at every such stage there was some feature apparently carefully positioned to take advantage of the site thus provided. At the turn below, a fruit-stall glowing with oranges and jack-fruit and bananas. At the turn above, the gates of the drive that led to the forestry bungalow. At this left-hand turn between them, half-veiled by the long grass and the overhanging darkness of the branches, a six-foot column of rough stone, so old and worn that its carving had almost eroded away, leaving only the elusive shapes of arms and hands that seemed to appear and disappear as oblique shadows gave them form, and to vanish completely in too direct a light. There had been a face, flattened away now into a featureless oval, and the scratched indications of turbulent hair. From the hips down – there was the negligent thrust of a hip still to be seen in certain lights – he was coated with an accumulation of dust from the roadside, clinging fast to his old and infrequent baptisms of reverential oil. His feet – he stood firmly upon massive and unmistakable feet – still glistened, protected by the long grass, and a sprinkling of coloured dye, red and orange, spattered his insteps. There was even a handful of marigolds, a day old and withered, nestling at the foot of the stele. He might have been any one of the pantheon, except that the blunt, truncated shaft of stone a yard or two away, oiled and garlanded even here in this remote place, was recognisably the lingram of Siva.

There had been more masonry here at some time, perhaps a small shrine, but only the dressed stone platform of its floor remained, affording a small dais in the shade, on which the sadhu sat. He was lean and muscular, long in the torso, and he sat cross-legged, the dusty, pale soles of his feet upturned, the pinkish palms of his long hands cupped in his lap. A length of cotton cloth in the familiar ochreous peach colour was draped over his left shoulder and swathed about his hips, and several strings of carved wooden beads and coloured cords hung round his neck. Tangled, oily curls of hair hung over his temples and shadowed his face, and on the ash-smeared forehead between the snaky tresses were drawn three horizontal lines, a vertical oval seal of red colouring uniting the three in the centre; one of many sect marks worn by the devotees of Siva. He was the colour of bronze, and as motionless as bronze, and the ceaseless faint quivering of the thick leafage that shaded him cast greenish lights over his oiled skin, and made him look like metal rather than flesh. His eyes, lowered beneath ash-bleached lids and thick black brows, gazed somewhere deep into the earth at the edge of the road, and his face never moved. In front of him in the grass his wooden bowl rested, empty.

The Periyar Lake lies about two thousand five hundred feet up in the Western Ghats, and about a hundred and twenty miles from the toe of India, but the road up from Madurai crosses higher ground on the way to it, and the altitude somewhat delays the hawk-like swoop of the night that drops abruptly, with only the briefest of twilights. It was during the curious, hushed pause before the transformation from daylight to dark that the Land-Rover came humming briskly up the serpentines from the plain, rounded the bend beside which Siva and the sadhu kept watch, and turned in at the gates of the forestry bungalow. The sadhu moved never a muscle, and gave no indication of having seen or heard its passing, as deep in meditation as the forest behind him in silence.

A few minutes later two girls came walking up the road from the fruit-stall at the turn below, with their arms full of bananas and small, rough-skinned green oranges, the kind that are still green when they are fully ripe and sweet as honey. One of the pair was Indian, in a plain green and white sari and a white cotton blouse, with her black hair plaited and coiled in a great sheaf on her neck. The other, slim and small-boned and blonde, was English even at first glance, and had sensibly not tried to conceal the fact inside a sari. Nothing could have disguised that fair complexion, or the pale, straight hair that hung limply to her shoulders, framing an oval face. Instead, she had compromised by adopting plain black trousers, worn with a short-sleeved shirt-dress. They were hurrying, because they wanted to get back to the bungalow before the darkness fell completely, for here between the thick swathes of forest the night would be velvet-black, almost palpable.

They drew near to the sadhu, and he was as oblivious of them as of the Land-Rover a few moments ago. The fair girl, who had noticed and remarked on him as they walked down to the fruit-stall, peered curiously into the shadows as they passed, and caught the faint gleam of oil and bronze, motionless under the branches.

'He's still there. Do you suppose he stays there all night, too?'

'I doubt it. It will be cold in the small hours, up here. They come and go as they please, there are almost no rules.'

Priya had the detached tone and ambivalent attitude of the Indian towards self-styled holy men. The basic equipment needed for the profession is simple and inexpensive; only one item, the holiness, need cost a man very much, and though some undoubtedly insist on and achieve it, many more, perhaps the majority, manage to make do without it. There is no immediate way of distinguishing the one kind from the other.

Patti hesitated, looking back over her shoulder. 'Is the bowl there for money?'

'For any sort of alms,' said Priya, 'but preferably money.'

'A chance to acquire merit,' said Patti, a little sadly, a little cynically, making fun of herself but still looking over her shoulder. Suddenly she stopped. 'Wait for me a minute, will you? Here, hold these!' She dumped her load of fruit into Priya's arms and turned impetuously to dart back towards the shrine, groping as she went in the depths of the big shoulder-bag she carried. The jingle of small coins came back to Priya's ears, and the darkness lurched a little lower, sagging towards them from the tree-tops.

Patti stepped delicately into the dry, bleached grass, and the rustle of her footsteps should have reached the sadhu's ears even in a trance, but he gave no sign. She stooped towards his wooden bowl, and he did not raise his eyes or rear his head. She stared intently, but all she could distinguish now was the faintly luminous shadow of a man encased in deeper shadow, as motionless and impervious as the Siva beside him.

'*Namaste!*' she said, touching her hands momentarily together over her offering; and she laid it in his bowl, and drew back. She thought the head moved a little, in distant acknowledgement, but that was all. She turned away with a sense of disappointment, and ran to rejoin Priya and relieve her of her load.

'Not exactly effusive, are they? Still – just for luck! Who knows! He may remember me in his prayers at the right moment.'

They walked on together quickly, and the next curve of the road carried them away out of the sadhu's sight, and cut off the fresh, intrusive voices that rippled the silence.

He still had not moved or uttered a sound.

The night came down like curtains of black silk, filling the trough of the roadway between the trees with fold on fold of darkness.

One

Thekady: Saturday Evening

There were two cars already parked in front of the long, low, ochre-yellow bungalow when the Land-Rover wheeled into line beside the porch; and at sight of the first of them, the ancient, sky-blue Ford with the grazed door and the re-touched wing, they all three uttered a hoot of recognition, at once derisive and appreciative.

'Here we go again!' said Larry Preisinger, switching off the engine. 'Didn't I say we would be running into the whole circus again before we reached the Cape? It's always the same. I drove this thing round Gujarat State, and the same folks I saw at the first halt haunted me all the way. Might skip an overnight stop here and there, but give 'em a few days and they'd show up again. An Indian couple from South Africa with three kids, visiting the home country, a middle-aged pair from New Zealand doing the world by easy stages and two young Czechs draped with about four cameras each. Now we've got the French for a change.'

'We might do worse,' said Dominic Felse thoughtfully.

'Yeah, we might, at that!' On the whole, in a wary fashion, they had approved of the Bessancourts. He looked doubtfully at the second car, a big black saloon, battered but imposing, but it told him nothing about its incumbents. A tourist car, probably, hired out for the weekend with driver, from Madurai. 'Looks like we'll be camping tonight. With two car-loads they *must* be full up inside.' Not that he minded; they were well equipped, with light sleeping bags, and a mosquito net that rolled up into the roof when not in use. Three can manage without too much discomfort in a Land-Rover, given a little ingenuity, and he had provided the ingenuity before he ever set out on this marathon drive round India, picking up co-drivers for sections of the route wherever he could, for company and to share the expenses. Dominic, acquired in Madras and on leave from some farming job, was one of the luckiest breaks he'd had so far, around his own age, a congenial enough companion, a good driver, and prepared to stick with him as far as Cape Comorin, and probably all the way back to Madras, too.

Lakshman unfolded his slender length from among the baggage, and slid out of the Land-Rover. 'I will go and talk to the *khanasama*.' He paused to look back and inquire, in his gentle, dutiful voice that balanced always so delicately between the intonations of friend and servant: 'If there are no beds, you would like at least food? It would be a change from my cooking.'

'It might be a change for the worse, but sure, let's risk it.'

Larry had been travelling with Lakshman Ray for nearly six weeks now, and had given up trying to get on to closer terms with him. Lakshman, whether he knew his place or not, certainly knew his employer's place, and firmly kept him there. With the greatest of deference, amiability and consideration, but implacably. He had done this sort of courier–interpreter job before, with other lone tourists, and had encountered, or so Larry judged, patrons with very different views on this relationship from those Larry himself held. Give him time, and he'd make any necessary adjustments himself; no sense in trying to rush him. Lakshman was the youngest of the three of them, barely twenty and still a student, until want of funds had driven him out to earn money for further study by such journeys as this. He had to get everything right, and he was taking no risks. Perhaps he didn't even want to slide unsuspectingly into a friendship for which he hadn't bargained. A cool young person, shy, soft-voiced, self-possessed and efficient, he spoke both Tamil and Malayalam in addition to his own

Hindi, so he was equally effective in the north or the south. Sometimes, Larry suspected, Lakshman had difficulty in remembering to keep Dominic at the same distance as Larry himself; Dominic wasn't paying his wages.

The bungalow, seen by the glow from its own windows and the Land-Rover's side-lights, was a pleasant, solid building of brick and plaster, with a deep, arcaded porch, and looked big enough to house quite a number of travellers, if the usual tourist bedroom-cum-livingroom in India had not been about as big as a barn, and with its own bathroom or shower attached. Three such suites, say, plus the kitchen quarters, and there would be no room left. No matter, the Land-Rover was good enough.

Lakshman came back gesturing mildly from a distance, and shaking his head; and behind his back the *khansama* stuck out a bearded head in a loose cotton turban from the kitchen door to take a look at his latest guests.

'The place is quite full, but he will feed us. And there is a *chowkidar*.' The security of the bungalow's grounds and the protection of its watchman were not to be despised.

'Good, then how about borrowing a shower, before the proper tenants get to that stage?'

'It can be arranged.' He was looking from them to the anonymous black car, and his smile was less demure than usual. 'Do you know who is also here?'

His look and his tone said that they were hardly likely to thank him for the information, though it might enliven their stay in its own fashion. It was not often that Lakshman looked mischievous, and even now he had his features well in hand.

'Sure we know,' said Larry obtusely, his mind on his shower, '*madame la patronne* and her *mari*.'

Prompt on the close of his sentence, as if responding to a clue, a high, clacking voice screeched: 'Sushil Dastur! *Sushil Dastur!*' from an open window, in a rising shriek that could have been heard a mile into the forest; and light, obsequious footsteps slapped hurriedly along the hallway inside the open door to answer the summons.

'Oh, *no*!' groaned Larry. 'Not the Manis! So *that's* the chauffeur-driven party, is it? We might have known! What did I tell you? Start touring anywhere you like, and within a hundred miles radius you keep seeing the same faces.'

'And hearing the same voices,' Dominic remarked ruefully. 'Poor little Sushil, he certainly hears plenty of that one. I wonder he stands it. And Bengali women *don't* usually squawk – they have soft, pleasant voices.'

'Not this one!' It was scolding volubly now in Bengali, somewhere within the house, punctuated by placating monosyllables from a man's voice, anxious, inured and resigned. 'Maybe he doesn't even listen, really, just makes the right sounds and shuts up his mind. Otherwise he'd go up the wall. And his boss is worse, if anything, even if he doesn't split the eardrums quite like his missus. Jobs must be hard to come by, or Sushil would have quit long ago.'

'I get the impression he is a relative,' Lakshman said with sympathy. 'Of the lady, perhaps – a poor cousin. And you are quite right, for a clerk with no paper qualifications it is not at all easy to find a good post. And perhaps he is more comfortable with this one than we suppose. It is security of a kind.'

They had run into the Manis twice since leaving Madras, once briefly at Kancheepuram, plodding doggedly round that fantastic city's many temples, and once at an overnight stop at Tiruchirapalli, where Mr Mani had constituted himself chairman of the evening gathering of guests at the travellers' bungalow, and unfolded his and his wife's life story in impressive detail. They were from Calcutta, where they had several textile shops, and they had come south to Madras for the first time to visit their married daughter, whose husband ran a highly successful travel agency. Thus they had the best possible help and advice in planning an extended tour of the south of India. Ganesh had made all the arrangements, Ganesh had ensured that they should not miss one famous sight while they were here. They had certainly missed none in Tiruchi. They had been observed in the early morning, before the stone steps were too hot for comfort, toiling dauntlessly all up the exposed face of the rock, Mrs Mani with her elaborate sari kilted in both hands, and Sushil Dastur scurrying behind with her handbag, her husband's camera and the scarf she had dispensed with after the first morning chill passed; and again later taking pictures of the budding lotus in the temple tank below. And in the afternoon they had taken a taxi out to Srirangam, and toiled relentlessly round every inch of that tremendous temple, with very little in their faces to indicate what they thought of its stunning sculptures, or indeed whether they thought at all.

Mr Mani's name was Gopal Krishna, and he was a firm, thickset, compact person of perhaps fifty, smoothly golden-brown of face, with crisp greying hair and large, imperious eyes that fixed the listener like bolts shackling him to his chair. He was so clean-shaven that it was difficult to believe he ever grew any whiskers to shave, and so immaculate, whether in spotless cream silk suit or loose white cotton shirt and trousers, or even, occasionally, a dhoti, that he made everyone else around feel crumpled, angular and grubby. He walked ponderously and impressively; one thought of a small, lightweight but inordinately pompous elephant. His voice was mellifluous but pedantic; it acquired an edge only when it addressed Sushil Dastur.

Sudha Mani was softer, rounder and plumper than her husband, and some years younger, and to do her justice, she was a pretty woman, with her pale gold cheeks and huge, limpid eyes, and curled, crisp rosebud of a mouth. But the eyes stared almost aggressively, and the tightness of the rosebud never moved a degree nearer blooming; and when the petals did part, she squawked like a parrot. She wore beautiful, expensive saris and rather too much jewellery, all of it genuine; but everyone here put capital into gold and silver ornaments. And she wore flowers in the huge knot of black hair coiled on her neck, but the flowers never seemed to survive long.

From her they had heard all about her first grandchild, and her troubles with servants, and the extreme sensitivity of her temperament. And from Gopal Krishna all about the state of the textile business, and his own commercial astuteness and consequent wealth.

Only almost accidentally had they ever discovered more than his name about Sushil Dastur, who fetched and carried, ran errands, took dictation, conferred long-distance with the management of the Calcutta shops and generally did everything that needed doing and many things that didn't around the Mani menage. His name they couldn't help discovering within half an hour. 'Sushil Dastur!' echoed and re-echoed at ten minute intervals, and in varying tones of command, displeasure, reproach and menace, wherever the Manis pitched camp. Private secretary, clerk, general factotum, travelling servant, he was everything in one undersized, anxious body.

In reality Sushil Dastur was not by any means so fragile as at first he appeared, but he was short, and seemed shorter because he was always hurrying somewhere, head-down, on his master's business; and the amount of prominent bone that showed in his jutting brow and slightly hooked nose contrasted strongly with the plump smoothness of the Manis, making him look almost emaciated. His brow was usually knotted in a worried frown above his large, apprehensive dark eyes, and his manner was chronically apologetic. Curly dark hair grew low on his forehead. Subservience had so far declassed and denatured him that it seemed appropriate he should always wear nondescript European jackets and trousers of no special cut, in a self-effacing beige colour. On the rare occasions when he appeared in an *achkan* he looked a different person.

'Looks like being old home week, all right,' Larry remarked glumly. For nothing was more certain than that all these people would be heading for the Periyar Lake in time for the early watering the next morning. There was nowhere else for them to be going in these parts. From the coast as from Madurai, from the west as from the east, the roads merely led here and crossed here; and few people passed by without halting at the lake to go out by boat and watch elephants. Other game, too, with luck, sambur, deer, wild boar, occasionally even leopard and tiger, though these last two rarely appeared; but above all, elephants, which never failed to appear, and in considerable numbers. 'You know, without wanting to seem intolerant, I'd enjoy my cruise more without the Mani commentary.'

'We could have a small private boat, if you wish,' said Lakshman tentatively. 'But it would cost more, of course.'

'Could we?' Larry perceptibly brightened. 'They have small launches there, too?' He looked at Dominic. 'How about it? We've stuck to our shoe-string arrangements so far, what about plunging for once?'

'I'm willing. Why not?'

'I'll go and telephone, if you really wish it,' offered Lakshman. 'It would be better to make sure.'

'Yes, do that! Let's indulge ourselves.'

The advantage, perhaps, of being a shoe-string traveller, is that you can, on occasion, break out of the pattern where it best pleases you, and do something unusually extravagant. The thought of having a boat to themselves, and all the huge complex of bays and inlets of the lake in which to lose the other launches, was curiously pleasing. Even on a popular Sunday they might be able to convince themselves that they were the only game-spotters in the whole sanctuary. Dominic was whistling as he reached into the back of the Land-Rover for his towels and washing tackle.

It was at that moment that the two clear, female voices

began to approach through the darkness from the direction of the gate, and there emerged into the light from the windows two girls, one Indian and dark, one English and pallidly fair, carrying nets of green oranges and bunches of rose-coloured bananas in their arms.

Two pairs of eyes, one pair purple-black, one zircon blue, took in the Land-Rover and its attendant figures in a long, bright, intelligent stare.

'Well, hullo!' said the fair girl, in the bracing social tone of one privately totting up the odds. 'You must be the outfit that passed us just down the road, when we were haggling for this lot. Staying over? I thought they were full up.'

'They are,' said Dominic. By this time he was well aware that Larry never responded to any overtures, especially from females, until he had had time to adjust, and to review his defences. Some girl must once have done something pretty mean to him, and all others had better step delicately. 'We sleep out in the moke. But yes, we're staying.'

'We came up by the bus. No use going on to the hotel, until tomorrow, anyhow,' she said simply. 'We couldn't afford to stay here, and it was too late for this afternoon's cruise when we got here. I suppose you'll be heading for the lake tomorrow morning?' Her eyes flickered thoughtfully towards the Land-Rover again; he didn't blame her for taking thought for the morrow, public transport was liable to be both unreliable and, on a Sunday, overcrowded. But she didn't ask, not yet. It was too early, and she wasn't going to be as crude as all that. As for the Indian girl, she stood a little apart, cool and still, watching them with a thoughtful and unsmiling face.

'So will everyone around, I imagine,' Larry said cautiously.

'You're American, aren't you?' she said, interested.

'That's right. My name's Preisinger, and this is Dominic Felse – he's English. As I think you must be.'

'Not much good trying to hide it, is it?' She shook her pale locks and laughed. 'I'm Patti Galloway, and this is my friend Priya Madhavan. If I had the colouring I'd like to sink myself into the background, and all that, but I decided long ago that it was no good. Priya's from Nagarcoil, we're making our way there gradually, and taking in the sights on the way. Where are you heading?'

'Oh, south. Down to the Cape, and then by Trivandrum and Cochin back to Madras. Dominic drops off at Madras. After that I don't know yet.'

Her eyes had opened wide. 'You must have a lot of time to spare. What do you do? Have you been working here? Or do you live here all the time?' She was restlessly full of questions, but there was something artless and disarming about her directness; and if it was disconcerting that she waited for no answers, at least that gave Larry time to make up his mind. Why not, after all? Lakshman was just coming out from the arcaded porch with a slight, contented smile that said he had been successful, and there would be a private boat for them tomorrow. And the girls had their own plans, which apparently involved the family of one partner, and therefore were hardly likely to be changed as the result of a chance meeting like this. He could afford to be generous without any risk of getting in too deeply.

'We were just going to sneak in and cadge a shower, as a matter of fact, before eating. If you two are on your own, and would care to join us, we should have a boat of our own for tomorrow morning. Why don't we eat together and fix everything up over the meal?'

The furniture of the bungalow's public room was of the simplest, but there were two tables, chairs enough and electric lighting that flickered alarmingly at times, but survived; and the *khansama*'s omelettes were good, and the fruit from the stall fresh and excellent. Since the tables were of the same size, it was natural to break up the guests into two equal parties of five; and that made it easy for the first on the scene – and inevitably that was Lakshman – to appropriate one of them for his employer's party and his employer's guests. Whether he approved of the addition of the girls to their number there was no way of knowing; his manners, as always, were graceful and correct.

Patti watched the other parties assemble with wide-eyed curiosity. Sudha Mani swept in wreathed in a nylon sari ('Not at all practical,' Priya said critically, 'synthetics slip terribly, and don't drape like live fabrics.') and a great many rather fine bracelets, forgot her handbag, and sent Sushil Dastur scurrying off to fetch it. Her husband was to be heard deploring in English, presumably for the benefit of the foreigners, the economic policies of the Indian government, and the burdens under which business suffered, but he ended, as usual, with the shortcomings of labour. And even this subject came down, inevitably, from the general to the particular, for it seemed there was a letter which Sushil Dastur should have written and dispatched, and had not, and a valuable order might be jeopardised as a result.

'If I do not supervise everything myself, nothing is ever done properly. Employees nowadays do not concentrate, they have no wish to work, only to pass the day and be paid. I was trained in the old school, hard I had to work, and by hard work I built up the business I have now.'

The Bessancourts spoke English reasonably well, a virtual necessity for other European tourists in India; and to judge by the conversation, they too had encountered the Manis previously in their travels, for the note of greeting was personal, even cordial. A familiar face in a strange land is a familiar face, and welcome, at least until you find yourself seeing altogether too much of it. Dominic could not imagine the Bessancourts and the Manis having much in common, or choosing to spend too much time together, but to have company over a meal is pleasant enough.

Madame Bessancourt was middle-aged, thick in the bust

and thick in the hips, with a heavy, shrewd, sallow face and black hair, barely beginning to turn grey. She had achieved something remarkable in her solution of suitable dress for this trek. She had taken to the *shalwar* and *kameez* of the Punjabi women, in dark colours and amply cut for comfort, and astonishingly she looked completely at home in them, and almost Indian. The yellowish tint of her cheeks, her black eyes and black hair, the heavy body that belonged by rights in the unrelieved, noncommittal black of the *patronne* of some small hotel in Artois, nevertheless put on this alien dress with complete authority. Maybe there wasn't really much difference between the French matron and the Indian matron, both masterful, practical and not to be taken lightly.

Her husband, on the other hand, had made no concessions. He was square and solid, with a balding head so uncompromisingly Alpine and a moustache so obviously French that any effort to conceal their origin must have failed from the start. So he wore suits exactly like those he would have worn at home, but made in lightweight cloths, and allowed himself an old Panama hat against the sun, and that was the extent of his special preparations.

'What do you suppose they *do*?' Patti wondered, watching them in fascination. 'At home, I mean? You just haven't a chance of guessing, have you? I suppose they could be retired, but they're not so old, really.'

'Heaven knows! Maybe a small factory somewhere – family business – and a son's taken over,' suggested Dominic, more or less seriously. Speculation is irresistible, and he had been wondering ever since he first set eyes on them. 'They bought that car in Bombay as soon as they landed, and God knows where they haven't taken it by this time. They both drive – well, too. They stay in dak bungalows or railway retiring rooms, and do everything as cheaply as they can – though that may be French parsimony rather than lack of funds – but they don't miss a thing. What they do, they do, a hundred and five per cent.'

'Perhaps,' Lakshman suggested, 'they won some big lottery prize, and this was a dream – and now they take possession of their dream.'

'Yes, but even so,' persisted Patti, still enchanted by Madame Bessancourt's ambivalent, Indian–French solidity, self-possession and repose, 'why *India*?'

'Yes,' agreed Larry pointedly, watching her sombrely across the table, '*why* India? Why in your case, for instance?'

'Me? Oh, I finished school two years ago, and didn't want to go on to a university – not yet, and anyhow, I'm not clever, I might have had trouble getting a place – and I was stuck full of youthful idealism and all the current jazz, and I thought India was just the groovy place, the place that had the answers. You know how it was! Maybe it isn't any more, I've been here two years.' She bit into the dimpled green skin of an orange, and began to peel it, frowning down at her fingers, which were thin, blunt-nailed and not particularly well-kept; even gnawed a little, Dominic noticed, alongside the nail on both forefingers. She had a nervous trick with her eyelids, too, a rapid, fluttering blink, but perhaps that was simply out of embarrassment, because all attention was now centred upon her. 'So I thought I'd volunteer to come out here and teach for a couple of years before I went to college, and though I'd missed the regular Voluntary Service Overseas draft – and anyhow, they might not have considered me the right type – I got this job in Bengal through one of Dad's business friends who had connections over here. Just an ordinary school that used to be a mission school, and there was teaching in English as well as Bengali, and I had to help all the classes with their English.'

'Did you learn any Bengali?' Dominic asked with interest.

She looked up at him quickly. Her eyes were really an

extraordinary colour, pale yet very bright, like a slightly troubled sea over sunlit sand. 'Some. I can get by, but I couldn't conduct a real conversation. Oh, it's been fine in its way, I'm not complaining. Only I came here thinking this was where the low living and high thinking was, and the way to understanding, and India was going to show me what was wrong with all the rest of us. And what do you know? – here they are, almost the most quarrelsome race I've ever struck, almost the most corrupt, and all the high thinking is just talk, talk, talk, and the government is as mixed-up and inhibited and old and tired as any of ours, and I can't see any end to it – or even any beginning of getting out of the mess. But maybe it's me,' she said disarmingly, and smiled up suddenly at Priya, and at Lakshman. 'Don't get me wrong! The best here are *the best* – the best you're going to find anywhere on earth. But as for the system – did we really ever expect so much of it?' She tilted her head, looking from Larry to Dominic, for plainly they were in this, too. 'I'm on my finishing leave now, I get two months paid, and I'm still travelling hopefully. But where to, God knows! How have *you* managed?'

Dominic waited for Larry to speak, and he didn't; for some reason Patti had shaken him, and his brooding face was the only thing about him that was going to be eloquent just yet. So Dominic filled the gap.

'I was lucky. Every time I hear anyone else talk about India I realise it. I got pitched in here on a special job, without any time to have preconceived ideas, and everything about the job came unstuck, and I was left living off the country. When there's a real crisis you find out who amounts to anything, and who doesn't. That's when I met the man I'm working for now – the Swami Premanathanand. You couldn't very well be any luckier than that, whatever the hole you're in. No, India didn't let me down. That's why I came back. But to work, not to meditate.' He was aware that that might sound a trifle superior, but that was something he couldn't help. 'That's the way it hit me, and I got hooked accordingly. And I've said I was lucky.'

'But where are they *going*?' persisted Patti fretfully. 'I can't see any future.'

'I haven't looked, I've been too busy with the present.'

'But what do you actually *do*, then?' she asked doubtfully.

'I work for the Swami's foundation, the Native Indian Agricultural Mission, on one of their farms near Tiruvallur. Doing anything – driving, messenger-boy, vet's assistant, whatever's needed. But mostly I seem to have become the district tractor-mechanic.'

'But isn't that sort of set-up just another way of being a big land-owner?' Patti objected warmly.

'Hardly! Everything we run is run on a co-operative basis. Each village is its own board of directors, and everything above a bare living for the central staff is ploughed back into the business.' But he was not particularly disposed to talk about it; he was on leave, and she already knew everything she needed to know about him.

'Do you think all that's really going to *change* anything?' she wondered wistfully.

'It already has. Since we set up this particular grouping we've nearly doubled our rice yield annually – partly by increasing acreage, and partly with better double-cropping. Did you know that Tamil Nadu is going to be a surplus state any minute now? Not just through us, of course, we're a very minor force, but we do work in with the government's intensive district programme, and that's far from minor.'

She looked reluctantly impressed, and at once sadly incredulous and warily hopeful. 'I suppose your people farm back home? I didn't have anything as practical as that in my background. My dad's a retired army officer. I was born into the establishment.'

'So was I,' said Dominic with a fleeting grin, 'only a

different branch. Mine's a policeman. Well, no uniform now, actually, he's deputy head of the county C.I.D. I haven't got anything more practical to offer than an arts degree, either, and that doesn't dig any wells here. Or at home, for that matter. Everybody thinks it entitles him to be a teller, when we've already got too many tellers and not enough doers. So I thought I'd come over here and see how the doers live.'

'Awful waste of a degree, though,' protested Patti, rather surprisingly reverting to type.

'Not a bit! It won't rot.'

She considered him thoughtfully for a moment, background, parentage, eccentricities and all, and looked more than half convinced. 'Well, maybe you've found something that'll stand by you,' she said handsomely. 'I wasn't that lucky. I never felt I was doing anything much, or getting anywhere. It seemed as if you'd have to smash the whole thing and start afresh before you'd see any results.'

'And what will you do now?' asked Larry, watching her soberly over the bowl of fruit. 'When your paid leave's over, I mean? Go home?'

'I suppose so. I've got some of my A levels to repeat if I want to teach seriously, but I haven't made up my mind yet. Yes, I guess I shall go home. Maybe try somewhere else. There's supposed to be a second country somewhere for everybody, so they say. Maybe the stars have to be right. How about you?'

'Me? Oh, I suppose I came here looking for the pure wisdom, like you. Though I ought to have known better. I'm an anthropologist by inclination, but a civil engineer by profession. I've been working on the plans for a small irrigation project up in Gujarat, but it looks as if various committees are now going to sit on the idea for years, and if they don't squash it altogether they'll probably alter it around until it's useless. I thought I might as well have a look around the country while they're considering the matter, so I bought the Land-Rover in Bombay, and set off more or less at random southwards. And Lakshman here comes along to take care of me.'

Lakshman gazed back at him serenely and amiably, but did not return his smile. Indian people, except those of the hills, do not find it necessary to smile whenever they catch your eye, but will gaze back at you directly with faces unyieldingly grave and thoughtful. In the hills they smile because they obviously enjoy smiling. And Indian people, Dominic thought critically, studying the two golden amber faces beside him, who can be the noisiest people on earth, also know how to be securely silent and to withhold even an eloquent gesture. Priya's delicate face, silken-skinned and serene, betrayed nothing at all beyond a general, detached benevolence. Suddenly he felt more curiosity about her than about her companion.

'Now we've all declared ourselves, except you, Miss Madhavan.'

'I am not at all novel or interesting,' she said in her quiet, lilting voice; and now she did smile, her chiselled lips curving and unfolding as smoothly as rose-petals. 'I am a nurse at the General Hospital in Madras. I have a large family of brothers and sisters, and my eldest sister happens to be a teacher in Bengal, and a colleague of Patti's. So now that I have my long leave, and Patti is free to visit the south, I invited her to meet me in Madras and come home with me for a visit. That is all about me.'

It was very far from all about her; there were reserves behind that demure face and those cool, thoughtful, purple-black eyes that would take half a lifetime to explore.

'So you've actually known each other, apart from letters, only a matter of days? We're all starting more or less equal,' said Larry. 'I picked up Dominic in Madras only five days back. We'd corresponded, just fixing things up for the trip, but we'd never seen each other until then.' He took a banana from Patti's hospitably offered bowl, a bulbous bow in an incredible colour between peach and orange and old rose. 'This at least I'll never forget about India, the fruit. Did you ever see such a shade as that in a banana before?'

'Never!' she agreed vehemently. 'And I've seen them all kinds and sizes, from the three-inch curvy ones like a baby's fingers, to hedge-stakes a foot long and pale, greenish lemon. I saw these when we passed the stall in the bus, and we simply had to walk back and get some.'

'Where was that?' Larry asked. 'I never noticed any stall as we drove up.'

'It was getting dusk then, and he hadn't lighted his little lamp, you wouldn't notice us. But we saw you go by. Two turns down the road – I expect he's packed up long ago, probably just after we were there, there wouldn't be much traffic up here after dark. One turn down the road there's what's left of a shrine of Siva. It looks pretty old, too, the carving's nearly worn away, but they still bring oil and marigolds.'

'No, really? As close as that? I might take a flashlight down and have a look at that presently.'

'Wouldn't tomorrow morning do?'

'Not a hope! We've got to be afloat before six, or we shall miss the best of the show. They might not hold the boat for us, either – don't forget it's Sunday. The best times, the two periods in the day when the animals come down to water, are from six on in the morning, and about half past three in the afternoon until dusk. And it takes a little while to get out to the best vantage-points – there's a whole lot of lake up there.'

The Bessancourts were withdrawing, with polite good nights to the Manis. They passed by Larry's table on their way to the door, and bowed comprehensively to the company, uttering in assured, incongruous duet: '*Au 'voir, m'sieurs, m'dames!*' Everyone turned to smile startled acknowledgement, for once united: 'Good night, *m'sieur, madame!*'

'The French,' said Patti with conviction, as soon as they were out of the room, 'are *formidable!*' It was a good word for the Bessancourts. 'What can they want here?' she demanded in a feverish whisper. 'What brought them here? I don't understand!'

Dominic, still charmed and touched by that courteous departure, so reminiscent of a respectable couple quitting a small restaurant in St Dié or Chaumont, wondered if it was so vital to understand. Wasn't it their business? Why not just be glad about that impressive, three-dimensional reality of theirs? But Patti wanted to recognise, to docket, to know all her landmarks.

'Where did you first see them?'

'At Mahabalipuram, among all that fabulous free sculpture. In the Mahishasura-Mardini cave, actually, standing like another rock, staring at the sleeping Vishnu. She looked exactly as if she was studying the joints in a butcher's window before buying, but I'll swear for ten minutes and more she never moved. Her old man stands just as still and gazes just as attentively, but in a different way. As though he were standing respectfully but impregnably in a church that wasn't his own, but still he saw the point for those who belonged there.'

'You like them,' said Priya suddenly, in her soft, detached voice, and smiled at him with her eyes as well as her lips.

'Yes, I like them.' Heaven knew he wouldn't have the art ever in this world to achieve communication with them, short of a miracle, but he believed confidently there was everything there to like.

The Manis were leaving, too, in a series of short, abortive starts and stops. 'Sushil Dastur, my bag – you have left it behind!' 'Sushil Dastur, please arrange about the breakfast and early tea ...' 'Sushil Dastur, don't forget you must see to that letter, there will be a post from the hotel... And the alarm at five, remember!'

('That goes for us, too, don't forget!' Larry warned in an undertone.)

They passed in procession, pausing momentarily to exchange valedictory compliments.

'You'll be making the morning run?' asked Larry politely.

'Ah, but not with the public launch!' Mr Mani wagged a triumphant finger and beamed his superiority. 'We have an introduction to an influential resident here. He has a villa on the lake, and the hotel places a boat at his disposal. He has invited us to be his guests tomorrow. It is a great honour.'

'A privilege!' sighed Mrs Mani, adjusting her green and silver sari over her plump and tightly-bloused shoulder. 'He is a most distinguished man – and wealthy!'

'A business associate of Ganesh, our son-in-law. Ganesh has very important connections. . . .'

They departed in a cloud of self-congratulation, and Sushil Dastur, trotting behind, turned his lustrous eyes in a timid smile and said : 'Good night, ladies – gentlemen!' with almost furtive goodwill, as if he feared he might be doing the wrong thing.

And with that the evening ended, since the next day was to begin at five. Except that Larry had sufficient energy left to light himself down the two coils of road between the black, perfumed walls of the forest, to examine the Siva stele. Lakshman felt it to be his duty to go with him, and even to repeat, very seriously, his warnings about never going out in the dark in open country without a strong torch, for fear of snakes.

When they came back, Dominic and the girls were still standing beside the Land-Rover, looking up at the immensely lofty black velvet sky coruscating with stars, and festooned here and there, as in India only the hill-skies and the shore-skies normally are, with coiling plumes of cloud.

'That's a find you made down there, Patti,' Larry said approvingly. 'I want to stop off before we go down again to Madurai, and get some slides. I'd need to consult somebody who knows more about style than I do, but my guess is that figure wasn't carved any later than about the seventh century. It could even link up with some of the stuff at Mahabalipuram, to my mind, only it's had a rougher passage.'

'I suppose the sadhu isn't still sitting there?' said Patti idly, withdrawing her zircon-blue eyes from the heavens.

'Sadhu?' said Larry in vague surprise, dropping his torch into the front seat of the Land-Rover. 'What sadhu?'

Two

Thekady: Sunday

The hotel stood on slightly rising ground, the length of a dark, moist drive from the road, and resembled nothing so much as an over-sized and under-maintained mid-Victorian rectory, complete with untrimmed shrubberies and too tall trees growing too close to the windows. Even the hard earth drive and the few slightly ragged flower-beds fitted into the image. And though they had climbed over the crest of the ridge and begun to descend again, there was still no sign of the lake; nothing but forest, sometimes thick as a creeper-draped stone wall on either side of the road, sometimes opening into what was almost park-land, with lush turf in which the trees stood gracefully spaced, waist-deep in grass.

Larry was a fanatical time-keeper, having learned the necessity the hard way. They had been the first party away from the bungalow and would probably be the earliest afloat here. The few people moving around at parked cars in the hotel grounds, or in and out of the open door, were almost all staff.

'If you will wait five minutes for me,' Lakshman said, scrambling out from among the gear stowed in the back of the Land-Rover, 'I must check in with the hotel desk, and find our boatman.'

By the time he emerged again they had secured the Land-Rover's steering with an ingenious padlocking device of Larry's own invention, briefly examined the palm-decked amenities within the hotel, still dim and almost unpeopled in the dawn, and moved round to the small terrace at the rear of the building.

And there at last was the Periyar Lake, or at least the first glistening reach of it, curving in to lip the soft green swell of turf some forty feet or so below the level of the terrace, and winding away in the distance to lose itself among folded green slopes of grass and trees. The far-off ranges modulated from green to blue, to smoke-grey, and dissolved into the pearly light of a morning as yet sunless. A flight of steps led down from the terrace to the grass, and thence a long, curving causeway swept away righthanded into the water, like a Devonshire hard, its coral-coloured surface breaking gradually through the green of the grass only to lose itself again beneath the quivering dove-grey of the shallow water. On the right flank of the hard, within its protecting curve, three or four white launches were moored; and from there a belt of stiller water, broad and pewter-grey, launched itself out across the lake-surface. To the left, where the bay rounded in a sickle of shore and curved away again, they saw the first ghostly gathering of dead trees, skeletons standing six feet or more out of the water, quite black, all their lesser branches long since rotted away. From the water's edge rose a band of about a hundred yards or more where the grass was pale, thin and low; then at high-water-mark the lush, man-high growth began, and the living trees, not jungle here, but fairly open woodland, through which the first rays of the sun filtered and found the mirror-surface, to splinter in slivers of blinding light when the fitful dawn-wind troubled the lake. There were clouds, soft, light and lofty, above the receding folds of the forest.

'No wonder the English felt more at home in the hills,' Dominic said, as they stood gazing in sharp, nostalgic pleasure. 'It wasn't only the temperature, it was the whole look of the place. You've only got to get high enough, and you've got English trees, English gorse and heather, even an English sky. You never realise how you've missed the variety of cloud until you see it again after months of staring at absolutely naked blueness.'

'Then perhaps they felt really at home,' murmured

Priya, with the first spark of mischief he had observed in her, 'when the monsoon rains began.'

'Personally,' Patti said sceptically, 'I can do with quite a lot of naked blueness before I start complaining. That's one of the things I *do* like about India, and one of the things I'm going to miss if I do go home.'

'You haven't made up your mind, then?' Larry turned to look at her with more interest than he had yet shown. She was duplicating, Dominic thought, a dilemma of Larry's own. Both of them were drawn, and both of them repelled; and both of them, each in a different fashion, held it against India that they did not know what to do.

'Oh, I don't know! – It's the parents, you know – I'm the only one, and they gave me the works, private schools, music lessons, riding lessons, the lot! I keep feeling I've got to give them some sort of return for their money. But then, even if I do go back and work at it, I sure as hell know the end product isn't going to be what they were bidding for. Maybe they'd be safer if I stayed here – I mean, you can do quite a bit of romancing about a daughter several thousand miles away, but it's no good if she keeps blowing in and smashing the image. And I do love this country – hate it, too!' she added honestly. 'Some of the components are marvellous, if only you could break the whole lot apart, and put them together again in some form that would actually *work*.'

'And couldn't you say that just as accurately about any country under the sun?'

'I suppose you could. I *know* you could. So why go home? Why go anywhere? Start from where you are.'

'I did,' he said grimly, focusing his Werra on the dead trees that spread their arms rigidly now over quivering silver water. 'I started practising shattering it to bits and rebuilding it nearer to the heart's desire right where I was, on a New England campus. I've had the New Left and the activitists – from mid- to extreme- to off-the-map and up-the-wall. They never changed a thing except themselves, and so far as I could see, that was no change for the better. And all they shattered were people – usually innocent people – as even policemen can be,' he added sourly, and turned his back on her abruptly, and the shutter clicked.

'Then where *do* you go after that?' she said, and she had been so startled by this burst of confidence from him that it was almost a cry of appeal.

'If I knew that, I should be on my way.' That was the most Dominic had ever yet heard from him about his own intolerable situation, and perhaps the most anyone was going to hear until he resolved it one way or another. 'Good, here's Lakshman, we can get off now.'

Lakshman came round the corner of the hotel in conversation with a young fellow of his own slender build, but taller and more muscular. He was dark-skinned and clean shaven, with a prominent nose and strong brows, above narrowed dark eyes that had the seaman's look of focusing upon distance. He salaamed briefly and cheerfully, and favoured them all with a broad and gleaming smile.

'Sir, I am Romesh, your boat-boy. Ladies, you please come this way.'

He pattered before them down the steps in his worn leather sandals, and led them down the tongue of grass and the curving causeway to the boats. His working wear consisted of khaki shorts and a tunic of white cotton, with a red sash round his waist, and a loose white cotton turban, with a short cockade of pleats over his forehead and a balancing fan of pleated folds on his neck.

Patti danced down the steps after him, Priya following more sedately. 'Romesh, you speak good English. That's lucky!'

'I speak a little, memsahib. Not good!' He turned upon her a flashing smile, half-bold and half-shy; she saw that he was quite young, probably only a few years older than herself. 'But I try to show you all game, very good. It will be fine morning, many elephants come.'

He loosed the rope that moored the smallest of the white boats; the canvas canopy slapped gently in the breeze, and then was still. The vast, bright body of the sun glowed through the trees, and the clouds, unbelievably high in a pale sky, began to sail slowly like boats on a reflected lake. Romesh drew in the line and steadied the boat, holding out a hand to help the girls aboard. There was comfortable room for them all, and seats to spare. The largest boat, rocking languidly to the motion they created, must hold as many as fifteen passengers without crowding.

Romesh kicked off his sandals and sat down to the motor, and in a moment teased it into life. They slid out into the deep channel, clear of the skeleton trees, and headed across the first bight of the lake. On either shore the bare, peeled area of grass rose, steeply or gradually, to the countour of the high-water-mark, and there the grass and bushes soared to a man's height, and the trees crowded close.

'The water is rather low,' said Lakshman, 'but that is good, because then the animals must come well clear of cover to reach the water, and we shall have a good view. Sometimes it is much lower even than this, and then it is more difficult for the boats, because there is so much dead forest.'

Close to the shore, wherever they turned, there was always at least one spectral tree to be seen. In the deeper passages whatever remained of the drowned giants – if anything remained – was far below the draught of motor launches. They looked back, and the hotel and the landing-stage were already out of sight. The note of the boat's engine was low, leisurely and quiet. Romesh scanned the shores as they moved, watching for anything living that might emerge from the rim of the trees.

'He is trained to catch any movement. If he sees something he will not make any sound, but point. Then he'll try to bring the boat in more closely and switch off the engine, so that we can watch without disturbing them.'

They had, as it seemed, an immense world to themselves. It was difficult to grasp the scale of these hills and these remarkably English-looking trees, until Romesh stiffened and pointed, and found them their first elephants. In a sheltered bay on their left hand, a whole ponderous herd winding its way down through the trees, across the open belt of spongy grass, and into the silvery shallows. Beside the boles of those trees the two big tuskers shrank to the dimensions of toy animals. There were seven or eight cows, and four calves, varying from a half-grown youngster to a small, skittish baby. They played and splashed and squealed like puppies in the shallows, sending up fountains of spray, while the elders wallowed blissfully, and heaved themselves ashore to graze afterwards streaming water like granite cliffs deluged by a flowing tide. Romesh, flashing white teeth in a delighted, proprietorial grin, shut off the engine and let the boat slide slowly inshore between the drowned trees, and they watched for a long time, until the herd moved off at leisure into the forest.

After that it was elephants all the way; they saw them pacing in line, far up on a half-cleared hillside, moving methodically down towards the lake. They saw them bathing in half a dozen sheltered coves, and paused each time to draw inshore and take pictures. Several times they saw deer, and once, where the shores opened out in grassland and they emerged into the widest part of the lake, a large sambur grazing, bulky as a bison. The sun rose higher, and the clear heat of the day came on, but the fresh currents of air across the water were cool and fragrant. Silver-blue before them, under a deepening blue sky only delicately dusted with cloud, the lake expanded broad and calm, and here the light was dazzling. They could see the long barrage of the Periyar dam far in the distance. After the enclosed, steep-shored bays the elephants preferred, this was a minor sea.

'It's time to turn back,' Lakshman said reluctantly, 'If we are to get the boat back on time.'

'What a pity!' Patti sighed. 'This is glorious. How long ago was the dam built, Lakshman?'

'Last century, it's an old one. I think about 1890. It turns the Periyar river through a long tunnel, and makes it flow east down into the Madurai plains. It used to go west to the Malabar coast.'

'And the wild life sanctuary, is that old, too?'

'Quite old, it was made while this was still Travancore State territory. It's been established so long that it has many, many herds of elephants.'

'You like to keep boat?' Romesh suggested hopefully. 'Come again in afternoon? Sometimes is better in afternoon. Maybe even see tiger.' He had brought the boat about, and they were heading gently back for the narrows.

'Oh, could we?' She looked hopefully at Larry. 'Is it very expensive? Couldn't you be our guests this time? If you don't have to rush away?'

They looked at one another, and apart from the question of who paid, which could be left in abeyance for the time being, there was no need for much persuasion. The beauty of the place and the fascination of the animals made departure seem a deprivation; at least they could have one more trip, for the late afternoon watering.

'All right, why not? If the boat isn't already booked for the rest of the day? After all, it is Sunday, there are sure to be a few trippers.'

'I take you,' promised Romesh heartily. 'I fix it for boat.'

'Good for you!' Patti was delighted. 'Romesh, you're a treasure. What's the rest of your name, may we know?'

He flashed his magnificent teeth at her in a pleased grin. 'It is Romesh Iyar, memsahib.'

'A good Keralese name.'

'Yes, memsahib, from Quilon.'

They were between the steep banks again now. Once or

twice they caught sight of buildings close to the water, one, as Romesh told them, formerly a palace. They were encountering, too, the boats which had set off later than theirs, and had just reached this stage in the pilgrimage. The big launch, packed with the Sunday whites of husbands and the fluttering saris of wives and flower-tinted dresses of children, ploughed steadily ahead into open water, passing them closely.

'I see the Bessancourts made it,' Larry said.

There they sat among the butterfly passengers, he in his sober grey suit and Panama hat, she in her black *shalwar* and grey and white *kameez*, with a white muslin scarf over her pile of black hair. They looked about them at the strange and beautiful world of the Periyar Lake with wide, attentive, appraising eyes; and when they saw their young acquaintances in the small launch they did not wave, but inclined their heads with the tightest of French smiles, as on an after-church promenade in Combeaufontaine or Oulchy-le-Chateau.

They were drawing near to the final inlet that would bring them back within sight of the hotel, when they met the smart white launch, as small as their own, but newer. Mr and Mrs Mani sat installed among its cushions in jubilant state, beaming like gratified children; and Mrs Mani, though somewhat taken aback at recognising her acquaintances in a private boat when she had certainly taken it for granted they were passengers among the rest in the communal launch, nevertheless fluttered a silk handkerchief at them graciously, and achieved a very accomplished smile for their benefit. Sushil Dastur sat in the stern of the boat, very neatly and nervously, his knees drawn up, hugging the inevitable briefcase that went with him everywhere. And opposite the Manis, lounging along the whole of one seat with a cushion at his back, sat a tall, bulky man in a tussore suit and a snow-white shirt, grey hair curled in tufts over his ears, and the sunlight glinting blindly from the lenses of his gold-rimmed glasses. They saw him briefly in passing as a sculptured mask in bronze, without eyes, with a heavy mouth and jaw and a thick, pale throat.

Romesh exchanged the smallest flick of a hand with the other boatman, and grinned to himself. When he laughed he looked even younger, and childishly mischievous.

'So that's the wealthy and distinguished business contact,' Dominic remarked, when the other boat was out of earshot. Romesh looked up brightly from the wheel. 'You know him, sahib?'

'Never saw him before. Never heard of him until last night. His guests told us they would be sharing his boat today, that's all. Do *you* know him?' He added with interest: 'He has a house somewhere here on the lake, hasn't he?'

'Quite close, sahib, over there, not far from the road.' He was shaking gently with suppressed mirth. 'I am laughing because Ajit Ghose, that boat-boy, he is new here one month only, he does not know! *I* was on list to take that boat today, and this Ajit, he thinks to himself, this client is very rich man! So he gets list changed, to have that boat for himself. I saw what he want, but I let him do it. Me, I know this Mr Mahendralal Bakhle. He is rich, but he is not generous. It will not be so fat a tip as Ajit thinks.'

'*What* did you say the man's name was?' Patti asked sharply, turning to stare after the diminishing boat with abruptly quickened interest.

'Mahendralal Bakhle. You know that name, memsahib?'

'Not exactly – it just sounds familiar, somehow. I think I've read it somewhere,' she said. 'Wasn't there something about him in the papers – about trouble on his farms, and some labourers who were killed? I'm nearly sure that was the name.'

'It is possible. He is a big landlord, own much land down in plains, near Sattur.'

'But surely,' Dominic objected, 'there's a limit to the amount of land any one person can own now – twenty-five acres, or something quite modest like that.'

'Oh, yes, sahib, that is true, but there are ways. Some landlords say that they part with their land, give it to their womenfolk, but often it is not true. Mr Bakhle, he still controls everything, all that land.' Romesh's English failed him, and he waved a frustrated hand, and addressed himself to Lakshman in Malayalam.

'He says,' Lakshman reported, 'that Bakhle was mixed up not long ago in some very nasty trouble with his Harijan labourers. That must be what Miss Galloway is thinking about. They wanted a rise in pay, and then there was an armed raid on their village, and several people were killed. Everyone seems sure that Bakhle had hired the strong-arm men to do the job for him.' He lifted his shoulders in helpless distaste. 'It could happen. Such things have been known.'

Priya, who was so silent and self-contained, and yet missed nothing, said simply: 'I have known such casualties come into our wards. There is very strong feeling among the Harijan labourers, and there is also great pressure being used against them.'

'Not, in fact, a very popular man, this Bakhle,' Larry deduced.

'With reason, it seems,' said Patti, casting a last long, dark look after his boat before she turned her back on it.

'Very much disliked, so Romesh says,' agreed Lakshman. 'But also very much envied and courted. Money is money, it talks loudly everywhere.'

'Prefer present company,' said Romesh boldly, and showed his teeth again in a bountiful smile.

'Well, thanks,' said Larry drily. 'Even if this doesn't turn out to be a very generous tip, either?'

'Even if there is *no* tip.' Romesh asserted firmly, and

brought the boat gently to rest, with a tiny hiss of compressed ripples, against the shoulder of the hard.

The Manis must have been invited to lunch at the villa, for they did not reappear at the hotel until nearly three-thirty, when it was time to embark again for the afternoon watering. Sunday whites and Sunday saris were assembling again in the party launch, and among them the sombre Bessancourts sat like monuments to France. And in from the gardens came Sudha Mani, the folds of her rose-coloured sari fluting round her plump ankles, her bracelets jingling with triumph, Gopal Krishna treading ponderously at her back, and Sushil Dastur at heel like a tired little dog.

'Sushil Dastur, go and order tea.' She sank into a cane chair among the palms and fanned herself gracefully. 'And see what kinds of sweets they have, and choose me some of those I like. Be quick! No, give me the flowers, you are dropping them.' She installed her booty on a spare chair, and beamed at Patti and Priya, who were just going out to the landing-stage. 'From Mr Bakhle's garden! So beautiful, aren't they? He has such a fine garden. Was it not wonderful this morning?'

'Wonderful!' they agreed truthfully.

The afternoon cruise was curiously different from the morning one; a completely changed light draped the hills, clear, yellowish, very still. The sky was washed nearly clean of cloud, and of a wonderfully pale, bright and remote blue. They remembered that dusk would come early here, and deceptively; there would still be full daylight in the open water when the many deep inlets were already drenched in darkness. But as yet it was bright sunlight, only just slanting towards the west.

'Look, Bakhle's out again!' Larry pointed a finger into one of the still, green aisles of the lake as they passed; and there was the immaculate white launch idling gently off-shore, with the silk-clad figure of Mahendralal Bakhle lolling at ease on his cushions, perhaps asleep, or near it. He had no voluble guests to entertain now, and the boat-boy was ready to respond to his every inclination, mindful of that fat tip he expected at the end of the day from a man so rich. The thought made Romesh chuckle happily and wickedly to himself as he observed them.

'That Ajit Ghose, he is so clever! Those people from Bengal, they think everyone in the south is stupid.'

'Their mistake,' said Patti drily. 'He's from Bengal, is he?'

'Yes, memsahib. He is not bad fellow, only he does not talk with us much, not friendly. Maybe only he is a long way from home.'

'And you don't know why he came south to work? I'd have thought the south had its own unemployment problem.'

Romesh shrugged and let that go, having nothing to say on the subject. 'See – elephant!' His pointing finger indicated them with precision, high on the steep hillside where the sun filtered through the trees and turned animals and earth to moving gold and static gold. In orderly file they paced after their tusker leader, the cows and calves following confidently; and though they seemed to move with the deliberation of doomsday, they covered the ground at an amazing pace, bearing obliquely downhill to the water. And now they were more playful and more relaxed than in the morning, scratching themselves meditatively on the ghostly trees, surging through the breast-deep water with a bow-wave breaking in phosphorescence before them, the little ones bouncing and frolicking in abandoned joy, the elders curling their trunks over them protectively.

Patti said: 'I love elephants!' And after a moment of silent watching she said sadly: 'Why can't we have a community like that, as placid and as natural and as perfect!' And indeed there was a conviction of untroubled happiness and kindliness here which at this moment seemed to justify her.

'Some worlds,' Larry said dourly, 'are simpler than others. You take what's dished out to you, and pay for it. Not like the Spanish proverb!'

'Look!' whispered Lakshman. The boat lay motionless now, and under the slope of trees it was premature dusk. 'They're going to cross!'

What moved them to it no one could guess, but the tusker and his younger fellow had waded far out into the water, and the cows were moving without haste after them, and marshalling the little ones with them. The whole herd was surging steadily into the lake, and setting course unmistakably for the other shore. Forward they lurched until tusks and trunks and massive shoulders and twitching ears had all vanished under the water, like ships sinking at their launching; but when only the domed, glistening tops of their heads remained visible, the lurching gait changed, and they swam. Like animated black stepping-stones, the herd sailed across the narrow arm of the lake with hardly a ripple, unhurried, majestic, oblivious of the boat that lay off in entranced silence, watching their passing from some thirty yards away. Occasionally a trunk came up for air, waved gently for a moment, and was again withdrawn, or the tip of an ear ruffled the surface. The watchers hardly drew breath until the cluster of rounded stones drew near to the steep shore opposite, and the leaders heaved their huge shoulders clear of the lake, streaming water and phosphorescence, and thumped imperturbably up the slope and into the tall grass, to disappear among the trees. The cows thrust up their heads one by one and followed, nuzzled by their calves, and all the glistening herd passed out of sight with hardly a sound.

Patti drew a long, awed breath. 'My God, and I never even knew they could!'

They looked at one another like people awakening from a dream. After that, anything was going to be an anti-climax.

Why look for more elephants? They had been so close that they could almost have leaned over and patted the littlest calf on its bobbing pewter head as it sailed by. And while they had been spellbound here, the day had lurched a long step towards its ending, at least here between the shrouding forested hills. In the opener water it would still be bright.

'Have we still got time to go on to the wider part?' Larry asked. 'It must look marvellous in this light.'

Lakshman conferred with Romesh, and Romesh in his obliging fashion hoisted a shoulder, and flashed his grin, and said that they need not worry about staying out beyond their time, they had plenty of fuel, and there would be no more cruises after this one. So they headed for the open water, silvery and placid mile on mile to the dam; and the day changed its mind and came back to full sunlight as soon as they were out from between the enfolding arms of the forest. Several times they saw elephants again, and several times deer, and the sky over them became the clear, pre-sunset sky of a summer day at home, shading down from deepest blue at the zenith to jade green at the rim of the world. The few feathers of cloud were coloured like roses, in variations of pink and gold.

They turned back at last. Romesh was just bringing the boat about in a long, sweeping curve, the water hissing along its side, when they all heard a distant, muffled report, not at all loud, but borne across the mirror of lake as though it came from everywhere at once, or from nowhere.

'What was that?' Larry demanded. 'I thought there was no shooting here. It isn't a hunting reserve, it's a wild life sanctuary.'

'That is right, sahib,' Romesh confirmed. 'But sometimes wardens must shoot injured animal, or rogue animal.'

'But it didn't sound like a gun to me,' Dominic said. 'More like what you hear at a good distance when they're blasting in a quarry. But I don't suppose there such a thing for a hundred miles around here.'

They listened, straining their ears, but the sound was not repeated. They had the broadest expanse of the lake to themselves, and the silvery hush of the hour was like a glass bell enclosing them.

'Ah, we're dreaming!'

But they had not been dreaming. Looking ahead as they sped towards the narrows, they saw a tiny puff of iridescent cloud rise and assemble in the sky far before them, and there hang shimmering like gilded dust for some four or five minutes before it disintegrated. In a countryside almost without aerial pollution, even a shot in a quarry would have produced little more than that. And before the arms of forest rose on either side to shut them in, it was gone.

The successive bends of lake became surfaces of steel mirror, reflecting pastel channels of sky, and shut in by black walls of forest. But wherever a wider bay opened the light took heart and returned. It was well after six o'clock when they came back to the place where they had seen the elephants cross, and instinctively looked again at the shore from which they had set out, where a few dead trees provided scratching posts in the shallows, and man-tall reeds grew, a paler patch in the dusk.

'What's that?' Larry asked, pointing. 'There in the reeds, look – something white...' Reddish elephants they had seen, but a white elephant would be too much to ask. Deer, perhaps? Anything pale would look white at this hour.

They peered, and caught the gleam he had been the first to see. Too white for deer, and too motionless; something low in the water, half obscured by the vertical stems of the reeds. 'Wait!' said Dominic sharply. 'Ease up, Romesh, there's something queer there— Take us in towards it a bit.'

Romesh slowed down, and obediently turned the boat's nose into the bay. They drew nearer to the pale patch, and it took on shape, veiled as it was, the curve of a white hull, a tatter of canvas trailing overside into the water.

'It's a boat – but it's foundered – it's filling!—' Dominic leaned over the side, and caught the quicksilver gleam of water inside the settling hull, and something else, pale wisps and bulges of cloth, awash among the bilge and hanging limply over the distant side. 'Something's happened— Closer, Romesh, get us alongside. My God, there's someone in her!'

They were all braced intently at his back as he kneeled on the seat and leaned far over to get a hand on the gunwale of the other boat. Patti's voice said, in tones of stunned and frozen unbelief: 'There can't be! It's only old rags – it's an old boat, it must have been abandoned here long ago....'

'Impossible, we couldn't have missed seeing it.'

The reeds rustled, brushing their hair and sleeves. Dominic got a hand on the rail and steadied them alongside; and now they could all see down into the unmistakable shell of Mahendralal Bakhle's smart white launch, awash from end to end with sluggish water.

All its seating nearest the engine was torn and splintered, and the motor itself hung drunkenly forward into the wash, a mass of twisted and fused metal. Every seam had been started, and oozed water and slime. The boat-boy lay with one arm trailing over the side, gashed by flying splinters and raked raw by blast, a few rags of his clothing dangling. And in the bottom, the water whispering from side to side over his shattered face as the boat swayed, lay what was left of Mahendralal Bakhle, in the muddy shreds of his tussore suiting. His chest was pitted with shrapnel wounds, and his gold-rimmed glasses, disintegrated into lethal slivers of metal and glass, had oblitered his eyes more thoroughly than the reflected light of the sun had hidden them at noon, and penetrated beyond into his brain. No bubbles arose through the water that covered his mouth and nostrils. The arms that lolled on either side his body terminated in the mangled shreds of hands.

Suddenly Patti uttered the most frightful sound Dominic had ever heard, a long, rending, horrified scream that rasped her throat and scarred their ears. And having once begun, she screamed and screamed, and could not stop.

Three

Thekady: Sunday Evening

They reacted after their kind. Lakshman caught the hysterical girl in his arms, turned her forcibly away from the horror and shook her until her broken cries gave place to blessedly subdued weeping. Priya, the nurse, kilted her sari to the knees, and was over the side as nimbly as a cat, standing on the broken stern seat of the other boat, with the water lapping her ankles. She leaned down to the lolling boatman, slid her arm under his shoulders, and turned up his head and face to what was left of the light. He was clear of the water, at least he had not drowned. But one arm was raw meat from the elbow, and he was bleeding fast into the debris of the boat.

'He is not dead – yet . . .'

Dominic climbed over into the hull to help her, knee-deep, and straddling Bakhle's body with one foot braced on either side.

'If we can get him into our boat, I might be able to stop the bleeding.'

Dominic got his arms round the man's thighs, and Larry came out of his daze with a shudder and a lurch, and leaned over to take from Priya the burden of the head and shoulders. It was astonishing what a weight this fragile-looking girl could lift, with one arm hooked expertly into the victim's surviving arm, the other hand steadying his rolling head. The white turban was a trailing rag, dirty and stained, but she did not discard it; it would serve as a tourniquet. They got the limp burden over the side and stretched out on a seat. She looked down briefly at Bakhle's body, and the green water lay motionless over the ruined face.

She looked up into Dominic's eyes. All the delicate lines of her features had sharpened and paled; she was a different girl. 'We can't do anything for him – he's dead.' And she turned to the one who was not dead – yet. On her knees beside him, blood and slime fouling the skirts of her sari, she rolled up the wet turban into a tight ball, and wedged it under the injured man's armpit; and the rags of his forearm smeared her breast as she did it, and she did not even notice. 'Romesh, give me your turban – quickly!'

He stripped it off with trembling hands, the whites of his eyes shining in the dusk, and long curls of black hair fell about his ears. She took it without so much as looking at him and bound her pad into place, securing the upper arm tightly over it. She knew how to handle a weight greater than her own, and what she was doing she did with all the concentration and passion that was in her.

Crouched in the stern of the boat, as far as possible from the horror overside, Patti sat limp and shivering with cold, her fist jammed against her mouth, her eyes immense with shock. And after a long, mute moment she turned and leaned over the side, and was direly sick. Lakshman hovered, alert and anxious, one eye on her and one on the boatman's limp body.

'We ought to take *him* in, too,' Dominic said, staring down into the bilge, 'if we can.'

'Waste of time, nobody's going to be able to do anything for him.'

'We could take boat in tow,' suggested Romesh, through chattering teeth.

'We'd lose it as soon as we got it off the mud. Pure chance it happened close inshore. Once in deep water she'd go down like a stone.'

'What *did* happen?' Larry asked feverishly. 'Could the engine have blown up? Is it possible?'

'Give me a hand, we'll try to get him aboard.'

But they were spared that, for as soon as Larry's weight

was added to Dominic's the boat began to slip away from shore and settle deeper. It was clear that without proper tackle they might only dislodge it and send it off again into deeper water, where it would certainly sink. Hastily they secured the broken hull to the nearest tree, and clambered thankfully back aboard their own boat.

'Get her going, Romesh, back to the hotel as fast as you can. We've got to get hold of a doctor, quickly.'

Romesh sat crouched over his motor, shivering but controlled, and set the boat moving at its best speed out of the bay and back towards the hotel landing-stage. On her knees beside the patient, Priya tightened her tourniquet, and watched the creeping streams of blood thin out and almost cease. But so much had been lost already. Dominic knew by her face that she had not much hope.

'He is so cold! If only we had turned back earlier, we might have saved him. Romesh, is there anything in the boat, a rug, anything to cover him?'

There was a thin blanket folded on one of the seats. They tucked that over him, and waited, silently, for the boat to round the last green spur and thread the last belt of dead forest to the hard. Patti, stunned and mute, sat with a handkerchief pressed to her lips, and made not a sound. Nobody had any longer anything to say. Not until they touched, and Romesh jumped ashore and made the boat fast. Then Dominic ordered:

'Run, go straight to the manager and tell him. Send for a doctor first, and send someone down with a stretcher or a door to carry him up. And blankets! After that, tell him to call the police.'

'The police?' said Larry, shaken. 'Yeah, I suppose they'll have to come into it, even if it was an accident —'

'It wasn't an accident,' said Dominic briefly, and stooped to lift the unconscious man's head and shoulders. 'Unless I miss my guess, it was a bomb. And we heard it go off – remember?'

They remembered; and now they understood. A distant, muffled report, like a shot in a quarry, and a puff of luminous dust hanging in the sky, a tiny cloud no bigger than a man's hand.

Exactly where the police came from they never discovered, but they were there within the hour. An inspector, his sergeant, and two uniformed men appeared in two cars; an ambulance was already there before them.

Most of the day-trippers had departed with the bus, but there were still a number of people around the hotel, and now no one could be allowed to leave until he had been interviewed and received police permission to proceed. The entire household was gathered withindoors under the supervision of a watchful and slightly officious Tamil constable, while the hotel's boatmen and the police officers salvaged the remains of Mahendralal Bakhle and his launch. Patti was clearly in no state to be of any assistance to anyone, she sat silent and cold with shock, staring before her; and since they had been six people in the boat, and five could give just as clear an account without her, the inspector, of his own volition, sent the doctor to give her a sedative, and bespoke from the hotel a room where she could be rolled up in blankets and left to sleep. By that time it was clear that they would not get away from Thekady that night.

'But it is terrible!' lamented Mrs Mani, dropping tears of alarm and indignation into her scented handkerchief. 'It is a dreadful thing! Poor Mr Bakhle! Such a tragedy – such a distinguished man!'

'A frightful accident!' her husband echoed, and there was no pretence about his agitation. Had they not been in that very boat all the morning? Suppose it had happened then? 'To think that only a few hours ago we were speaking with him! He showed us his garden... And what do we know? Why must we be kept here? Now we have to pay for our car an extra day, with the driver, and we had intended to be back in Madurai tonight. . . .'

A frightful accident. That was what they were all thinking, no doubt, and that was bad enough.

The Bessancourts sat patiently among the palms, rock-steady, waiting to be interviewed when their turn came. Their programme was not so rigid that a day's delay could upset it. They had nothing with which to reproach themselves, and nothing to fear; they would tell what they knew, which was merely their own movements during the day, and that would be that. And since they were not players in the drama, but merely caught up accidentally in its fringes, they did not expect the police to give them a high priority in their list, and were resigned to a long wait, but a dignified one. Madame Bessancourt, from some survival kit of her own, had produced a large, half-finished sweater, and was doggedly getting on with her knitting.

They were kept waiting more than another hour before Inspector Raju came into the main lounge, where the guests were assembled.

'I should like first to see Mr Preisinger and Mr Felse and their party, who found the damaged boat. Also their boat-boy. If you will come this way.'

A small office had been placed at his disposal; with chairs enough to accommodate them all, the room was full, for one corner was already occupied by Sergeant Gokhale and his notebook. The sergeant was young, alert, and spruce to the point of being dandified, and apparently quite prepared to take down statements given in English. Like his superior officer, he was in plain clothes; evidently they were dealing with the detective branch. Romesh came in last, summoned from somewhere behind the scenes, his face wary and tired, and a little frightened.

Inspector Raju was tall and lean and greying, a man perhaps in his early fifties. He had a thin, lined face and intelligent eyes that missed nothing, from the stains on the sari Priya had as yet had no opportunity to change, to Romesh's shrinking uneasiness; and his complexion was no darker than a sallow European tan at the end of an average summer.

'Now – I had, of course, a brief verbal statement from Mr Felse on my arrival. It was laudably concise and accurate, everything I needed at that time. But now I want you all to think back and give me a full account of your day, in detail. There is time. And what one omits, another may remember. Perhaps Miss Madhavan could give her account first, then she may go to join her friend. There is no need for me to see Miss Galloway tonight; by morning she may be more herself. It was, I know, an ugly experience.' His eyes flicked one appraising and appreciative glance at Priya, who had also suffered the same experience, but sat here composed and calm. 'You do understand that you will have to pass the night here? I have asked that arrangements shall be made for you.' Another thought struck him. 'But perhaps you have not your luggage with you, since you were not expecting to stay?'

'We have everything in the Land-Rover,' said Larry. 'We'd intended driving back to Madurai this evening, so we settled our account at the forestry bungalow.'

'Good, then we shall not be putting you to any great discomfort, though I am sorry for the delay. Yes – very well, Miss Madhavan?'

Priya accounted for her day briefly and thoroughly, taking time for thought. When she had finished she said punctiliously: 'I am trained, of course, to be able to deal with casualties. It is an acquired skill, not a virtue. I think Miss Galloway has really lived a very sheltered life, though I am sure she would not think so herself. Could I ask you, Inspector, if my patient – if he is still alive?'

If he hesitated, it was only momentarily. 'So far, he is, and that is thanks to you. But I would not hold out too much hope for him. It was necessary to risk rushing him down to hospital, he needs surgery at once, and of course they are already giving him blood, but—Well, we shall see! Thank you, Miss Madhavan! You can go to your friend now.'

Priya went; and one by one the others added what they could to the picture of the day. Raju called on Dominic last of all.

'And what was it that made you think this might not be an accident, Mr Felse?'

'I didn't see how it could be. I could imagine a minor blow-out from an engine, but nothing of this kind. This had wrecked the whole boat, every seam had started. And the violence of the injuries ... it looked more like some kind of explosive gadget, deliberately planted. And that made me think of the sound we'd heard, and the cloud we'd seen. It would have been somewhere over those stretches of the lake.'

'And the timing? You did not notice the exact time of the report?'

'By pure chance, yes, I did. Not because of the explosion, but because we'd just decided we ought to start back, and Romesh was actually turning the boat then. I did a sort of mental check on how long it would take us to get back. It was then ten minutes to five.'

'Thank you, that is useful. Very well, now you may all go. But you will not leave the hotel until given permission.'

But as they were filing out at the door he suddenly called: 'Mr Felse!' And when Dominic obediently turned back he added in a lower tone: 'Come back for a moment, Mr Felse, and close the door. Sit down again.' He sat back in his chair and sighed, and then smiled at Dominic very persuasively: 'May I say that you have been most useful to us in this case? But for you I doubt if we should have been called in so quickly, and but for your party, and especially that admirable young woman, we should not have stood even the slim chance we stand now of ever getting a statement from the boat-boy Ghose. I don't rate it high, but at least it exists. I think I owe you a little information in my turn. You may like to know that you were perfectly right. We have been going over the boat very carefully – that is why we delayed so long before seeing you. There was indeed an explosive device planted in it. As far as we can judge up to now, it was taped under the engine. From the position of the bodies it would appear that Mr Bakhle was at the wheel himself when the explosion occurred, and Ghose was behind him, in the stern. The firing mechanism was a small clock, and we have found the dial and parts of the bomb. It would seem that it was timed for five o'clock.'

'Then it fired in advance of the time,' said Dominic.

'So it seems. A faulty device, but it was effective, all the same. You see the force of the timing. If the boat was taken out during the afternoon watering period, it was likely to be wrecked somewhere at the extreme of its range, well away from any inhabited place, and therefore, in all probability, from all help. It was an entirely professional job, Mr Felse – well put together, and no bigger than a medium-sized torch. And an important land-owner – and let me be frank, one much disliked locally – has been wiped out.'

'It seems,' said Dominic carefully, 'that Mr Bakhle preferred to stay somewhat nearer home than usual this afternoon. He had guests this morning, and perhaps he was tired, and didn't feel like going far. If the boat had really been at the limit of its range for the usual time allotted, it would have been where we were, out in open water. And it would have sunk totally, probably without trace.'

'That is indeed the probability. Though with explosives there is always an element of chance. In our country, as in yours, Mr Felse, there are certain categories of people, distinct even among terrorists, whose favourite tools are the gun and the bomb. I am interested in your attitude to this affair, and I feel it only right to suggest to you that you and your friends, merely by virtue of being the first arrivals on the scene, and close and intelligent witnesses at that, may be at some risk yourselves. The evidence, as you have said, was most probably meant to disappear into deep water. But it did not, and you have become closely involved with it. I don't say there was much for you to deduce – I do say that the Naxalites would have preferred not to run that risk.'

'Naxalites?' Dominic looked up at him sharply. 'You really think they could be in it? Here?'

'Here and anywhere. They may have originated in Bengal, they certainly have not stayed there, though they are less organised elsewhere. One of their weaknesses, indeed, is that the strings have almost always to be pulled from Bengal. But they extend everywhere, from Darjeeling to the Cape. "Death to the landlords!" is as valid a rallying-cry in the south as in the north.'

There was more than that; Dominic could tell by something withdrawn and watchful in the deep-set grey eyes. They had recovered part of the mechanism – the strings were almost always being pulled from Bengal – there could be ways of identifying where that bomb had been manufactured, perhaps even by whom.

'Then the probability,' he said slowly, 'is that we have an agent from the north working here – not necessarily a Bengali, but sent from there. And you, I think, were already looking for him before this happened.'

The inspector smiled. 'Mr Felse, you will do well not to enlist in our police, and not to learn any more.'

Dominic smiled, too. 'I'm halfway there, as luck will have it. My father is a detective-inspector in England, I grew up in the tradition, even if I didn't join the force. I grudge it that the lunatic Left, in any country, should discredit the legitimate Left by trying to turn killing into an approved weapon, and I hate it when their phoney grievances alienate sympathy from the genuine grievances that are there all the time, and need to be noticed and taken seriously. I don't say even Bakhle was expendable – but surely Ajit Ghose wasn't. One more life, a perfectly innocent one, is all in the day's work, it seems.'

'One or a hundred, I assure you. It's all right – in this room we are quite private, I have seen to that, and Sergeant Gokhale here, though an impudent and insubordinate young man, is perfectly discreet.' Sergeant Gokhale cocked one dark eye at his superior and smiled faintly, undisturbed at being discussed in this manner; they had evidently worked together amicably for some time. 'But I should not theorise outside this room, not even among your friends. Here you may.'

'I was thinking of the bomb,' Dominic said. 'If it was set to go off at five, then it was planted – or at least activated – since five this morning. I don't know if the boat was used yesterday . . .'

'It was, both morning and evening. And in the evening it was refuelled and serviced by the head boat-boy here, who is absolutely reliable – a local man who has worked here for many years. No, I think we can ignore the possibility that someone affixed that device at one visit, and then came back today to set it. We can concentrate on the time since five this morning . . .'

'Then who had access? Judging by the time when we met Bakhle's boat this morning, it was rather late in leaving . . .'

'You are right, it did not leave until well after seven, and it came back about eleven. So from five until seven-twenty-five it was at the landing-stage, and again from eleven until three-fifteen. During the first period access would be very easy for anyone connected with the boat service or the hotel. Possibly even for outsiders. During the second there would be quite a number of people around, and though access would be easily possible, it would also be risky, since anyone unauthorised might very well be challenged if he approached the boat, and would in any case run the risk of being noticed, remembered and identified afterwards. One would choose the early morning in preference, I think. And then there were the morning guests, Mr and Mrs Mani and their servant. I shall be seeing them, of course. They are from Bengal . . .' He let that tail away gently into silence, one eye on Dominic. He didn't believe in it very seriously, but he had an open mind.

'They were very flattered and excited about having an introduction to Mr Bakhle,' Dominic said. 'But I suppose that would be the line to take if they wanted the introduction and the invitation for a special purpose. Not very likely Naxalites, on the face of it, they have a lot to lose, and nothing to gain, which is usually the determining factor. Though not always, I suppose. But more important, all the letters of introduction in the world couldn't have *guaranteed* them an invitation to share his boat.'

'That is true. Also terrorist agents do not commonly proceed in threes, and for one to be such an agent without the risk of being suspected by the others might be difficult. Still, there could be vital secrets even between husband and wife, much more between master and servant. And as for possessions – have you noticed that the tenets of a creed are sometimes religiously observed by the rank-and-file adherent, but do not seem to be binding on the leaders of the cult? There are Naxalite bosses who are themselves greedy and tenacious landlords. Well – and you cannot think of anyone else who had ample opportunity, and was also from Bengal?'

'Yes,' said Dominic, after a long pause during which they looked each other measuringly in the eye, with a degree of wonder and curiosity. 'Only it makes no sense. Yes, I didn't miss the connection. Nobody had more opportunity than Ajit Ghose, nobody could hop in and out of that boat with as obvious a right as he could. For him it would have been easy, he was taking out that boat today, nobody would think of questioning him. And he comes from Bengal, and he's been here only a short time. Romesh told us. And he told us more – that originally *he* was down as Bakhle's boat-boy for today, and Ghose contrived to have the duties changed, so that the job went to him instead. I haven't forgotten. But it would be crazy! He stood to blow himself up, too. *If* he did it, he *did* blow himself up.'

'He may not have intended any such development. Terrorists have died by their own bombs before now.'

'Not with that much room to manoeuvre. He could have fixed it to go off when he wasn't aboard —'

'How? You think a man like Bakhle would ever go aboard first and wait for his boatman? At the landing-stage, whatever pretext he might have made to absent himself, it would not have been a practical proposition. He would have been under suspicion immediately. No, if it was to happen in the boat, it had to be well out on the water, and therefore he had to be there. But don't forget the circumstances. They were close to shore, and it would appear that Bakhle himself was at the wheel at the time, apparently quite a frequent habit of his, and perhaps not difficult to contrive more or less at will. Thus Ghose would be behind him, while Bakhle's attention would be focused ahead. I have already confirmed that Ghose is a strong swimmer. May he not have intended to slip overboard shortly before the hour, and swim ashore? The boat was to founder. What would the boatman be then but a lucky survivor who happened to be blown overboard, and had no chance to help his passenger? If he wished to continue here and behave as an innocent victim, I think his chance of success would be pretty good. If he wished to disappear, having accomplished his immediate mission, that, too, would be easy. *But*...'

'But,' said Dominic flatly, 'the timing mechanism was faulty, and the bomb went off ten minutes early.'

'It is possible. I don't say more. We shall be examining his belongings, and tracing his antecedents. As we shall in the case of everyone else concerned.' He rose to indicate that the interview was over. 'Meantime, remember only that your position, and that of your friends, just *may* be a slightly exposed one, if someone fears that you may have noticed too much and too accurately.' And he added: 'A last point – your really devoted Naxalite might well contemplate the sacrifice of his own life with equanimity, if it was a necessary risk in the cause of taking Bakhle's. I don't say he would surrender it gladly, or refrain from all possible precautions; but he would not let that consideration stop him. As usual, it is only among the top ranks of the hierarchy that total cynicism prevails. The rank-and-file can be truly dedicated.'

Dominic was halfway to the door when he halted and looked back. 'But if you're right, then the terrorist is already *hors de combat* – even if he's still alive.'

'So?'

'So there seems no continuing threat to any of us.'

Inspector Raju said gently: 'It is not yet certain that the solution I have outlined is the correct one. But even if it is ... Mr Felse, Ajit Ghose, though literate, is almost without education. He may have planted the bomb – he certainly did not make it. Someone supplied him with it, and taught him all he needed to know to make it effective. Someone, somewhere, will be busy observing the results.'

Four

Thekady: Monday Morning

Patti came out of her sedated sleep reluctantly and sluggishly, to sense the white of day outside her eyelids; and for a while she lay without opening them, unwilling to face the world. But even inside her own closed mind she could still see the obscene horror of abrupt death, the mangled body stirring rhythmically and helplesssly in the water, the upturned face, with blood and mud for eyes. A man who, according to Romesh, had hired thugs to attack and kill, simply to suppress a demand for better pay. Remember that, too ... This is a dirty world, and nothing is ever simple. But to kill that way, from a safe distance, and not caring in the least about the wretched, innocent boat-boy, who had never hired thugs to kill anyone, and owned no land. There are things which can never be justified ...

She knew she would have to open her eyes at last, and get up and dress, but she waited until she heard the soft rustle of Priya's cotton sari, and knew that her friend was already up and busy, and maintaining this considerate silence only on her accoont. Then she lifted her lids resolutely, and sat up in bed. Priya was standing in front of the mirror, braiding her long black hair. She had on a low-necked white blouse and an amber-and-gold sari this morning; and the soiled sari she must have washed last night, and draped in the shower-room to dry. She turned quickly at the slight sound, and smiled at her room-mate composedly, if a little anxiously.

'Good morning! How do you feel today?'

'Doped,' said Patti truthfully. But not, she thought, heavily enough; I can still see him. 'And stupid. And ashamed. I'm sorry I was such a dead liability yesterday.

But I'd never seen – never imagined – anything like that. Even if you tried to describe it, to someone who'd never actually seen such a thing, it wouldn't mean anything. But when you run your nose right into it. . . .'

'I know,' said Priya warmly. 'It was not your fault at all. Don't think about it any more – at least *try* not to think about it.'

'It'll be a long time before I stop,' Patti said wryly. 'Priya – how do you ever manage? I mean, in a casualty department, when these things are brought in – hit-and-run victims, gang killings, knifings in fights – all that . . . How do you set about keeping your cool? Or do you just get used to it in time?'

'No, you do not get used to it,' Priya said almost with asperity. 'Or rather, perhaps you do and you don't, because if you don't – in one way – you can't bear to go on being a nurse, and if you do – in the other way – you had much better stop, because you're not fit to be a nurse. Your mind gets used to it, and then you can use your faculties to try and combat it. But your heart never gets used to it, and you never stop being hurt.' She added deprecatingly, suddenly aware of her own warmth: 'It is not for everyone, of course, why should it be?'

'Not for me,' said Patti with decision. She swung her feet to the floor, and sat on the edge of her bed. In the corner of the ceiling a tiny jade-green gecko clung upside-down, motionless but for the slow lift and fall of transparent eyelids, and the pulse in his throat, which vibrated almost too rapidly to be seen. Harmless, mysterious, jewel-like little things. The more I see of men, the more I like animals! But we're all caught, aren't we? You can't resign, once you're born.

'He seems to have been guilty of some deaths himself,' Priya said, attempting comfort that seemed to her quite irrelevant, but might make a difference for Patti. 'It is not only Romesh, I have been asking. Everyone knows the story, and most people believe it was he who was responsible for that attack. And it was a very bad case – one family was burned in its hut. But the raiders got away, and no one can prove anything.'

'No,' Patti agreed, reviving, 'I gathered he wasn't a very nice man.' She got up and pattered across barefoot to the shower-room, suddenly brisk and resolute, as if she had made up her mind about facing both today and yesterday, and had to take the plunge now, and violently, or lose the initiative altogether. 'Do you suppose Inspector Raju's still here? I've got to see him . . .'

'Just a minute,' Priya called back from the bedroom. 'There's someone at the door.' And she went to open it, to find herself confronting a sleepy but still debonair Sergeant Gokhale. Even after a sleepless night he was not so tired that he could not take pleasure in the sight of a good-looking girl fresh and spruce from her morning toilet, and not so devoted to duty that he could not make use of his eyes and his smile to convey his pleasure.

'I hope I'm not disturbing you too soon, Miss Madhavan. Inspector Raju would like to speak to you in his office – the room he was using last night. But at your convenience, there is no hurry.'

'Thank you, it's quite convenient now. I will come.' And she called towards the shower-room: 'The inspector wants to see me. I won't be long. Do take down that sari, if it's in your way.'

'I already have. All right,' said Patti's voice, half-resigned and half-relieved, 'after you!'

She was dressing when Priya came back. She came in very softly and quietly, as was her way, and began to collect up her night things without a word, her hands competent and quick as ever; and it took Patti several minutes to realise that there was a different quality about this silence, a private tension, not at all out of hand – she had never seen any emotion get out of hand in Priya so far – but nevertheless troublous and dismaying. Then, looking up with carefully screened attention through the drift of her fair hair as she brushed it, she saw tears overflow slowly from the dark eyes. She dropped her brush and was across the room in an instant.

'Priya, what is it, what's the matter? What did he want with you?' She flung an arm round the slender, straight shoulders, and then, in terror that her touch was too familiar and would be unwelcome even in these circumstances, snatched it away again. And Priya smiled faintly but genuinely, and smudged the tears away again. No new ones followed them.

'It's all right – that is, it isn't anything unexpected. I didn't look for anything else. But I told you, it never gets any more bearable when you lose one . . .'

'But what's that inspector been doing to you?'

'He is very kind, and it was nice of him to think of telling me. Of course he knew it was what I really expected, but how did he know, then, that it still mattered so much?'

'But what did he *say* to you?' Patti persisted furiously.

'He sent for me to tell me that Ajit Ghose is dead.'

'Oh, *no*!' Patti whispered.

'But of course! It was foolish to consider any other possibility, because practically speaking there *was* no other possibility. But still one tries. He died on the operating table. They got him so far alive.'

'Then he never spoke? He never had the chance to tell them anything?'

'He never recovered consciousness at all.' She went on assembling her belongings in a neat pile, and looked round the room to make sure nothing had been forgotten. 'After breakfast I think he means to let us all leave. I mean the inspector, of course. He was most kind. He tried to comfort me by telling me something more – that it is perhaps as well that Ajit Ghose died. He said I could also tell you, if I thought it would help to compose your mind.'

'I shall be seeing him,' Patti said, staring sombrely into her own thoughts.

'He says it isn't necessary, unless you wish it. Besides, it really does seem unnecessary now. He told me that Ajit Ghose came from Bengal only a month or so ago, just as Romesh told us, and it was true that he asked for the duties to be changed so that he could go with Mr Bakhle's boat. Romesh thought it was for the sake of a big tip, but now it seems he may have had other reasons.'

Patti's eyes changed their focus, stared at the incredible idea, and turned then to stare at Priya. 'You mean that *he* planted . . . ? The boat-boy himself? Of course I see he was the only one who could do it without any difficulty or risk at all, but then. . . . *No risk!* My God, I'm crazy! Why, it would be suicide!'

'Well, not quite, as they see it. Though if they're right he must have been willing to accept the risk of suicide. They say he was a fine swimmer, he may have intended to slip overboard and swim clear before the explosion, but he would need to leave it until the last few minutes, you see. And as it turns out, the bomb was a little faulty. It went off ten minutes before time.'

Patti pondered, wide-eyed, wringing her hands restlessly in the lap of her demure shirt-dress. Her face was quite blank, her pale pupils fixed. 'But they must have more than that, to be so sure. There must be something else they know.'

'Yes, there is. They've been going through his things. People like Ajit don't have much – a few clothes, a blanket, a bed-roll, maybe a pot or two, a few books if they're literate. He was – barely, but he had one or two books. One was "Shakuntala" – you know it? In among the pages they found several Naxalite leaflets and some Maoist literature. It is what they expected. What they were looking for.'

Patti sat quite still and silent, gazing before her. 'And you think,' she said, 'that it's really true? They're sure of it?

He threw his own life away to make sure of taking Bakhle's life? Then he wasn't just the pathetic, innocent victim I thought he was? My God!' she said, more to herself than to Priya, 'It's terrifying!'

'He thought it would put my mind at rest,' Priya said with a rueful smile. 'The inspector, I mean. So that I should know that, too – that he wasn't just an innocent victim, that he died as the result of his own act. He thought it would make a difference!'

'Doesn't it?' demanded Patti, astonished. 'It does to me.'

'It doesn't to me, not very much. I told you, you never get used to losing one. What he may have done doesn't make much difference. Except that he might have lived to die a worse way. Shouldn't we go and see if the men are up? They were going to sleep in the Land-Rover – there weren't enough rooms.'

Patti rose slowly, like one still in a dream. 'You are incredible! I'm frightened of you, and I envy you, you know that? I can believe in *you* dying for a cause – without any heroics, either, just in cold blood – like Ajit Ghose!' A sudden thought struck her, and she halted with her hand on the handle of the door. 'He was telling you quite a lot, wasn't he, this inspector! Do you think he's going to let everybody know? That his case is successfully closed already?'

'I think,' said Priya, considering, 'that he may. Perhaps for a reason of his own.'

'Oh? What do you mean by that?'

'I think,' she said carefully, 'that Inspector Raju has his reservations. Yes, he surely believes that this is the truth about Mr Bakhle's assassination. There seems no doubt about that. But not the whole truth. You see, this was only a half-educated man, however intelligent he may have been...'

'And however fanatically devoted. Yes, I see that. It takes specialist knowledge to make bombs.'

'Yes. Could Ajit Ghose have done all this quite alone? So by letting it be known that the case is closed, I think Inspector Raju is setting out to put someone else at his ease, too – and off his guard.'

At breakfast in the hotel dining-room, when most of the delayed travellers were already present, Inspector Raju made his announcement. First in Tamil, then in English, for the benefit of the foreign element, which even included a couple of innocent Germans, late arrivals and pathetically ignorant of all that was going on. In halting German Larry translated for the hapless engineers from some northern hydro-electric undertaking:

'Everyone present is now at liberty to proceed, subject to leaving with the police particulars of exactly where he can be contacted in the new few days, if it should be necessary. The case is now satisfactorily concluded, but we may need to get in touch with certain witnesses in connection with the detailed documentation of the events of yesterday. Will everyone who is ready to leave please report first to the police office on the premises. Thank you!'

Madame Bessancourt, without a word, rolled up her knitting and put it away in the capacious black bag that never left her side. Monsieur Bessancourt, with the same deliberation, picked up his Panama hat in one hand and their overnight portmanteau in the other, and they were ready. The first to be ready, as they had been the most patient and imperturbable during the delay. Police matters were to be accepted and respected in every country, but no need to waste time once the release was given. They passed by the table where Larry's party sat at breakfast, and performed their ritual bow as gravely as always.

'Are you heading back towards Madurai?' Larry asked, by way of making conversation in passing.

'No, we are going on to Kottayam, and then down the coast to Quilon and Trivandrum.' Monsieur Bessancourt glanced down at the folded map in his breast pocket as if for confirmation. 'And on to the Cape afterwards. And you?'

'The other way. We go back on our tracks nearly to Madurai, then south towards Tirunelveli. Later we shall be going on to the Cape, too.'

'Then perhaps we may meet there,' said Madame graciously. Inevitably, Dominic thought. Nobody is going to be touring this near to Cape Comorin, and not go the rest of the way, and by any route the distance is much the same. The odds are we shall all meet there.

'We must go and tell our plans to the inspector. It is tragic that this beautiful place had to be spoiled by such an act. And for your so terrible experience I am sorry. I hope you can forget what you could not help. *Au 'voir, messieurs – mesdames!*'

They all murmured their thanks and appreciation, and wished the departing travellers: '*Bon voyage!*' And the indomitable pair disappeared duly into the little office, recorded their time-table, walked out to their battered blue Ford and drove away.

The Manis had come in too late to hear the announcement; only Sushil Dastur, fussing anxiously about their table and exerting himself to make sure the tea and eggs should be just as they preferred them, listened with patent relief and gratitude, glad to have good news to relay to his employers as soon as they appeared. Theirs, after all, had been the worst situation; had they not spent the entire morning in the boat in which the bomb had been planted? Naturally they had all protested their horrified innocence, and exonerated one another, but all the same they must have spent an acutely uneasy night.

'Even we,' Larry remarked, 'should have been feeling pretty queasy, if all five of us hadn't spent the entire day together – barring the odd private moment, of course. An example of safety in numbers.'

Sudha Mani fluttered into the dining-room at last looking the worse for a restless night, her pretty face rather puffy and pale, her husband treading heavily after her, as though unusually deflated and tired. If he had not had good news to relay, Sushil Dastur would probably have been suffering for their discomforts. As it was, the watchers could see from across the room the sudden glow of relaxation and ease as Mr and Mrs Mani heard that they were free to leave; and in a very few moments the old assurance and self-esteem began visibly to re-inflate their sagging curves. Sudha reached for the tea-pot, and with recovered appetite they attacked the eggs that were set before them. To judge from their distant exchanges, seen but not overheard, they even had heart to reproach Sushil Dastur for the cook's shortcomings before they dispatched him, fairly obviously, to see their luggage portered back to the hired car, their bill paid, and the Tamil driver aroused from his semi-permanent repose in the back seat. They meant to lose no time in getting away from this place which had promised so radiantly and performed so viciously. No doubt they regretted ever hearing the name of the distinguished Mahendralal Bakhle, let alone bringing a letter of introduction to him.

'I suppose we'd better pack up and get out of here, too,' Larry said.

'I'll go and settle the bills,' said Lakshman, rising.

The girls, in slightly embarrassed haste, began a duet of insistence on paying their share, but Larry quashed that at once, or at least postponed all consideration of it. 'Later – don't bother now. Lakshman will pay everything, and we can think about it later. After all, there's no hurry, you're coming down with us as far as the railway. Go ahead, Lakshman, and we'll go and check out with the inspector.'

They had to pass close by the Manis' table on their way across the dining-room, and Sudha, just recovering her volubility in full, halted them with an appealing hand.

'Can you imagine what people are saying! – Think how terrible for us! It was that boatman! – Yes, right in the boat with us all that time, and looking like any other boat-boy, so quiet and willing. And we could have been blamed – such a dreadful position we were in.'

'I'm sure the inspector didn't suspect you,' Dominic said soothingly. 'Naturally he had to question all of us.'

'Yes, but even now we must tell him where we are going, where we can be found ... Why should that be, if it was that boat-boy?'

'That is mere routine,' said Gopal Krishna comfortably. 'Even if there is no arrest and no trial, because the man is dead, still they must file the records of the case. And suppose they should want to confirm some detail of the time with us? Or with Mr Preisinger here? It is the same for all.'

'That's it exactly,' Larry confirmed soothingly.

'You are going on towards the coast?' asked Mani.

'No, back towards Madurai.'

'We, too, of course, the car we have hired there, we must return it. Then we think of going out by train to Rameshwaram for one or two nights, before going on south.'

'I am so thankful,' Sudha said fervently, 'that they found out so quickly it was that boat-boy. Imagine, he had Naxalite propaganda hidden away in his belongings. I ask you, did that man look like a terrorist? You cannot any longer trust anyone or anything.'

'Hush, my dear, don't distress yourself,' murmured Gopal Krishna, patting her plump amber hand. 'It is all over now. You must forget about it.'

'That is so easy to say,' she protested fretfully, 'but it is not so easy to forget one has sat in the same boat with a murderer.'

'Two murderers,' Larry corrected cynically, but only in a whisper, and not until they had moved on from the table and could not possibly be overheard. 'One with money, one with none. One who hired thugs to do the job for him, the other who did it himself, and felt so strongly about it that he made sure by killing himself as well. But you know which of the two *she*'d retain some respect for, don't you?'

'Ah, so you're off already,' said Inspector Raju, looking up at them over a table strewn with papers, the debris of a hasty breakfast, and the cigarette-butts of a sleepless night overflowing from two glass ashtrays. He had discarded his tie and his jacket, and his lank, greying hair stood on end in all directions from the activities of his long, thin fingers. Even Sergeant Gokhale looked less immaculate than on the previous evening. 'No doubt you have heard by now how this affair has come out? Now it only remains for me to wish you a good journey wherever you are going, and happier arrivals than this one has been.' He did not look at Dominic with any more pointed significance than at the rest of them; the conversation of yesterday might as well never have taken place.

'Is it quite certain that this man Ghose was responsible?' Larry asked curiously.

'Miss Madhavan did not confide in you all?' The inspector looked at Priya with a small, glimmering smile. 'What admirable discretion! But yes, it is generally known by this time. Why not? We have found ample evidence in the dead man's possessions that he was deeply involved with the Naxalite terrorists, and the head boatman confirms that it was at Ghose's request that he changed round the duties for yesterday. There is not much room for doubt.'

All very decisive and satisfactory, Dominic thought, meeting the placid grey eyes. A case quickly and tidily solved, and a nice clear field ahead for that other person, the one who supplied the bullets but did not fire them, to lower his guard and emerge from cover, like the animals crossing that treeless belt of scrub grass to reach the water. Where, if he happens to be anyone present here, someone who has appeared only as an innocent bystander in this lake atrocity, he will not only afford the police a good view of him, but will also be on a long lead and ready to be hauled in at will. Because they're going to know where every one of us is – or says he's going to be – for the next few days, longer if they feel like continuing the supervision; and they're going to be checking that we really are where we say we are.

'I think,' said Priya, looking hesitantly at Patti, 'that Miss Galloway wanted to speak with you, Inspector.'

'At your service, Miss Galloway. I hope you are feeling better this morning?'

For once Patti looked disconcerted, even stammered a little. 'Thank you, I'm quite all right. It was only that I rather thought *you* would want to talk to *me*, since I made such a fool of myself keeling over like that last night. I don't suppose I can add much to what the others told you, but I thought you'd probably want to see me, anyhow.'

'That was very correct of you. But I think there is no need to trouble you any more. Now if you will give us particulars of your future movements, Sergeant Gokhale will note them down.' He pushed back his chair from the table, and stretched out his long legs with a tired but well-satisfied sigh. 'You are all going on together for the time being?'

'From here, yes,' Priya said, after a pause to allow Patti to take the initiative if she chose, and a quick, shy glance at Larry. 'Mr Preisinger has been kind enough to offer us a lift down to the railway line at Tirumangalam, and from there we are going to take the train to Tenkasi Junction. By this evening we shall be in Kuttalam – Patti wanted to see the resort there, and the Chittar Falls. But we don't yet know where we shall be staying. If there is room at the travellers' bungalow we shall stay there overnight, perhaps tomorrow night, too. We could report there to the police, if that will do, and say where we are living. Then the next day we shall go by train to Tirunelveli, and by the bus to

Nagarcoil, and there we shall be staying with my parents. I will give you the address.' She recited it gravely, and Sergeant Gokhale wrote it down.

'Thank you, that is quite sufficient. And Mr Preisinger and Mr Felse?'

'After we drop the girls,' Larry said, 'We're going on by the Tirunelveli road to a spot near Koilpatti. It's a village you reach by a minor road, slightly higher up in the foothills. What's the name of it, Dom?'

'Malaikuppam. It's on my account that we're making this detour. I have to visit somebody there, and we're invited to stay a couple of nights. We ought to reach the place early this evening, with any luck, so we shall be there tonight and tomorrow night. I don't know what he calls his house, but it's the main house of the village. Our host's name is Purushottam Narayanan.'

'I see. And you will be there two nights. And then?'

'Then,' said Larry, 'we go on to Nagarcoil and the Cape. Probably in one day, it's no distance, not more than a hundred and twenty miles. We shall stay at the Cape hotel at least one night, maybe two. If you could give us a telephone number, we can report any changes direct, or go to the local police as you wish.'

'No need to do either until you leave the Cape, but in any case I will give you the telephone number of my own office, in case *you* need *me*.' He smiled as he quoted it for them to take down; a slightly oblique and unamused smile. 'Thank you, that is all. I wish you all good travelling and safe arrival.'

'Just a minute! Please... !' Patti broke in quickly and eagerly. 'Could I... If Priya doesn't mind, I should like to change our plans. But it depends on Mr Preisinger, really.' She turned to look appealingly at Larry. 'Could you bear it if we asked to travel on with you, instead of going by train? I know I did say I wanted to see the Chittar Falls, and this Kuttalam place in the hills, but after what's happened here, honest to God, I'd be so much happier with a safe escort. And you see, I didn't realise until now that you were actually going through Nagarcoil. If you can possibly put up with us for a couple of days more, and take us all the way to Priya's folks, I'd gladly do without the Chittar Falls.'

'But, Patti, they are going to stay with a friend,' Priya objected, mildly shocked at this bold asking.

'I know, but surely there'd be a dak bungalow or a rest house somewhere near, where we could bed down. We wouldn't be in the way, honestly.'

There was no way of knowing whether Larry objected bitterly or welcomed the suggestion, for his face was never particularly expressive, and at this moment he was caught at a disadvantage. They had, after all, joined forces more or less by chance in the first place, and none of them had expected the alliance to continue. More embarrassing still was the fact that Priya had entered her protest so promptly, and deprived him of the opportunity of appearing genuinely warm about the prospect; he should have spoken up immediately or not at all. Not that it made any real difference, except to his self-assurance, for there was still only one thing he could do, and he did it with the best grace he could achieve.

'Of course, we'll be delighted to take you. No difficulty whatever about the transport end of it. And if accommodation is short, we can always camp again. How about it, Dom? Do you think this friend of yours would be very much put out if five of us descended on him instead of three? He never turned a hair at taking on Lakshman and me.'

'He isn't exactly a friend of mine,' Dominic said scrupulously, 'not yet, anyhow. I've never set eyes on him. But his father was a friend of my boss, and the son's asking for our help and advice with his land, not being in the least prepared for the job. His father was only in the late forties, he didn't expect to have to give his mind to running the estates for years and years yet. From all I can gather, a dozen people could descend on the place and hardly be noticed, but perhaps I'd better call him up and explain the situation first.'

'Oh, no,' protested Priya, colouring to a warm peach-colour which was her version of a blush. 'Please, you must not ask him for hospitality for us, that is too much.'

'I won't ask. Except, perhaps, whether there's a travellers bungalow or a small Indian hotel anywhere within reach. But you mustn't grudge him the possibility of offering,' he said, half teasing her, something he wouldn't have ventured to do yesterday. And she smiled briefly but brightly, instead of remaining grave and slightly distressed; another thing which would not have happened yesterday. They had travelled a long and by no means obvious way in twenty-four hours.

'Settle it with Mr Narayanan,' said Inspector Raju tolerantly, 'and let me know.'

Dominic was back from the telephone a few minutes later with the answer he had confidently expected.

'We are all invited most warmly.' Purushottam's words, not his own, delivered with both constraint and ceremony in the purest of pure English, straight from Cambridge but rooted deep, deep in the soil and rock of India. He had heard the voice once before, but as yet had never seen the face and form that went with it, and he wondered often and curiously what he was going to find in the flesh. All he knew was that Purushottam Narayanan was a year or so his junior, and had been studying in England until his father died, and tipped him headlong into the vexed affairs of a large, wealthy, but recently somewhat neglected estate. To judge by his telephone manner, classical English was something he lived with intimately, awake and asleep, but colloquial English had made no mark on him so far. 'Don't worry about anything, Priya, he means it and he'll enjoy it. Don't forget he's just bereaved, newly home after several years in England and he must feel like a maladjusted alien. A little company will do him good.'

'It is most kind of him,' said Priya, not altogether happily, but with a reconciled smile. And her peach-bloom blush deepened to a dark rose-colour. 'He must have much on his mind. We shall try not to disturb him more than we need.'

'Good, then that is settled,' said Inspector Raju briskly, 'and we can contact you all at Malaikuppam.' Sergeant Gokhale amended his notes accordingly. 'A good journey! I hope you may also have an uneventful one from now on. One such experience is more than enough.'

They went out to the freshness and radiance of a fine morning, and the Land-Rover standing waiting with a bonnet starred and sticky with honeyed droppings from the flowering trees.

Dominic came round from the kitchens with a box full of prepared food and fruit he had taken thought to order on rising, in case they should find it more convenient to picnic on the way. There were little three-cornered pastry cases stuffed with vegetables, and crisp pancakes sprinkled with paprika, the dough-cake type of bread called *nan*, and joints of chicken fried in golden batter. And fruits of all kinds, and a bottle of boiled water. No need now to go in to the railway junction at Tirumangalam; they would save a little time, and eat better with these provisions than at any restaurant they were likely to encounter on the way, not to mention being able to choose the place, the shade and the view.

Outside the back door Romesh Iyar squatted on his heels, strapping up a meagre bed-roll which presumably contained all his portable goods. Today he was not in his white tunic and turban, but wore khaki shorts and a bush shirt, and his curly hair fell in black ringlets over his intent forehead. As Dominic's shadow fell upon him he looked up, and showed a resolute but thoughtful and wary face, which mellowed into an ingratiating smile of recognition.

'*Namaste,* Felse sahib! You go Madurai now?' He had been well tipped, and was well-disposed, but he did not look particularly happy. 'I go away, too. I go by the bus soon.'

'You're leaving here? Leaving your job?'

Romesh rotated his head fervently from side to side in violent figure-eights of affirmation, and showed the whites of his large eyes. 'I not stay here now, this is bad place. I not stay here where boat-boy gets killed. I tell inspector sahib, tell boss, too. This place no good for me any more, so I go.'

'But it's over now. It's all over, nothing more will happen. It was a good job, wasn't it? I shouldn't quit just for that.'

Romesh hoisted his wide, lean shoulders under the baggy bush-jacket and set his jaw. 'No good here for me now. I not stay here, not like it here. Must go.'

'And Inspector Raju knows you're leaving?'

'Oh, yes, sahib, I tell him, and he say O.K. I report to policeman night and morning, then everything O.K. I tell him where I go, and he say all right.'

'And where will you go? What will you do?' Dominic fished out the small coins from his pocket. 'You're going to need bus fare. Here, put this away!'

Romesh pocketed the coins in his turn with a slightly brighter smile and a bob of thanks. 'I go see my brother in Tenkasi, maybe they got job for me on railway. If that no good, I try in Quilon or Trivandrum. Every day I tell police where I stay, do everything they say. Only I not stay here.'

He had made up his mind, and nothing would change it. He squatted patiently and doggedly beside his bundle, and settled down to wait for the daily bus, his back already turned on Thekady and the Periyar Lake.

'Well, good luck!' said Dominic, and went on to join his companions.

On the way down the forest serpentines on the eastern side of the range they made a brief halt below the forestry bungalow, so that Larry could get his slides of the Siva stele among the trees. The light was clear and brilliant, the conditions perfect; and now that they were clear of the lingering shadow of the tragedy at Thekady they were all recovering their spirits and beginning to look forward again instead of back. Only Patti was rather quiet; still slightly dopey after her sedatives, she admitted, and perhaps also anxious to make it clear, since she had more or less extorted this invitation, that she intended to be as unobtrusive and as little trouble as possible.

The fruit-stall was there in its usual place below, lavish as a harvest festival. Only the sadhu was missing; there was no one sitting beside the lingam in the shade of the trees, and not even a flattened patch in the grass to show he had ever been there.

Five

Malaikuppam: Monday Evening: Tuesday

They halted for lunch on a strip of sand beside a stream, just off the road, where they had a patch of shade from a clump of young coconut palms, and a wonderful view of the distant, convoluted blue heights of the Western Ghats, out of which they had come, and which, under a variety of local names and shapes, accompany the southbound road almost to the Cape. And in the afternoon they passed through Sattur, and remembered Mahendralal Bakhle, whose disputed lands lay somewhere in the neighbourhood. From Koilpatti they soon turned right, at Dominic's somewhat hesitant direction, into a minor road, white as flour, climbing gently between paddy fields greener than emeralds, and tall palmyra palms, with the half-veiled blue complexities of the hills endlessly changing shape before them. And by the first downward swoop of evening they reached Malaikuppam.

It lay on a gentle slope, facing south-east, and the rice here had become a different strain, a hill-rice, the upland crop almost golden in colour, and in one field being cut. Groves of trees framed the village as they approached it. There was a pond on one side, and two boys were splashing along its edges, minding the water-buffaloes that wallowed in its coolness with their blue-black hides gleaming and their patient, placid faces as near expressing happiness as they would ever be. In one place they saw tobacco growing, its huge leaves shading from pale green to yellow, its stems five feet tall. It did not look rich country, but neither did it appear depressed or poverty-stricken; and yet life in rural India is commonly lived on a knife-edge of debt and destitution, and they all knew it.

There were women just gathered at their evening chore of drawing water from a big, stone-rimmed well on the dusty village square. One of the girls stood aloft on the four-foot-high rim, outlined against a sky turning to orange and gold, and the others handed up their brass pots to her to fill. Poised with thin brown toes gripping the stone, she dipped and raised the brimming pots, her anklets and bangles gleaming, and all her gestures were pure and graceful and economical, a lesson in movement. Larry halted the Land-Rover, and all the dark female faces turned to stare at them in candid curiosity, and laugh aloud in frank appreciation of their oddness and incongruity. It was a disconcerting experience which all the foreigners among them had suffered several times before. But when Lakshman leaned out and asked for guidance in fluent Tamil, the nearest woman approached willingly and cheerfully, and pointed them the way. Higher than the village. A little way uphill, and they would see the gates.

They saw the wall first, lofty and white, capped with crude red tiles, and it went on almost as far as they could see. Then they came to the gates, wrought iron gates that stood wide on a short, dusty drive and a broad central court, round which the various buildings of the household were grouped somewhat haphazardly, many of them having been added at different times. Everything was low, one-storeyed and white, and shaded with overhanging eaves; and the first buildings they passed were clearly the dwellings of farm-servants and household retainers, of whom there seemed to be a great many. Then there were buildings that appeared to be barns and store-rooms, all space around the broad open area of trodden earth that gave place, a little higher, to a paved court. The end of the vista was filled in by a wide terrace, with steps leading up to it, and crowned by a long, low, single-storey house, white-walled and red-tiled, a little like a ranch-house but for the strong batter of the walls and the shaping of the roofs. Over the tiles the ornamental bushes and fruit trees of a garden peered, and beyond was a grove of forest trees looking over the boundary wall.

'Riches without ostentation,' Patti said critically. 'I sort of knew it would be like this. At least it doesn't look English. Have you ever been in the Nilgiris, and seen all those dreadfully unsuitable houses that look like something left over from Queen Victoria's jubilee, and are all called "Waverley" or "Rosemount" or "The Cedars"? You wonder whether you've slipped through a crack in space and time, and ended up somewhere quite different. At least this *is* rural India, not suburban Cheltenham.'

'I was once invited to a Women's Institute meeting,' Priya said unexpectedly, 'in Bangalore.' Everyone turned, even at this vital and anxious moment of arrival, to gape at her in astonishment, the statement came so startlingly, not in itself, but from her. 'I didn't go,' she said demurely, 'I had an extra duty. I was nursing there then. But I would have gone, if I'd been free.'

'Isn't it marvellous?' Patti said, gratified. 'You know when the real imperial rot set in? When the British memsahibs arrived! The men were quite willing to learn the ropes and go quietly and discreetly native, and no one would have been any the worse for it. But once the wives were let in, and the families, and the damned establishment, it was all over. Everything had to conform to the home life of our dear queen, and everybody stopped learning anything about the home life of the native Indian, and profiting by it. It didn't matter any more, it was just something to be brought into line. Which of course it never was. Thank God! You can't just run around the world trying to teach other people respectability, when what that really means is respect for an Anglican doll in a crinoline!' She caught Dominic's eye, dwelling upon her consideringly as Larry brought the Land-Rover to a halt close to the terrace steps. 'Yes, you're right, I'm talking too much because I'm nervous. I invited myself here. I know it.'

'You talked a blue streak of truth there,' Dominic said honestly. 'I wouldn't worry about your rights and titles. This sort of caravansarai absorbs visitors wholesale. Come on, let's go and find the host.'

They clambered out, shaking the dust out of their clothes self-consciously. Lakshman withdrew into the background here; this was no duty of his. It was Dominic who led the way up the staircase to the terrace, and crossed to the open door under the wide eaves.

And suddenly, none of them ever quite knew how, there was a young man standing under the lintel, waiting formally to welcome them. They had heard nothing; he moved gently and fastidiously, after the manner of his race and the code of his aristocratic line. But he had heard the Land-Rover arrive, and needed no other summons, being the punctilious host he was. Probably he had been listening for their engine for an hour and more, whatever he had been doing in the meantime. He stood quite still in the doorway of his house to welcome his guests, the least pretentious figure in the world, and the gravest, a slim, neatly-moulded young man in thin grey flannels and an open-necked white shirt, with short-cropped black hair that waved slightly on his temples, and a spark of something remote and touching, hope of companionship, recollection of gaiety, faith in the possibility of friendship, something intimately connected with England and the English, in his large, proud, aloof and lonely dark eyes.

'I'm Purushottam Narayanan,' he said, in a clear, courteous, almost didactic voice. 'Everything's ready for you. Do come in!'

The hospitality of the Narayanan household was absolute but not elaborate, the furnishings of the rooms comfortable but simple, and Indian style, like the dinner they presently ate in a large and rather bare room overlooking the terrace and the small, glimmering fires and lamps of the village below. Cutlery and some nine or ten dishes of various vegetables and curries were set out on a large table, and everyone on entering was handed a warmed plate and turned loose to charge it as he felt inclined. The host, attentive, grave and reserved as yet, told them what each dish contained, and added punctilious warnings where he felt the contents might be rather highly spiced for their tastes. Then they all sat down with their selections at a smaller table set in the window, and two servants hovered in the background, ready to offer replenishments at a nod from their master.

Afterwards the servants brought bowls of a creamy sweet made with rice, its surface covered with tissue-thin sheets of silver foil, which were also meant to be eaten; and fruit, in a bowl of water, and rich, strong coffee.

By this time they had exchanged all the courtesies, the host expressing his gratitude for their company and his pleasure in it, the guests their thanks for his kindness and their appreciation of all the thought he had given to their comfort; and still they were no nearer knowing whether his pleasure was personal or formal, his gratitude heartfelt, even desperate, or merely an acceptable phrase. He sat among them, cross-legged at one end of the long seat built into the window, talking intelligently about merely current things, such as the Indian scene, and their journey, and their intended onward journey, his large, unwavering dark eyes moving intently from face to face, and no gesture missing and nothing undone that could contribute to their well-being; but some inward part of him might as well have been, and probably was, a million miles away from them.

He was by no means a small man, being fully as tall as Dominic, though still a couple of inches short of Larry's gangling height; but he was built in the slender South Indian style, with light bones and smooth, athletic flesh, and in repose he looked almost fragile; an impression reinforced by the refinement and tension of his face, which was clearly but suavely cut, without any of the hawk-likeness of Lakshman's Punjabi features. The moulding of his lips was fastidious and reticent, the poise of his head very erect, even drawn a little back, as though in insurmountable reserve. And out of this austere countenance the melting southern eyes gazed doubtfully, withholding communication, even while he discoursed politely and plied them with favours.

But there was nothing indecisive about the face, and nothing to suggest that the part of him he kept private was not engaged at this very moment in furious and resolute activity of its own.

'I must apologise,' he said, when even the coffee had been cleared away, 'for being such a poor host. I have been too preoccupied with this responsibility here, to which I'm not accustomed at all. Give me a few months, and when I have all this moving as I want it to move, then you must come again, and let me have more time to show you the countryside.' Not a word of his father's death and his own recall to take over the household; such family concerns must not be inflicted upon girl guests. 'I realise that you have made your own plans, too, of course. But you will at least have tomorrow? You need not leave until the next day?'

'No, Wednesday morning we'd planned on moving,' Larry agreed.

'And at what hour ought you to set out?' For the first time he smiled, a little self-consciously. 'I'm sorry, that sounds terrible. I would be happy if you need not leave at all that day, but you see, my father's lawyer is coming that morning to help me clear up all the affairs my father left in confusion. He was ill for some time before he died, though we never realised how ill, and things were a little neglected, not to mention a law-suit he had with a cousin over a plot of land lower down in the plain. That's why I have been locking myself in his office all day and every day, trying to get everything sorted out for when the solicitor comes. I would like to arrange my meeting with him for an hour that won't inconvenience you at all.'

'We ought to make an early start,' said Larry. 'We have to drop the girls in Nagarcoil, and then go on to Cape Comorin. I think we should say seven in the morning.'

'Then I shall arrange for Mr Das Gupta to come at eight. I shall send my car down to Koilpatti to fetch him, after you have left. He drives, but badly, and our road up here is not good, he will be glad to have transport. Now we need not think any more about departures. You have tomorrow, and we can do quite a lot with that.' He looked across at Dominic. 'You will come out with me and have a look at the set-up here? I should be grateful. I have some ideas, but you will know better than I if they are practicable.'

'I'm only a herald for the Swami,' Dominic said, 'he's coming down himself as soon as he can. But naturally I was hoping to get a look at things while I'm here, and let him have an outline of what you have in mind. There'll be a good deal of ground to cover?'

'We can put in all day on it, easily. Perhaps we could borrow the Land-Rover for the day?' He turned to flash a sudden engaging smile at Larry. 'And Dominic tells me – he mentioned it on the telephone – that you are a civil engineer, and have been working on an irrigation scheme up north. Is that right?'

Larry admitted it, without bothering to add that he feared for his plan's survival.

'Then you're just the man we want! Please come out with us. You see, further up here towards the hills we have a small river which is a tributary of the Vaipar, and centuries ago there was a whole system of tanks built down its course, with earth dams. They've been out of use and overgrown – oh, three hundred years, I'd guess – but I believe it wouldn't be impossible to reconstruct the whole system. With earth dams they were a poor risk in the rains – if the top bund went, the whole lot went, that's why they were abandoned. But it wouldn't be so difficult, with a little capital, to put in a more durable system now on the same line. Come with us, and see!'

'Sure I'll come, glad to!' And Larry would have been willing and ready to launch into a whole technical discussion of the water situation in Tamil Nadu, and the possibility of harnessing more of the rivers of Kerala, on the narrower, better-watered west of the Ghats, to irrigate the drier plains on the east; but Purushottam diverted the flow. It was necessary to make plans, but as briefly as possible. Tomorrow they could talk water, and rice, and terracing, and the mysterious ancient tanks of Malaikuppam, the whole day long. Tonight they must devote themselves to making the girls' stay here pleasant.

'And for you, Miss Galloway and Miss Madhavan, I think we can arrange something more interesting. I hope I have done the right thing. Dominic mentioned when he telephoned that you had originally intended going to Kuttalam. It's less than forty miles from here, so why should you miss it? My car will take you there tomorrow, if you would like that, and Lakshman will take care of you while we are busy. In the evening we shall all be together again.'

'It sounds perfect,' said Patti dutifully. Too perfect, she thought, exchanging a glance with Priya, we're being disposed of while the business men confer. And suddenly she would have liked to think of a way of piercing through that impregnable defence, that barrier of attentive politeness that fended them off so successfully and yet left them no ground for complaint. 'I don't suppose Inspector Raju would mind if we make a day-trip, Priya, do you?'

'Inspector Raju?' said Purushottam, drawing his fine black brows together in a frown of inquiry.

'Oh! – I see Dominic didn't tell you everything on the

phone. So he didn't explain how they came to acquire two girls as well as the original party. I'm sorry, I didn't realise.' But she had realised; how could Dominic possibly have put over that entire long story in the few minutes he had taken over his call from Thekady? 'It isn't such a pleasant story, I'm sorry now I spoke. We got mixed up with a police inquiry, that's all, and we're supposed to be on call if needed. But we shall be back here by evening. And I would like to go, very much.'

She knew, of course, that it could not rest there; once she had said so much, somebody had to tell all the rest, otherwise no one would have any peace of mind. It was Dominic who took on the job of filling in the gaps, since Purushottam was primarily his concern.

'I didn't go into it on the phone because the inspector was waiting, and time was precious. But I should probably have told you tomorrow in any case.' Tomorrow again, when they would have got rid of the women, and have the whole day for their own concerns, thought Patti. But instead he told it now, briefly but accurately. Purushottam listened with close and shocked attention, and his brows levelled into a ruled line across his forehead. Once he looked at Priya, and not involuntarily or fleetingly, but a long, straight, piercing look, as though he saw her for the first time. In the face of his own overwhelming preoccupations, it was an achievement to have astonished Purushottam.

'And you think there may be other Naxalite agents active in these parts? It wouldn't be the first time, of course, there have been cases here before. A couple of them were picked up near the Nepalese border a week or so ago, so there doesn't seem to be much of a limit on their movements. I'm so sorry that you had to go through an ordeal like that.'

Patti asked, with wincing curiosity: 'It doesn't make you wish you hadn't come home? Or that you were in some different line, and not stuck with all this big estate? It's such a vulnerable position once you've got a revolutionary

Left with members prepared to throw away their own lives for a cause – like this man Ajit Ghose.'

He gave a brief, almost scornful heave of his shoulders, and his mobile lips curled in what was not quite a smile. 'I've got work to do here, and I'm going to do it. I want to see this land twice as productive and twice as effectively run as ever before, and chalking up a substantial profit annually to prove it. I'm going to make two crops of rice grow where only one grew before, and where we're already getting a *thaladi* crop of sorts, I'm going to boost it by at least fifty per cent. And I don't want this to be a monoculture farm, either, I want banana plantations and some other crops, so that we can provide better than just casual work. I'm going to see this land paying and producing the way I want it to – or die trying. You know what it says in the Baghavadgita: Do what you must, and give no thought to the consequences. "But if thou wilt not wage this lawful battle, then wilt thou fail thine own law and thine own honour, and get sin." '

'The trouble is,' Patti said after a moment of silence, 'the Naxalites probably quote the Baghavadgita, too, and I bet Krishna says exactly the same to them.'

The three of them came slowly down the long hillside together, to where they had left the Land-Rover parked in the meal-white dust at the side of the track. Behind them the ground rose in broken folds, and there were the sparse beginnings of the forests that proliferated, far above, into dense jungle. Before them the open, rolling land lay outspread, fields and groves and villages, threads of shrunken water, standing crops and grazing cattle. They walked alongside the almost dry watercourse, marking at each decline the ridges in the ground where once the bunds of the irrigation tanks had been, mysterious hummocks under the grass.

They were talking hard enough now, with animation and

point. The tanks could, Larry was positive, be put back into operation at comparatively little expense, given ample and willing labour. And much could be done at the same time to level some of these bordering fields, and conserve water and soil by discreet terracing.

'Ours isn't a delta economy, we're never going to get three crops off our ground. But we can get two, given these quick-maturing new hybrids the government are producing at Adutharai.'

'We've been doing some work along the same lines ourselves,' said Dominic, 'in our own laboratory. And our situation isn't very different from yours here. The Swami will probably bring Satyavan Kumar along to have a look at your land, as soon as he can. He's the man you want on seeds.'

'You know what we could do with most of all? Some sort of small, agriculturally-based industries. Something that will give a chance of steady employment, instead of casual. Capital isn't going to be a problem so much. My father left a great deal of money. And you've seen my place – what do I want with all that accommodation? It will make central stores and offices, and there's plenty of room to build more plant and workshops as we grow. And we've got plenty of skills, and some good, shrewd heads among the village councils. Three of the villages are bold enough and clever enough to come in from the start, two more will probably follow them in. The others will take a season or two to make up their minds, and all we've got to do to get them in is show an improved profit. Once they see their neighbours growing more prosperous, they'll want to come in, too.'

They had reached the road and the Land-Rover. Purushottam stooped and took up a few caked fragments of the brown earth, and crumbled them in his fingers, frowning down at them thoughtfully.

'I was very fond of my father, but I never did see eye to eye with him. That made me feel terribly guilty when he died, and I had to come home. Not that coming home is very easy, in any case, after living such a different life there in England. You feel a stranger here and an alien there. But I couldn't live anywhere else than in India, not permanently, so the thing to do seems to be to settle down as fast as possible. Not by following up what my father was trying to do, though. That would be a thumping lie for me. He tried to hang on to every acre, you know – he was a good landlord, mind you, and what he felt was partly out of loyalty to his tenants, but he didn't know how to change. He was a bit of a litigant by inclination, too, in his middle years, and there've been complications. Now I've got the clearing up to do, and I know what I want, and with the Swami's help we may be able to strike an agreement with the authorities.'

'His credit's high, in the state and centrally,' said Dominic, 'and he'll do everything he can, you can rely on that.'

'I've no ambition to be a landlord, none at all, but I do want to see all this land being put to the best possible use and paying good money to everybody who farms it, and it seemed to me that a co-operative grouping was the best way. And if the co-operative does get floated, and will find me a useful job, I'll be satisfied. I'm ready to plough as much as possible of my father's money into the funds.' He ran the fine brown dust through his fingers and let it sift to the ground. 'Water's the main need. Not much use looking for ground water here, though. Pity!'

'Those tanks can be brought back into service,' Larry assured him, 'and once you've got your fields levelled, contour channels will cost you very little. You'll get your water if you get your labour. And if they don't make you chairman of the co-operative, there's no gratitude or justice.'

Purushottam tilted his head back and laughed aloud. It was the first time they had heard him laugh, and it was a gay, impulsive, almost startling sound. Only now did they realise that something of the quality of defensive isolation had been banished from his eyes, and the pale, finely-drawn tension had left his features as the formal self-consciousness had been shed from his gait and gestures. It was an unobtrusive transformation, but a complete one. For these two or three weeks, since his homecoming to perform the son's part at a funeral, he must have been the loneliest young man in India, and suddenly he had companions, even allies.

'I don't think I'm cut out for a chairman, somehow. I'll probably end up as general dog's-body and mechanic, like Dominic. Do you think I can keep up a household like mine on that? At least until we convert them all into agricultural workers?'

They drove back to the house in the early evening in high content, and the light grew rose-coloured in the sky to westward. Patti and Priya and Lakshman were home before them from Kuttalam, and the servants were keeping watch on the dinner with one eye and the courtyard with the other, waiting for the last of the company to return before serving the meal.

During dinner Purushottam made a valiant effort to keep the conversation general, and defer to everything the girls had to say; but once the big table was cleared it was not long before the large-scale maps came out to cover it again, and the men gathered round with heads bent seriously together, tracing the fall of the land and the course of the meagre rivers, and marking out the possible immediate scope of the new farm.

'You cannot farm this land by smallholding, and that is what people here are still trying to do. The result is debt everywhere at the first monsoon failure, or the first blight, because there are never any reserves. It can only be made effective on a large scale.'

'And with a diversified economy.'

'Exactly. And we are not dealing with a silt-fertilised soil like the deltas, where even on a big scale hand-labour pays off better than mechanical methods. We have less to lose and more to gain.'

They called in Lakshman to view the land they had surveyed during the day, and left the two girls to the newspapers and the radio. Patti watched the hands of the clock slip slowly past the hour of nine, and asked Purushottam resignedly: 'Have you got a typewriter, by any chance? If you wouldn't mind, I should like to write a letter home. What with all the trouble at Thekady, I haven't written for a while, and they do rather tend to expect them every few days.'

He jumped up remorsefully from the table. 'I'm so sorry, we're neglecting you terribly. Yes, there's a typewriter in the office, but it's a huge old table machine. I could have them bring it up here for you...'

'No, really, there's no need, if I can borrow the office for an hour or so. I won't disturb anything there. It's just that there really hasn't been a chance until now, and my mother is the worrying kind.'

'Of course, if you'll be comfortable enough there. It might be quieter for you, that's true, it's right across at the edge of the yard. I'll come down with you.'

She protested that she would find it, but he came, all the same. Above the beaten earth of the lower yard the sky arched immense and full of stars, the darkest of blues, and yet so clear that it seemed to have a luminous quality of its own. The low white buildings gathered out of the air whatever light remained, and shone faintly lambent, hollow-eyed with deep windows and doorways, with here and there the murmur of voices and the spark of a lamp. The office, as he had said, was the most remote of all the buildings, even its windows turned away from the yard which all through the day was the centre of activity in the household. It was thick-walled and not very large, one wall stacked high with cupboards and filing cabinets, a big desk set near the window. Both it and the typewriter on it were littered with papers and folders.

'You were in the middle of something. I'm sorry!'

'No, I'm nearly straight now. When Mr Das Gupta gets here tomorrow morning I shall be ready for him.' He swept up the scattered papers and moved them out of her way, and whipped the current sheet out of the machine in such a hurry that he tore it. She exclaimed in regret, and he laughed. 'It doesn't matter. I left it so hurriedly this morning that I should have had to do it again in any case, I've completely lost the thread. It isn't more than a quarter of an hour's work, I'll do it early in the morning.'

'A lot of money certainly makes a lot of work,' she said, so gravely that there was no offence in it. 'Don't you ever want to drop the whole thing and just walk out?'

'I never walked out on anything yet. You can't abdicate your responsibilities, whatever they are.'

'No,' she agreed, 'you can't do that. Krishna was right.'

Purushottam shook up the cushion to make the typing chair a little higher for her, and looked round to make sure the light was adequate on the carriage. 'My father hated figures so much – on paper, that is, he was clever enough with them in his head – that he made this office right away in the corner by the kitchen garden to be free from distractions while he struggled with them. I've had cause to be glad about that myself now. You're sure you have everything you need? There are stamps here, do take whatever you want.'

He left her to it; and only a few paces from the door she heard him break into a light, fleet run, so eager was he to get back to the plans for his super-farm. She sat down at the desk, and fed a clean sheet of paper into the machine, and began to type her letter home.

By the time Priya and Dominic came to look for her, more than an hour later, she had finished not one letter, but two, and was just folding the second into its envelope.

'One to my grandmother in Scotland, too. They're both edited rather radically – I could hardly tell them we were so close to what happened in Thekady, could I, they'd be having fits! There,' she said, thumping down the flap of the envelope, 'that's duty done for the next two or three days.' And she reached into her big shoulder-bag, which was slung over the arm of the chair, for her own store of stamps. She was glad it was not Purushottam who had come to fetch her back to the house; he might have been hurt at seeing her use her own stamps when he had offered her his, and she would have been sorry to hurt him.

Six

Malaikuppam: Wednesday Morning

They were up for breakfast at six, but Purushottam had been up for an hour and more by that time, first superintending the preparation of a supply of food for them to take with them, then re-typing the memorandum he had spoiled the previous day. He was a rapid but erratic typist, and by the time he was called to breakfast he had finished the job, and turned to arranging everything relevant in order, and tidying away everything irrelevant from sight. A quarter of an hour's strenuous work after the Land-Rover had departed, and everything would be ready.

A dark-brown maidservant, too shy to speak, brought morning tea to Patti and Priya in their room. She drew the curtains, and there on the table beside Patti's large bag were the two letters, ready stamped and labelled for air mail.

'Purushottam will send them to the post for you,' said Priya.

'Oh, I'll take them with me. We can drop them in a box in the first town we pass through. You got on to first-name terms with him over the maps, did you?' she said carelessly.

'No,' said Priya composedly. 'I just thought of him so. I have not called him so as yet.'

They dressed and packed briskly, forewarned by now of Larry's strict time-keeping. In four hours or so they would be in Nagarcoil. Home, for Priya; and even for Patti, in a sense, home.

India had not quite grasped the vital nature of time to a western mind, and both the tea and coffee came rather late; but in spite of that, it was only just after seven o'clock when they all walked out to the terrace, and down the steps to where the Land-Rover waited. The servants had collected all the bags from their rooms, and waited to stow them wherever Lakshman indicated. Larry had the bonnet of the Land-Rover up, intent on the engine. Purushottam and Dominic found themselves standing together in the soft morning light, with nothing left to be done. They looked at each other and smiled.

'Please give my reverences and regards to the Swami, if you should see him again before he finds time for me. Tell him I rely on him to smooth my passage with the state government. If they agree to let me do it this way, nobody in Delhi will raise any difficulties. I've thought about this ever since I got the news, in England . . .'

He had never felt alone or lonely in England until then; never until his widowed father died in his prime, and left to a virtual stranger – yes, however loving and bound, still a stranger – the estate he had tried to hold inviolate against the tide of events. Then in an instant he had known how Indian he was, and felt the tendons of his heart contracting and driving him back here, where he had been raised, where he knew every soul in the nearest three villages, every tenant for ten miles around, and felt for them as his father had felt, but had other means of expressing his membership.

'No, before then, really. Ever since I began to grow up and think for myself, and not just as I was taught. We could be almost self-supporting here. They all keep two or three buffalo, the women take care of them, they want them for milk, and labour, and manure. Give us time, and we might have a dairy, too – not a huge affair like Anand, just a small district Anand. And we have smiths, good workmen, we could be the district tool-shop and repair station within a year. From that it isn't so far to a small factory for specialist tools – why not?'

'Why not?' agreed Dominic. In India there is one factor

which is never missing and never in short supply: manual skill of all kinds, prepared to copy anything, prepared to improvise anything, given the idea. Something not to be found in repetitive processes, production belts and modern organisation of labour.

The two girls stood a little apart, ready to get aboard when everything was loaded. They had done everything they had to do, and now there was nothing whatever to distract them from listening.

'Do you really think they'll buy the idea?'

'I don't see why not. They've been known to say that the co-operative is the hope of rural India, why should they back out on it in this case? And if the Swami and the Mission come in on it, that should clinch it.

'There'll be some tricky relationships to be settled, of course, what with hoping to bring in the small cultivators and the Harijan labourers on a fair footing, but that's for the legal men to work out. It can be done all right, given the goodwill, and I do believe we shall have that. Just as long as they accept the idea in principle!'

'They'd be crazy if they didn't,' Dominic said, 'considering you're offering to give them the central base, a good deal of equipment, all your land and pretty well all the capital you possess.'

'Well, not quite all, you know. I've got some industrial stock and a bit of money my mother left me, I'm keeping that for insurance. But what do I need with a plantation establishment like this? My generation doesn't want to live this way. I don't really need any more, basically, than any man down there in the village – less than those who've got families to feed. I rather look forward to working my own passage on the same terms as the rest. Not that it will work out that way,' he added honestly. 'The name counts for a lot, and there's no way of altering that even if I wanted to. I shall be voted in there somewhere among the management, I know that. And I shall enjoy it, too, making this district work for every soul who lives in it, more efficiently than it's ever worked before. But at least I shall have to be *voted* in! If there'd been anyone left in the family but myself and one decrepit old great-aunt,' he admitted, 'it wouldn't have been so simple. But there's no one now to object if I choose to give away everything I've got.'

He would not have said that so simply if he had remembered that the girls were only a couple of yards away; but he had forgotten them utterly, he was speaking only to Dominic, who already knew his mind.

The luggage was all stowed. Lakshman opened the door for the girls to climb aboard, and Larry shut down the hood, and drew breath to make his farewells.

'You've been immensely kind to let us all descend on you like this —'

Patti, who had opened her shoulder-bag and was rummaging frantically in its tangled interior, suddenly exclaimed: 'Damn! I knew I should leave something behind. Is the office open, Purushottam? I went and left my diary in there last night, I remember now . . . I must run and fetch it!'

'I'll go!' he offered immediately, but she was already in flight.

'No, I know exactly where I left it. I won't be a moment!' Back over her shoulder floated a long-drawn: 'Sorry, everybody!' She ran, the bag bobbing under her arm, all down the gently sloping court, little puffs of dust dancing at her heels.

'Just like a woman,' said Larry philosophically, and glanced at his watch. 'Oh, not so bad! Only eight minutes late.'

'After some months in my country that's extraordinarily good time-keeping.'

'Look, you've got my address – let me know if you get started on the work here, and if I'm still around I'd like to be in on it.'

'I shall be glad if you can! In any case, come again before you leave India.' They stood and waited. Patti had vanished into the deep doorway of the distant office. Still they waited, and she did not reappear.

'So she knew exactly where she'd left it!' said Larry resignedly.

'I'll go and help her look,' Priya offered.

She had taken no more than two or three steps away from the Land-Rover when there was suddenly a curious quiver that shook the outlines of solid objects, and made the earth seem to heave with an imprisoned and contained life of its own. Then a muffled reverberation like a great, smothered gust of air caused the shape of the office to bulge and quiver, the thatch lifted and lurched drunkenly aside, borne on a wave of dust, the splintered door sagged outwards and fell from its upper hinge, and from the windows at the rear two clouds of dust and debris billowed, dissolving slowly into air. The sound of the explosion was strangely deadened and contained within the yard-thick mud walls, but the blast came undulating like a snake across the earth, smoking with dust-devils, whipped at the folds of Priya's sari and slashed her ankles with gravel. Her eyes were blinded, and the wind pressed against her, holding her motionless. She felt someone's arm take her about the waist, and someone's body intervene between her and the tearing force that assaulted her; and she clung with closed eyes to this sheltering body until the ravaging wind had spent itself and left them still upright. She heard someone's voice saying, even before the sound of running feet began:

'Oh, my God, my God, not again!'

And another voice, her own voice, saying, not entreatingly, but with fierce professional authority, as she looked up into Purushottam's face:

'Let me go! Let me go to her! This is my job!'

The office, when they groped their way into it through

the dense fog of dust and the particles of paper, wood-splinters and debris from the burst thatch, was a scarred shell, windows and window-frames blown out and scattered over the kitchen-garden at the rear, where three terrified but undamaged children crouched screaming hysterically, the door a tangle of sagging planks, the floor deep in wreckage. What was left of the typewriter, a skeleton of torn-out keys and twisted metal, lay under the shattered windows. The desk, every joint ripped asunder, lolled against the wall.

They stumbled over the body of Patti Galloway as they fumbled their way blindly within, and at first they did not even realise what it was. Papers and dust covered her, she was a roll of matter powdered over with dissolution. Tatters of clothing draped her, once they brushed the dust aside, but she was ravaged and disrupted like a rag-doll torn up in a temper. Dominic retrieved one sandal from the far corner of the little room. The tight enclosure of this place had magnified the effect of the explosive far beyond what they had seen in the open at Thekady. And yet there seemed to be some things that were almost untouched, the soft, pliable things that blew in the wind and made no resistance, like the long, straight fair hair that slid fluidly over Priya's arm as she raised the mangled head.

Patti was dead before they ever reached her.

Seven

Malaikuppam: Wednesday Evening

None of them, until some time afterwards, really got the events of that day into focus, or could link them into any significant sequence. They reacted rationally, answered questions coherently, even remembered abstruse and advisable precautions, and took them as a matter of course; but all in a haze, like automatons responding to automatic stimuli. Too shocked to feel, they could still think and reason, and do what the circumstances demanded of them.

So they left Patti lying where they had found her, because even her position might mean something to the trained observer, something to indicate where the explosive had been placed, and how fired. There was nothing they could do for her, except, as soon as it was bearable and time had allowed them to thaw out enough to recognise the necessity, to let her parents know what had happened to her, and perhaps, also, inform whoever had been more or less responsible for her in this country, her head teacher, or the business acquaintance of her father who had got her the job. No one could help Patti herself any more. If there is such a thing as instantaneous death, that was what had happened to her, and nobody could undo it.

So they set a guard on the doorway of the wrecked office, and another of Purushottam's servants in the garden at the rear; and Priya, still blindly following her own nature, retrieved the screaming children from among the vegetables, and made sure they had not a scratch upon them before she handed them over, now shaken only by hiccoughing sobs, to their distraught mothers. After that they went back to the house, all of them walking rapidly and mechanically like somnambulists, chilled of face and unnaturally wide and fixed of eye, and the telephoning began. First the local police; and they were not so far gone as not to realise that Purushottam's family name would count for a great deal there. Then to Mr Das Gupta in Koilpatti, to tell him that no car would be coming for him today, that no meeting was possible today. Not the reason, however; not yet. Later they might well feel that they needed his legal advice, but first they must let the police have their head. Touch nothing, alter nothing, inflect nothing. The loaded Land-Rover still stood below the terrace; they had forgotten it, until Purushottam sent out a servant to bring in the bags and remove the food before the heat of the day began. They all knew there would be no departure now.

'We ought,' said Dominic, expressing what they were all feeling, 'to let Inspector Raju know what has happened, too.'

For this could hardly be anything but a corollary of the affair at Thekady. Either one more in a series of outrages which had begun there, or else a move to eliminate witnesses of the first crime. They hovered between the two opinions, but the one thing they could not believe was that this was an unconnected incident. They had blundered into a labyrinth, perhaps merely by reason of being on the boat that discovered the murdered body of Mahendralal Bakhle; and now every move to find the way out might be the wrong move.

'It is a delicate matter,' said Purushottam. 'We are in Tamil Nadu, and the lake is in Kerala, and the state police can be jealous of their rights. We must wait until they come. But as it does seem to be a continuation of your Inspector Raju's case, they may even be glad to call him into consultation. We should be diplomatic.'

They could use such terms, and consider such niceties, while all the time within their shut minds the frantic thoughts kept running round and round in circles like shot animals trying to reach their own pain: 'Patti's dead. She left her diary in the office, and she remembered it and ran back for it, and the office blew up in her face and killed her. Ten minutes more, and the Land-Rover would have been on its way, and she would have been safe on board – but then Purushottam would have shut himself in there with his accounts – Patti delayed the departure, and it's Patti who's dead . . . *But which were they after?*'

'But we could call the Swami,' said Dominic.

'In Delhi?' It seemed almost as far away as America.

'Why not?' He wanted to hear the sanest, most reassuring and detached voice he knew. It had a way of settling things into a true perspective, even death. This was not the first time he had faced the Swami Premanathanand across a murdered body, and perceived in consequence that death is only a part of the picture, however inevitable and omnipresent. 'He'll need to know what's happened, since he sent me here, and he's quite certainly concerned about you.'

'Yes,' agreed Purushottam, faintly encouraged. 'I suppose it might be a good idea at least to let him know what's happened.'

It took Dominic some little time to get his call through and even when he reached the number that belonged to the haphazard little central office of the Mission, buried in the narrow complexities of the Sadar Bazaar, it took him longer still to get hold of the Swami. There was a minor policy conference in progress over the projected purchase of some new agricultural machines, and the Swami could leave the council only for a few hurried minutes. Dominic could picture the earnest heads bent over coloured brochures, and all the ardent faces, young and old, so lit up with partisan enthusiasm that the sharp western mind would never recognise their angelic shrewdness and practicality until they had beaten down his prices and extracted from him his most effective lines. They had a small factory in Andhra where they were making their own, working them out to specification according to regional needs, but they couldn't yet do everything themselves. And angels need to be both practical and shrewd, in order to hold their own with fallible mankind.

The distant voice, gentle, courteous and abstracted, said in his ear: 'I have only a few moments, I am sorry. You are at Malaikuppam?'

'Yes, Swami, we're here. Since the day before yesterday...'

'And all is well with you and Purushottam?'

'No, nothing is well. We need your advice.'

'Tell me,' said the Swami alertly, and composed himself to listen in silence. When the brief but shattering recital was completed, he continued silent for a moment, and then he made utterance twice, with a thoughtful pause between, and very gently hung up the receiver.

Dominic came back into the room where the others waited; all their eyes were on him, and Priya at least seemed to see in his face something heartening, as though he had been given a promise, and carried the sheer relief and reassurance of it in his eyes.

'What did he say?'

'He said,' Dominic reported faithfully, '"To the born sure is death, to the dead sure is birth; so for an issue that may not be escaped thou dost not well to sorrow."'

'Helpful!' said Larry sourly, his New England mentality outraged.

'And then he said: "I will think what is best to be done." And hung up.'

'And is that all?'

'You don't know him,' said Dominic.

Strangely, as if a strangled spring had been released to gush freely, Priya bent her shining black head and began to cry, freely and quietly, not like a heart breaking but like a broken heart beginning to mend. And Purushottam, far too Indian to put an arm round her, nevertheless leaned forward with a gesture of fastidious delicacy, almost of fear, as though he had astonished himself, and took her hand in his.

The Tamil inspector of police from the district H.Q. was a strong contrast to Inspector Raju, a highly-strung, insecure man who made a fair amount of noise over his activities; but luckily his insecurity prompted him to accept a highly-convenient let-out when it was offered. After lengthy discussion by telephone with his District Superintendent he gave it as their joint opinion that the Keralese authorities should certainly be called into consultation, since this appeared to belong to Inspector Raju's prior case. The probability must at least be examined. Meantime, all the witnesses were kept waiting in suspense inside the house, while Purushottam showed the police officers the scene of the tragedy. Then he, too, was dispatched to wait with the others.

It was no wonder that they had a long time to wait. They had seen the desolation of the office, every shard of which would have to be examined; for somewhere there were the fragments, such as remained, of the second bomb. And they had seen the violation of Patti, with which the police doctor was now engaged. What they had to tell was of secondary urgency. They waited now in a very slightly relaxed but still numbed quietness, chilled with shock for all the growing heat of the day. The servants brought food, but no one did more than play with it, if this helpless distaste could be described as play. Only late in the afternoon did Inspector Tilak get to them, and even then it was to inform them that Inspector Raju had been notified several hours previously, and was on his way. The satisfaction in his voice was carefully suppressed but none the less present. The death of an English girl in a terrorist outrage was a very hot potato, which he was by no means sorry to be allowed to drop in the lap of the police of the next state. What he wanted to hear from them first, therefore, was the whole story of the events at Thekady; and they told them separately, each of them remembering in isolation. Their statements regarding the new outrage were left to wait until Inspector Raju arrived, as in the early evening he did, driven by Sergeant Gokhale in a rather unexpected Mercedes.

Mindful of his duties as a host, Purushottam had made provision for them. A meal was waiting, and there were rooms prepared, since clearly they could not return to their own state this same night. The two inspectors had a lengthy session together before they interviewed their witnesses, and it was past nine o'clock by the time they had all made their second statements, and were assembled again in conference. It seemed that Inspector Raju, in view of what they knew already, saw no point in concealing from them those aspects of this case which linked up only too surely with the previous one.

'Mr Bakhle was killed by a bomb, deliberately planted on board his boat. I can tell you now that the bomb that killed Miss Galloway, of which we have found fragments – more fragmentary, unfortunately, than in the last case – seems to have been manufactured in a similar way, with the same materials, probably by the same hand and at the same time. The connection is clear. We cannot reconstruct the dial of the firing device this time, and we don't know for what hour it was set, for there is a possibility that it may have gone off through some unexpected shock or vibration. So we can't deduce from the time of the explosion anything precise about the person for whom it was meant. But I'm sure you will not have missed the implications. In five or ten minutes more the party would have left, and it seems obvious from your statements that after your departure Mr Narayanan would have gone back to his work in the office, in preparation for his lawyer's intended visit.'

He looked round them all, and his lined face was a little grey and tired after his journey, but there was nothing wrong with the sharpness of his eyes.

'Yes, it is true, not everyone could have known that fact, though all this household could, as well as yourselves. But that is less significant than you may think, for the fact seems to be that ever since his father's funeral rites Mr Narayanan has spent much of his waking time in there, and that may be well known by now to most of the district. It could also very easily have been learned by anyone making a private study of Mr Narayanan's habits. I have seen for myself that though there may be a watchman during the night, this house is virtually open twenty-four hours a day. The gate is almost never closed, but even if it were, the wall would be very easy to scale. In short, the bomb could easily have been planted during the night by someone who had watched Mr Narayanan's routine for some days, but perhaps had not even realised that he now had guests. The necessary observations may well have been made before your arrival. But in any case another death, the death of an innocent bystander, quite uninvolved in any ideological struggles in India, would not worry the people who plant bombs to do their work. To them Miss Galloway, I'm afraid, merely represents the loss of a little explosive. They have more.'

Quietly and carefully Dominic said: 'You're saying, Inspector, that the attack was meant for Purushottam. Not for Patti.'

'I am saying that quite clearly that is the inference you have all drawn from the occurrence. It is, indeed, the inference anyone would draw. So much so, that now I am only wondering, and perhaps asking you to consider the possibility, too, whether that is not what we are all meant to think. Here is another landlord, a vulnerable target, obviously the bomb was meant for him.'

Purushottam's sombre face did not change; the idea was not new to him. Nor did it seem to impress him very much, after the day they had spent here together, and the sights they still carried burned within their eyes, and could not stop seeing.

'But,' said Inspector Raju, 'There are many landlords, some more obvious targets than our friend here. Here is a new bomb outrage, at the home of the land-owner who *happens* to be entertaining the witnesses closest to the Bakhle killing at Thekady, and that bomb outrage just *happens* to wipe out one of those witnesses, instead of the host. I am not very fond of coincidences. I always tend to look round behind them – almost to believe that they are not coincidences at all. Therefore I would like you to consider the possibility that an agent of the Naxalites may very well have moved here from Thekady to Malaikuppam, not because his next victim had already been marked down here, but *because he was following you, the witnesses.*'

'But in that case,' said Larry, galvanised into speculation almost against his will, 'if he wanted to get rid of *us*, why not plant his bomb in the Land-Rover, and time it for when we were well away from here? It would be the safest method I can think of.'

'Because, Mr Preisinger, for the past two nights Mr Narayanan's watchman has been making your Land-Rover his base. He is a romantic, and to him a Land-Rover is an exotic wonder. You may be sure no one has had the opportunity of violating that sacred vehicle. Moreover, supposing there was a choice among witnesses – some, say, who knew virtually nothing, one who had some special knowledge – they would have preferred to aim, at least, at getting the vital one, and letting the others go. Many deaths are acceptable in a pinch, but need not be wastefully incurred where they are not necessary. And Miss Galloway had made use of the office yesterday evening. She may have been under observation then – even so closely that someone knew she had left her diary there. I do not say it is so. I say only that it is something to be considered, and I ask you to consider it.'

'She wrote two letters,' said Priya suddenly, raising her

heavy dark eyes. 'She had them sealed and stamped in her bag, ready to post. If she had any knowledge – if there was anything troubling her – may she not have put it into her letters home?'

'We had already thought of the same possibility, Miss Madhavan. The bag is virtually undamaged. We have opened the letters. They are exactly what would be expected of a young girl's letters home – quite straightforward accounts of her travels, only omitting, understandably, the ugly experience at Thekady. There is nothing there for us. Naturally they will be passed on to her family. But what made you think of that? Had she behaved as if she had some secret and dangerous knowledge? Her collapse at Thekady now almost suggests that she believed she knew something of perilous importance, and was frightened to confide it – frightened to a degree which cannot quite be accounted for by the shock of the discovery, which was common to you all. And under which, I must say, you yourself behaved with exemplary fortitude.'

She hardly heard the compliment, though if she had it might have given her both pleasure and pain. She was peering into pure air before her, frowning anxiously.

'I don't know ... She'd had such a sheltered life until she came to India, naturally she was very much upset by the manner of Mr Bakhle's death. She had never known anything like that. I don't know, it would be easy to misinterpret what was no more than the after-effects of shock. What can I say? I hardly knew her. Surely you must have looked through all her belongings. Was there nothing?'

'Nothing. For of course you are right, we have looked.'

'And the diary she left behind – it was very important to her, she ran at once to recover it – like the wind she ran.'

'Ah, the diary!' Inspector Raju drew a long breath. 'What has become of that? Who will tell us? We have sifted through every scrap of paper that remains in that office, Miss Madhavan. But we have found no diary.'

In the hours before dawn, when at last he fell asleep after long contention with wakeful images that would not be shaken off, Dominic dreamed of hearing a car's engine climbing steadily up the track from the main road, endlessly climbing and climbing and refusing to give up or be discouraged, though every yard gained was replaced by an equal distance unrolling ahead. A part of his mind was still awake enough to realise that this was one of those frequent frustration dreams that come between waking and sleeping, usually in the last hours before arising, and go on for an eternity that turns out to have been contained in the twinkling of an eye. The frustration is there because the minuscule particle of time involved compresses the eternity too strictly for any fulfilment ever to be achieved. The car would never complete the climb, never arrive anywhere. He knew that as he slid away into deeper sleep.

But when he opened his eyes on the rose-radiance of dawn, and his ears to the chattering of the sparrows on the verandah, and the passing scream of parakeets come and gone like a flash of light, he felt in his bones and blood that something was changed since yesterday. He showered and dressed, and went out through the quiet house, where nothing stirred but the distant soft movements of barefoot servants, to the terrace, and straight across it to the top of the steps.

Below him the Land-Rover still stood forlornly waiting; but beside it was parked, with almost pedantic neatness, an elderly black Morris. It seemed the car of his dream had completed the climb, after all, and arrived at its destination. He was not aware of ever having seen this car before. It had the discreetly old-fashioned, anonymous, average look of the hired car, and betrayed nothing whatsoever about the man or woman who had recently driven it.

Dominic went looking for him. The terrace continued round the corner of the house and all along the north-east wall; and at an hour when everything that wakes turns its back on the chill of the night and looks eastward into the first rays of the sun, this jutting corner seemed to be the place where anyone already waking would naturally go. There was a stone seat just round the corner, draped with a hand-loomed rug. And there was a man sitting cross-legged on the seat, his hands cupped in his lap, his face upturned to the rising sun.

His colour was pale bronze, and in the reddish, gilding rays of dawn, launched horizontally like lances along the mist-blue and dust-amber land, he might have been indeed a bronze, made not so far away in Tanjore in the high period of the art, three centuries and more ago, for all his clothing melted into the same range of glossy metallic shades. Not even the darkness and texture of hair broke the unity, for his head, with close-set ears and beautiful, subtle shaping of the skull beneath the skin, was shaven naked as his face. Lofty, jutting bronze brows arched above large, closed eyelids; the long lips were folded together peacefully in the faintest and purest of smiles, and the thin, straight nose inhaled so softly and tranquilly that not even the act of breathing seemed to inflect his charged stillness.

But he was not asleep. As soon as Dominic's advancing figure cast a shadow on his nearer shoulder, the bronze cups of his eyelids lifted from exceedingly bright, mild, knowing eyes, dark brown and deeply set; and when two more steps had projected the shadow across his body he dwindled magically but gracefully into a middle-sized elderly gentleman wearing a saffron robe with a frayed hem kilted comfortably round his loins, and a fawn-coloured trench coat draped over his shoulders. His naked feet – his sandals lay beside the bench – were slim, bony and whitened with dust. He looked way-worn, but not tired. And he looked up at Dominic with a bright, gratified smile, and joined his palms gently under his chin in greeting.

'*Namaste*, my son!'

'*Namaste*, my father! I'm glad you are here.' His very

presence resolved everything into a matter of serene understatements.

'You are not surprised?' remarked the Swami Premanathanand, with a distinct suggestion of disappointment.

'Never surprised by you. But very glad of you.'

'I flew from Delhi to Madurai – it is a tedious business, thought it is so quick. And from Madurai I have driven that hired car – a car quite unknown to me, I am used only to my own.' His own was a forty-year-old Rolls, visually reduced by sheer hard labour to a flying scarecrow, but mechanically nursed like an only child. He was slightly surprised by his success with this modern degenerate, and a little proud. 'I arrived nearly an hour ago, but I did not wish to disturb anyone. I am afraid this is a house not well-blessed at present with dreamless sleep.'

'I dreamed I heard you coming,' said Dominic.

'That was not a dream, I was thinking of you. As I promised,' he said, 'I gave thought to the problem of what might best be done. And I thought that my responsibility in this matter is very great, and that I ought to be here with you.'

He rose, and slipped his feet into his worn sandals, his long, prehensile toes gripping the leather thongs.

'Shall we go into the house?'

Eight

Malaikuppam: Thursday

Purushottam, puffy-eyed from want of sleep but eased and heartened at the sight of his visitor, made his ceremonial greeting, and bent to touch in veneration the Swami's hands and feet. Larry hovered, long and dubious and aggressively American where his scepticism was called into resistance, everything about him from his bristling crew-cut to his thick-soled travelling shoes making a point of its complete un-Indianness. Priya offered her *namaskar* shyly but with composure, and answered the grave smile with a pale, withdrawn smile of her own. Lakshman was respectful, dutiful and more obstinately the paid courier than at any time during the last few days, so that there should be no mistake as to where he stood, and how immovably he stood there.

And the police, after an hour or so of cagey assessment, maintained with scrupulous politeness and reverence, opened their ranks and let the newcomer in. That was perhaps the greatest compliment paid to the Swami Premanathanand that day.

It was Inspector Tilak who called the afternoon conference, and presided at the head of the table, with Inspector Raju tactfully on his right hand; though as officer in charge of the original case the direction of the discussion was smartly and gratefully handed over to the Keralese officer as soon as proceedings opened. The Swami took his place at the foot of the table; but Dominic, seated halfway between, found himself experiencing repeatedly the kind of optical illusion in which up becomes down, out becomes in, and the foot of a table is translated into its head. It did not disconcert him; he had seen it happen before where the Swami was concerned, even when, as now, that enigmatic person was doing his best to suppress the tendency. His face was attentive and respectful, his eyes mild, and his voice asked gently for guidance rather than making suggestions; and with his usual timeless but astute courtesy he listened carefully to everything everyone else had to say, as they went over once again the entire history of the case.

'So as I understand it,' he said diffidently, when he had absorbed everything, 'we have here two deaths which are certainly closely connected, and there are some facts about them which need not be questioned. That they are the work of experienced terrorists, most probably Naxalites. That the bombs were made by the same hand, almost certainly in Bengal, and therefore that someone brought them south to the agent chosen to use them. Now the agent at Thekady is known – unhappily after the event and after his own inadvertent death. Whether he was to be used again for the same role is something we do not know; but since he was killed by his own act, clearly he cannot be responsible for what has happened here. There remains the supplier. I am not so naive as to suppose that other Naxalite agents may not be available in the south; but they are unlikely to be experienced with such comparatively sophisticated weapons as these. And also it is wasteful to acquaint too many people with the plans for such an act. Even those who sympathise are safer knowing nothing. One person, the messenger who brought the bombs, was already in the secret, and is the most probable person to have pursued the intent to the end. Have I followed you correctly?'

'Perfectly,' said Inspector Raju.

'And is it established that this person must have brought the bombs south only recently?'

The two inspectors glanced at each other, and Inspector Raju said, after only a momentary hesitation: 'In the first one some folded sheets of newspaper had been used as wadding inside the case. We have identified a Calcutta newspaper, dated not quite four weeks ago.'

'So we are looking, in effect, for someone who has come from the north since that date. Someone who does not belong here. A stranger. It should not escape us, of course,' he said mildly, 'that there are several such in this room now, including myself. Naturally those of us who have known one another for some time will feel that that line is hardly worth pursuing, but we must not ignore it altogether. There were also, at Thekady, a number of such people, visitors to the wild life sanctuary. And those, I know, are being kept under observation since that time. But none of them, as far as we yet know, has been anywhere near Malaikuppam.'

'As far as we know,' agreed Inspector Raju drily. 'But some were as close as forty to fifty miles on Tuesday night, and with cars it is not so difficult to move from one place to another. The Manis, for instance, decided after all to keep their hired car and driver rather than go by train over these last stages of their tour. They spent only one night at Rameshwaram. On Tuesday night they were at Virudhunagar, and last night at Tirunelveli. From either it would be no great journey here. Oh, they have reported their presence everywhere scrupulously. But there are still eight hours in the night. We shall check on everyone.'

'We are fortunate in having an officer who knows the district as Inspector Tilak does,' said the Swami warmly. He already knew from Purushottam's cook and watchman that the inspector was a native, born and raised not twenty miles away. 'So he will have everyone's goodwill and assistance in his inquiries about any strangers recently seen in these parts.' That hardly followed, Dominic thought, until he remembered that the stranger they were looking for was a Naxalite terrorist. In theory the extreme left-wing Marxist forces were on the side of the great suppressed majority; but in practice the members of that submerged class were the most likely of all to die in the ideological carnage, and nobody knew it better than they did, or resented it more bitterly.

'May I continue? I am talking chiefly to clarify matters in my own mind. Then we have the present outrage, and this unknown person who is responsible for it. It seems that we are confronted with two possible theories: one, that X was following up a pre-arranged pattern of events in attempting the murder of Purushottam, one more representative of "the chief class enemy": two, that he followed Miss Galloway here in order to wipe out what he had cause to believe might be a dangerous witness against him in the previous case. In short, in the first case the bomb was meant for Purushottam, in the second for the victim it actually claimed, Miss Galloway. Let us take the second case first.

'If it was Miss Galloway he wanted, then he must have followed the Land-Rover here, otherwise there would have been no way of tracking it afterwards on a cold scent to this particular place. Then again, X must have observed Miss Galloway using the office for her typing, and supposed – perhaps because of the diary she left behind? – that she was likely to do so again, or why plant the bomb there? But if he was there watching her during the evening, why risk the bomb at all? Why not a knife on the spot, or his hands? The office is one of the remotest buildings, with windows away from the court. Entry and exit would not be difficult, a cry could be cut off quickly, there was darkness to cover his retreat. He would have been a fool to take a more devious but extremely haphazard way. This militates against the theory, but does not altogether invalidate it, for we all know that sometimes men under pressure *are* fools, and *do* take the most inept ways of achieving their ends. And perhaps this one, previously merely the messenger, was too afraid of being personally responsible, too wary of ever actually showing his face. Better an inefficient attempt from a safe distance than a possibly disastrous direct confrontation. So let us still bear the theory in mind as a possibility.

And what is in its favour? The matter of the diary, which Miss Galloway discovered she had left behind, but which was not in her handbag when she was found, nor anywhere in the office. So perhaps, after all, someone *was* watching, someone who wanted that diary removed and destroyed. Someone who both planted the bomb that night, and stole the diary. Miss Madhavan, did you ever notice this diary? Can you tell us what it looked like?'

'She had a little red leather address book and stamp-case,' said Priya, 'and a big red leather writing-case. The diary could have belonged to the same set.'

'This we have found,' said Inspector Tilak. 'But no diary.'

'I don't actually recall seeing her writing up a regular entry in any book. But that needn't mean anything. It would be only a matter of a few lines, perhaps not even filled in each day. After all, I was with her for such a short time, only about ten days.'

'Nevertheless,' the Swami maintained, 'it remains a possibility that she had written down in it something of vital importance – perhaps something she did not even realise to be important at the time. If so, it can only have been something connected with the bomb outrage at Thekady. Now you were all together there, as we know. Even before the two parties joined, at the forestry bungalow, Miss Madhavan was with her, travelling with her, sharing a room with her. Now what can Miss Galloway have seen or realised that the rest of you did not?'

They could think of no possible juncture at which Patti's experience at Thekady had been different from theirs.

'And yet,' said Larry slowly, 'when we found the boat she did come to pieces – to a rather surprising degree. I mean, it might be only a temperamental difference – I was knocked pretty useless myself at first. But she went down for the count, they had to give her a sedative and let her sleep through until next day.'

'Yet she had seen only what you saw. So it was not something *witnessed* then. Could it have been something *recognised and made sense of* then? Something that linked up with something else she already knew, and had not realised she knew? Go back, Miss Madhavan, to the journey up to Thekady. Go over it in detail in your mind, and see if there is not at some point something which she did, and you did not do, something she saw, and you did not see.'

Priya opened her tired eyes wide, and stared back into the recent past, and began to recount the whole commonplace detail of that bus trip into the hills, proceeding with a patience which expected no excitement on arrival.

'We got off at the bungalow, and took a room. No one else left the bus there The French couple were already there, and the Manis arrived just as we came out to walk down to the fruit-stall below. It was while we were at the stall that Larry's Land-Rover passed on its way up to the bungalow, but it was nearly dusk then, especially there among the trees, and they didn't notice us. Then we walked back. There was nothing else, I think – except that Patti looked to see if the sadhu was still sitting by the lingam, and then she went back and gave him some small coins. For luck, she said.'

For luck! Whatever force had been allotting Patti her luck had made sure that all of it was bad.

'Sadhu?' said Inspector Raju, taking his long, worrying fingers abruptly out of his tangled grey hair. 'What sadhu?'

'Just a sadhu. He was sitting by the Siva lingam, one bend of the road down from the bungalow. I don't remember noting him when we drove past in the bus, but we saw him as we went down to the stall, and then on the way back Patti turned back to give him some money. Suddenly she said: "Wait for me a moment!" and gave me her parcels to hold, and she walked back to him. I saw her reach in her bag for some coins, and heard her put them in his bowl.'

'Now this,' said Inspector Raju, unsheathing his pen, 'is interesting. I know that road as I know my hand, and never yet have I seen a sadhu choose that particular place to sit. Did your friends also see him?'

'No, he wasn't there when we drove back to Madurai,' Lakshman said for them all. 'And we hadn't noticed him on the way up.'

'So only you two girls saw him face to face, and might know him again?'

Priya hesitated. 'I shouldn't know him again – I don't think I could ever be sure. He wore a devotional mark like this . . .' She drew the three lines and the small upright oval joining them. 'But he was sitting back among the trees, and it was getting dusk. I didn't go near, I just waited for Patti.'

'So she was the only one who got a close look at him?'

'Is he so significant?' Larry ventured. 'I thought they were liable to turn up pretty well anywhere, come when they chose and leave when they chose.'

'That is very true, but nonetheless this is curious. Consider this spot of which we are speaking! One bend of the road below the bungalow, where buses stop and a few people alight – one bend above the fruit-stall, where some at least of the passing cars might be expected to make a stop. But not *at* either of them. At a spot where no one is going to halt but the occasional archaeologist, and only if his attention has already been called to the meagre remains there. Those who live by alms must go where people are expected to be.'

'But there must be times when they're not concerned solely with extracting money from people,' said Larry.

'Those who sincerely desire a solitude where thought is possible will not be found sitting, from choice, beside a motor road. No, this is not a proof of anything, but it is a most curious detail.'

'It is also,' the Swami pointed out delicately, 'an apt

occurrence of just what we were looking for – a stranger in the picture, however briefly. Someone who did not belong to the staff or the visitors at Thekady, or the bungalow, or the bus, or any part of that ordinary weekend excursion. Is it possible that she saw that face again elsewhere and recognised it? Perhaps at the lake, in quite a different connotation? He may be irrelevant, of course. But it would be no harm to inquire if such a Saivite devotee has also recently been seen near Malaikuppam.'

'We will see to that at once,' said Inspector Tilak, making notes with great vigour.

'Then, if I may, I would like to consider the other possibility. For in this case we must find the right course of action, in addition to taking thought. If the bomb was meant for Purushottam, and not for Miss Galloway, many things are simplified. The Land-Rover need not have been followed here. The terrorist came here because this was where his assignment awaited him, and the arrival of Mr Preisinger's party was merely coincidental. As we have said, a little reconnaissance would show that Purushottam has been spending his days in trying to make sense of his father's affairs. In short, a bomb planted in his office and timed to go off at almost any time during the day, between meals, would have an excellent chance of securing his death. It was meant for him, and only by reason of the slight delay in the Land-Rover's departure, and perhaps also of this idiosyncrasy of exploding ahead of the fixed time, did it kill Miss Galloway instead.

'Those are the two theories. Either is possible. But the reason we must take this last one seriously has little to do with which will eventually turn out to be the right one. It is simply this: In the one case, if they meant to kill Miss Galloway, they have succeeded, therefore they will wish only to disappear into the landscape and not be traced. In the other case, if they intended to kill Purushottam, they have failed.

'Therefore,' said the Swami, calmly and distinctly, 'they will try again. So the question is, how are we going to ensure his protection?'

Purushottam, who had been all this time listening with only half his attention, and with the other half pondering some gnawing anxiety of his own, apparently in some way connected with Priya's clear profile, jerked up his head with a startled and almost derisive smile. As though, Dominic thought, he still doesn't altogether believe in the danger to himself, or, more perilously still, has no respect for it.

'My protection? What can one do except take all sensible precautions, and then simply go ahead with living? I shan't go looking for trouble, you can be sure. And we have a pretty large household, all of whom are to be trusted.'

'Yet still Miss Galloway is dead,' Inspector Raju reminded him austerely.

He flushed deeply. 'I'm sorry, you're right. I'd overlooked the fact that by attracting danger to myself I may have cost one life already. But that situation can easily be altered if you, sir, are prepared to let my guests proceed with their journey. Then I shall no longer be putting them in jeopardy.'

'How can we go?' Priya protested. 'We have sent a cable to Patti's parents, and we must be here to make arrangements – to do whatever they may wish. They may even fly over here to take her home. How can we abandon them now?'

'As far as the police are concerned,' Inspector Raju said, after a brief, consulting glance at his colleague, 'the party is at liberty to proceed on the old terms. Provided they will keep in touch, and be available at need, they may leave in the morning.'

'And I advise that they should,' said the Swami. 'I will remain here to receive Mr and Mrs Galloway, or their instructions, and will do whatever little can be done to make this loss easier for them. But that would not in itself solve the problem of Purushottam. No, don't refuse me yet, first listen to what I suggest.' He leaned forward, his linked hands quiet and still upon the table, and his brown, shrewd eyes surveyed them all at leisure, one by one. He had put on his wire-rimmed glasses, which sagged drunkenly to the right of his nose because the right lens was thicker and heavier than the left; and through the weighty pebble of glass his right eye put on its cosmic aspect, magnified out of reason and unnervingly wise. It lingered upon Priya, and passed on tranquilly enough; to Larry, on whom it pondered but briefly thoughtfully; to Lakshman, on whom it rested longer.

'We have here a party of guests expected to drive on to Nagarcoil and the Cape. It is only too well-known to our enemy by now, of course, that only one young lady will be going home to Nagarcoil. But three young men came, and three will leave. Now I admit that if a close watch has been kept on this household during the past few days, the probability is that Purushottam may now be known by sight to those who are seeking his death. But on the other hand, there is quite a good chance that he is not. He has been back in India only a very short time, and so deeply preoccopied during that time that he has hardly been out of the gates until Tuesday. Lakshman is about the same build and colouring.' The large, bright eye remained steadily trained upon Lakshman's face. 'Lakshman will remain here with me, in Purushottam's clothes. He will become Purushottam. And Purushottam will go with the party in Lakshman's place, as courier. Thus we can get him away safely from this house, on which the terrorist will be concentrating. It will gain us the time to take further measures, and allow the police to proceed more freely. And naturally,' he added, 'a very careful watch will be kept, twenty-four hours a day, upon Lakshman's safety.'

It was done with such gentle assurance that only

Dominic, who knew him so well, realised what an astonishing suggestion it was to come from a man like the Swami, to whom the humblest of lives ranked in value equal to the loftiest, and indeed would probably take precedence in its claims on his protection and solicitude. Nor had it even the remotest hope of being accepted. He looked curiously at Purushottam, whose mouth had already opened with predictable hauteur, to veto the proposition. He was probably the last young man in the world to allow himself to be smuggled out of his own house because of a criminal threat to his life, especially if it meant leaving someone else to bait a police trap in his place. Dominic waited confidently for him to say so, and for some reason the words had halted on the very tip of his tongue. He cast one brief, piercing side-glance at Priya's profile, and another, as it seemed, back deep into his own mind, where he hid that private preoccupation which had been distracting him earlier. And he stopped to think before speaking. And then it was too late, for Lakshman had spoken first.

'I am quite willing,' he said, 'if you think it will be helpful.' His face was inscrutable, aloof and unsmiling, most markedly maintaining that ambivalence of his between servant and equal. There was even something of the proud forbearance of the servant assenting to something which should only be asked of an equal. And as though he had sensed it, Purushottam found his voice the next moment; a more subdued voice than anyone would have expected, and a more reasonable.

'You can hardly ask me to duck out now, if it means leaving one of my friends standing in for me here, where the danger is.'

His choice of phrase was not calculated; he was not, in fact, a person who ever did much calculating. Lakshman's face lost its chill of correctness. He repeated firmly: 'I am quite willing. I shall be well protected.'

'But whatever could be done to protect you could also be

done to protect me. Why should not I be the bait to catch this agent? For I take it that's what you're hoping for? Since I'm the one he's after, I could serve the same purpose, surely, and serve it better.'

But it would not serve the same purpose at all, Dominic realised in a sudden rush of enlightenment. Not the purpose the Swami had in mind, not the purpose Inspector Raju had instantly perceived and approved, though he kept his mouth shut. The Swami had looked round the entire party with a detached eye, excluded Dominic because he knew him, and Priya – yes, quite positively he had acquitted Priya – for reasons of his own. That left Larry and Lakshman, who had travelled down here from the north together. On balance he had considered Lakshman, as an Indian, more likely to be involved in political mysteries than Larry, and there was also the point that the suggestion he had made could apply reasonably only to Lakshman. How seriously he rated this possibility there was no knowing; but it could not be excluded. The suggestion had been made primarily to see how Lakshman responded to it; and he had settled that without delay by his proud assent. Did that let him out altogether? Not necessarily. There might be Naxalites here, too, who could be contacted and used, and need not, in the last resort, be confided in. So the Swami would persist in his proposition. His design was to get Purushottam away from this house without his departure being known, and to hold Lakshman here in his place; and then to mount constant guard on him night and day. If he was innocent, and exactly what he seemed, he should be protected from harm. If he was guilty, he should be so lovingly watched and guarded that he should have no chance to smuggle out a word or a sign to any outside contact, to send other agents in pursuit of Purushottom. If he was innocent he would certainly be acting as bait for a police trap, and the few days' grace they would be buying by the exchange might produce a satisfactory capture. If he was guilty, and clever enough, they would have purchased nothing but stalemate. He would sit tight and take no action, and they would make no discoveries. But it was worth a try.

'And besides,' Purushottam went on reasonably, 'if they have decided on my execution, it's because I'm a land-owner. So my best defence is surely to go ahead as fast as I can with my plans to turn the estate into a co-operative farm, and stop *being* a land-owner.'

'You are making the mistake,' said Inspector Raju with a sour smile, 'of expecting logic and principle to have some part in your enemies' motivation. Fanatics recognise neither. They can decree hatreds; I doubt if they even know how to revoke one.'

'Moreover,' the Swami pointed out gently, 'even if your faith was justified and they called off the hunt in your case, this same killer of men and girls would be free to turn his attention elsewhere. We are asking you rather to help us to capture him, and save the next life, not merely to conserve your own.'

'Yes, I'm sorry, you're quite right. But if I stay, and Lakshman goes on, how will the position be different?' But he asked it as in duty bound, not vehemently; there was even a faint suggestion in his tone of reluctance to argue further.

It was Lakshman who provided the reasonable answer, and saved the Swami the trouble of finding plausible arguments to back his suggestion. Lakshman did it in the pure warmth of his response to being categorised ingenuously as a friend. Some answering gesture seemed called for, even if it had to be rather more self-conscious.

'I think,' he said, smiling, 'that the Swami feels he would have a more tractable subject in me, one more likely to obey orders and be cautious about his own life. Perhaps we should all breathe more freely in feeling that you are safely away from here.'

'In any case,' added the Swami smoothly, 'in a few days

Lakshman also could be quietly dispatched to join you. It is simply a matter of covering your immediate retreat. The right number of people must be seen to leave, and someone must be seen to remain, to represent the master of the house. If no one is watching, well, we shall have taken pains to no purpose, but does that matter?'

'I will stay,' said Lakshman decisively.

Everyone looked at Purushottam, and Purushottam looked no less intently at the Swami, with a slightly baffled and curiously gratified expression, as if he had been conned into something he now realised he wanted to do.

'Very well, if that's what you wish, I will go.'

Inspector Tilak withdrew, no doubt gratefully, as soon as the conference broke up, and Inspector Raju departed with him, leaving two men under Sergeant Gokhale to spend the night on the premises. Dominic went down with them to their car.

'Manpower with us is as much a problem as with the police elsewhere,' said the inspector ruefully. 'We can't do more. It would not be wise, in any case, to draw attention to your party by attaching a police guard to it, even if we had a man to spare.'

'We're warned,' said Dominic. 'We shall be keeping a sharp look-out, But it seems we shall be leaving the centre of action here with you.'

'If there is to be action. Too often the leopard withdraws into the jungle and is no more seen.'

'Do you know where the French couple are – the Bessancourts?'

'Last night, at Trivandrum. The night before they were at Quilon. Everyone appears to have done exactly what he proposed to do, and everyone has kept me informed.'

'And the boat-boy? The one who wouldn't stay at Thekady after the explosion? I think he expected to be the next!'

'Romesh Iyar? He has been reporting regularly to the police at Tenkasi. In any case, of all of you who left after that murder, he has been under the most constant observation, for he has been working at the junction there, portering on a casual basis. This evening he will be told – by now he *has* been told – that he can move on if he wishes, and need not report any longer. Why check on him further? He was working fifty miles away when the bomb that killed Miss Galloway was planted.'

'And the Manis are at Tirunelveli. Only we,' said Dominic sombrely, 'were here.' He thought of the Swami's practical and necessary realism, and wondered if they had really travelled in company with the murderer's accomplice who had now himself become a murderer. Useless pretending it was impossible, however hard it might be to believe. Useless to take it for granted that Lakshman's convincing display of innocence and co-operation could necessarily be accepted at its face value. He hoped fervently that there would be some move soon which would enable the police to produce the veritable culprit, alive, identifiable beyond question as guilty, and a total stranger.

Purushottam came in the dusk to where the Swami sat on his stone bench on the terrace quiet, rapt and alone. The young man brought a low stool and sat down at his feet. For a few minutes neither of them spoke. The very brevity of the twilight made it precious, a luminous moment held suspended in air, delicately coloured in gold and crimson and transparent green, soon to dissolve into the clear darkness of the night.

'And are you seriously interested in that young woman?' the Swami asked at length, in the same matter-of-fact tones and with the same aplomb as if he had been asking the time.

'How did you know that I wanted to go?' Purushottam demanded.

'I did not, until you showed me. I thought we might have considerable difficulty, my son, in persuading you to comply. You saved me a great deal of trouble.'

'I like her,' said Purushottam cautiously, and looked down frowningly at his linked hands, aware both of the inadequacy and the ambiguity of words. 'Swami, I am the classical Indian problem, and you must know it. I am the foreign-educated Indian youth coming home. I have two cultures, and none, two backgrounds and none, two countries, and none. You know the saying: He is homeless who has two homes. *I* am real, I am more real than ever I was, but nothing now has a real relationship with me. I am without parents now, without close family, and therefore, in a sense, freer than most young men coming home, but in many ways it is an illusory freedom, because it has to deal with the possible lack of freedom of others. And even in me there is still a great deal of respect for tradition, whether I like it or not. People in my situation come back agonisingly aware – almost morbidly aware – of the complexities and rigidities of Indian marriage. And I can see that any orthodox family might well hesitate at attempting to assimilate anything so bizarre as I have now become. And even worse, in this situation – in this shadow and uncertainty....'

'You need have no doubts concerning Miss Madhavan,' the Swami assured him tranquilly. 'I have known students, secretaries, clerks, cooks, housewives, artists, all manner of women who have at some juncture turned to terrorism. But never yet, in any country, have I known a case of a nurse who became a terrorist.'

'I didn't mean that. I haven't any doubts, of course. But if I am to continue as a target for assassins, how can I cause her to be involved with me? I have no right. Yet if I let her go now, I may never meet her again. And I know nothing at all about her family, the plans they may have for her, or what, for God's sake, they'll make of me!'

'There is a very simple cure for that,' said the Swami,

watching the stars burst out, sharp and brittle as frost, in the distant sky, where the fading green of the afterglow ended. 'Go with her to Nagarcoil, and find out.'

'Three strange young men arriving out of nowhere? It will not be like that. We shall put her down a little way from the house, and she will take good care to wait for us to drive away before she goes in.'

'You will be making a very stupid mistake,' said the Swami reprovingly, 'if you begin by under-estimating the lady.'

Priya appeared in the doorway, the green of her sari outlined in silvery light from the room within.

'Purushottam, may I use the telephone?'

'Of course!' He was on his feet in a moment. 'You would like to call your home?'

Her white teeth showed in an amused smile. 'Ours is a very modest house, we have no telephone. But there is a silversmith at the corner of the street, a friend of my parents, he will take a message if I ask him. I want to let them know we are coming, so that they can prepare. I think we should be there by one o'clock? You are all invited to my home for lunch. My family will be very happy to welcome you.'

The Swami admired the stars, and said nothing.

Nine

Nagarcoil: Friday Morning

They drove out from the gate in the early morning, Priya between Dominic and Larry in the front sea, Purushottam among the luggage in the back, where Lakshman would be most likely to ride. Lakshman himself waved them away from the terrace, realistically enough. If there was a watcher, the picture was there for him to see. But it was hard to believe in it, except when the ruins of the office fell away on their left side, and the edge of desolation touched them afresh, and made the morning air seem suddenly preternaturally cold. They were all thinking of Patti, who had been so challengingly alive, and was now a mere broken body, not yet released from police custody. In a moment, in the twinkling of an eye. 'To the born sure is death, to the dead sure is birth; so for an issue that may not be escaped thou dost not well to sorrow.'

Priya had said earnestly to the Swami, before they climbed aboard the Land-Rover: 'They must not see her. It would be better to take home only her ashes and her belongings.'

And he had said: 'I will take care of everything.' For Priya had seen her, and Priya had strong feelings about what bereaved parents should and should not be asked to endure. It was a field in which he had some experience, too, but he respected hers.

To Dominic, and privately, he had said: 'Telephone me each evening until we meet again. And if anything occurs, *anything* that seems to you significant, or to have anything to do with this matter, then telephone me at any time, as soon as possible. We do not yet know whether the thread will stay here with us, or go there with you.'

But when they were through the gates, and Dominic was driving down the dirt road from the village, in the astonishing brightness of early morning, it was more than they could do not to turn their heads and their eyes away from the wreckage behind, and towards the world ahead, which was varied and beautiful, and had a welcome waiting for them.

They passed through Tirunelveli at about nine o'clock, and they were in the most Christianised district in the whole of India, though until they crossed the bridge over the Tambrapurni river, and saw the tall spire of the C.M.S. church soar in front of them, there was nothing to make them aware of the characteristic. From Palamkottai southwards they were on the main, unmetalled road to Cape Comorin, and the landscape was a sequence of palm groves deployed among rice paddies, thatched villages, the occasional gopuram of a minor temple, and always the accompanying shapes, misty and deeply blue-green under their jungle growth, of the Western Ghats on their right hand. Monkeys crouched under the trees along the road, unstartled, peering at them with their sad, wizened faces, and jack-fruit like huge, lumpy, holly-green Rugby footballs dangled on their thin, drooping stems from the branches.

'Soon,' said Priya, her face brighter now and her eyes wide with anticipation, 'we must turn off to the right for Nagarcoil.'

They were no more than eight or nine miles from the sea now in either direction, south-east or south-west. At the fork they took the more westerly road, as Priya directed. India had already demonstrated in its invariable manner the nearness of the ocean which its people, apart from a few fishing communities, do not love. The sky was almost an English sky, no more than half of it blue, the rest scudding cloud, driven fast, though there was no wind at ground-level, and forming and re-forming in constantly-changing masses and temples and towers. The light had become a maritime light, moist and charged with melting colours, scintillating instead of glaring.

The road widened at the same time as it seemed to narrow, because lines of small houses had begun to frame it on either side. It acquired the texture of a street, and other and taller buildings sprang up behind the first, and became the beginnings of a town of more than a hundred thousand souls. A nondescript textile town, where among other things, they make hand-loomed towels of all kinds and sizes. A town with Jain associations, and Christian ones, too, of several persuasions; and in its way a pleasant place, more spacious than most of its kind, and with something of the air of a country market town, with energy and time to spare.

'Now we are coming into Nagarcoil,' said Priya.

The house lay off one of the quieter and narrower streets at the edge of the central shopping area. There was a space of beaten earth drawn back in an open square from the street, with a solitary tree at one front corner, and in its shade a patch of bleached grass. Each of the three closed sides of the square was a little, deep-eaved, whitewashed house one storey high and overhung by a red-tiled roof. They were as neat and clean as brand-new dolls' houses, and not much larger. Purushottam's ranch-like dwelling would have contained ten of them, and his compound at least fifty. And the children who came tumbling out of the house on the right, as soon as the Land-Rover turned into the yard, were as bright and spruce and petite as dolls. Little girls in minute cotton dresses, western style, little boys in cotton shorts and white shirts; all of them huge-eyed and smiling and excited, but perfectly silent, and all the girls wearing little crowns of flowers. The moment they had fully taken in the Land-Rover, and confirmed for themselves its veritable arrival, they shot back into the house as precipitately as they had frothed out of it, and the voices that had been mute outside were loosed in a torrent of shrill Tamil, speading the news. Before the travellers had all climbed out and shaken off the dust of their journey, Priya's parents appeared in the deep doorway at the head of the five shallow steps. They marshalled before them the three littlest girls, who held up at the full stretch of their short arms dewy garlands of lotus buds and roses and jasmine. With formidable solemnity they descended the steps, taking passionate care not to trip over their burdens, and advanced upon the visitors.

'Good God!' said Larry blankly, between consternation and delight. 'What *have* you got us into, Priya?'

'You have never been garlanded before?' she said innocently. 'In my family we do things properly.' And she went to meet the little girls, lifted the necklaces for them, and hoisted the first over Larry's head, and the second over Dominic's. But Purushottam, his face brighter than they had ever yet seen it, sat down on his heels to be on a level with the panting littlest, and let her hang her garland round his neck with her own hands. He had an unfair advantage, for he could talk to his hostess, who chattered back to him in high delight.

'All the ones who go to school know English,' Priya said reassuringly. 'Come, I would like to introduce you to my parents.'

Mr Madhavan was probably in his late forties, no more; a short, square, muscular man with crisp hair just greying at the temples. His wife was plump and round, with a cheerful face that smiled even in repose. Their best festival wear was plain, practical cotton, whites for him and sensible wine-coloured sari for her, laundered many times but laundered superlatively. There was no wealth here, only a hard-won and shrewdly-planned living, and a great deal of good humour as oil for the machinery of making-do. There was a cheerful flurry of greetings, blessedly in English; and with ceremony which hardly seemed ceremonious because it was so exuberant in its warmth, the visitors were brought into the cool of the house.

'Not all the children,' Priya said, reading their minds, 'are ours. Two of the littlest belong to my eldest married brother, and two to my married sister – they both live quite close – and one or two from the neighbours seem to have joined the party, too. You are a great event, you mustn't grudge them gate-crashing.'

There was also a beautiful girl of about seventeen, a plain but engaging one of fifteen and two boys aged eleven and nine. They were so many and so colourful and the little ones so light and rapid in movement that it was like being surrounded by a cloud of butterflies.

How even the ones who belonged in the house ever found room there remained a mystery. So far as they saw, it consisted of only two rooms, though the kitchen was obviously elsewhere. The room into which they were brought was furnished very simply with a couple of cushioned benches which must also have done duty for beds, a large table and a few chairs, a chest of drawers against one wall, covered with an embroidered cloth and proudly presenting the parents' wedding photograph, two or three other family pictures, a carved box, and a bowl in which flowers floated. A curtained doorway led through into a second and smaller room with two charpoys draped with bright covers, and a little table loaded with family ornaments and souvenirs. The bright calendar hanging on one wall showed a blue, effeminate, mischievous Krishna leading a timorous Radha through the grove. But on another wall there was an unexpected reproduction of a modern Christian nativity, romantic and sugary-sweet, complete with ox and ass. Purushottam studied it with dazed interest, and turned to look wide-eyed at Priya.

As for Priya herself, she was perfectly at her ease, composed, even a little amused, certainly proud of her poor, prolific, hospitable and gracious family. She helped her mother to settle the guests comfortably, relieved them of their garlands, and brought, before everything else, glasses of cold water. Then the women vanished to the sacred and invisible kitchen. They also herded the small children out into the yard to play, though until their curiosity waned they tended to creep back and stand in a little rainbow cluster in the doorway, frankly and greedily staring.

'My daughter tells me,' said Mr Madhavan, sitting down with his guests, 'that you will go on to Cape Comorin. It is only about eight miles from here. But you are a South Indian yourself, Mr Narayanan, and doubless you already know it.' He was feeling his way towards a subject which must be mentioned, to set everything in clear order, but equally must not be allowed to cast too long a shadow upon this gathering. 'You will understand, we were expecting Priya to bring her friend with her. All my girls were looking forward very much to her visit. Priya has told us already, by courtesy of our good friend, Mr Achmed, who has a shop close by, what has happened. It is a terrible tragedy, and we are deeply sorry. For her parents especially. Such a dreadful loss for them. Death is not an ending, of course, but it is a separation.' It did not sound so far from the Swami's: 'To the born sure is death ...' But it caused Purushottam to cast a fleeting glance at the pretty, Christmas-card Bethlehem on the wall.

Mr Madhavan followed the look, and smiled understandingly. 'Perhaps Priya did not explain us. We are Salvationists. Oh, yes, you will find we have quite a strong community here. Since my grandfather's day our family has belonged to the Salvation Army. There is an excellent Army school here, all our children attend it.'

It seemed utterly fitting that the good friend Mr Achmed, who took the telephone messages for the family, should be a Muslim, Purushottam breathed deeply, and warned himself, half-heartedly, not to expect too much; but so much had been lavished already that he found it difficult not to feel encouraged. Instead of the orthodox, narrow Hindu family he had feared, all the more insistent on the proper procedures because they were not rich, adamant about suitabilities of caste and background, here was this cheerful, exuberant, free-thinking tribe with a door wide open to friends of all creeds, and professing not merely Christianity – which after all might have been a disadvantage rather than otherwise in some of its manifestations – but the most down-to-earth, hearty and extrovert brand of Christianity possible. Exotics themselves in this conformist India, they were surely capable of assimilating even such an exotic as Purushottam Narayanan, half-westernised, a non-believer in caste, and about to beggar himself – comparatively speaking – by turning his lands into a co-operative farm, if the state authorities did not block his plans out of spite towards the central government, which was always a possibility. He had not admitted to himself until then how much he valued and wanted Priya, with all her quietness and her dignity, her courage and self-respect, the occasional spark of demure mischief in her eyes, and in particular, and most daunting of all, her sturdy ability to stand on her own feet and be independent even of him, in a world heavily weighted against feminine independence. Now he had qualms on only one score, that as yet he did not know whether she felt the same way about him. But one fence at a time!

'My middle son plays the trumpet in the Army band,' said Mr Madhavan, confirming with every word the good impression he had already made. 'My eldest son – he will probably come in for coffee afterwards if he can get away from the shop where he works – has on the other hand reverted to his great-grandfather's Vaishnovite persuasion. It is a change without a difference, don't you think so? Largely a matter of what label one uses. But if a man feels more at home and more suited with one than with another, and finds the kind of help he needs, that is what matters.

We get on very well together.'

Faced with so interesting a set-up, Larry came out of his shell and began to ask question after question, none apparently being barred, and none that he was likely to frame resented. It was not often he had such an opportunity, with someone at once as articulate and as artless as Mr Madhavan. And the children gazed and listened in fascination until the women reappeared in procession from some outhouse kitchen, and shooed them out again to play.

The fifteen-year-old spread the table with a cotton cloth, and the seventeen-year-old brought in four huge, glossy green banana leaves, delicately holding two, folded edge-to-edge, between thumb and forefinger of either hand, and laid them for plates. They were newly washed, and drops of water sparkled in the veins that ran down into the stems. Then Priya and her mother brought in the dishes, and stood and served as the men ate. There was rice, spiced and tinted with saffron, a variety of vegetables, and a chicken curry; and afterwards, some of the ultra-sweet Indian sweets made with coconut, which treacherously soak you with a fountain of syrup unless you know how to eat them. Forks had been thoughtfully provided for the foreign guests, but both of them chose to eat with the fingers, like the rest of the party. The two teenage daughters went off to feed the gaggle of hungry children in the kitchen, and the feast overflowed into the yard and into the street.

When everyone else was taken care of, Mrs Madhavan and Priya also helped themselves and sat down with the menfolk. And by the time the younger girls brought coffee Mr Achmed the silversmith had arrived, and the eldest son with his wife, and the married daughter with her husband, to meet the visitors and to reclaim their various children. The walls of the little house bulged.

Out in the centre of the open square the Land-Rover stood all this time, a magnet for the interest of the whole district. Word went round from one to another, and half the neighbourhood came to see.

Priya emerged from the kitchen with a new pot of coffee, and crossed to the steps of the house. The Land-Rover had nearly disappeared beneath a cloud of gaily-coloured children; but they were in pride and awe of it, more concerned with being seen to belong to it than anything else, and there seemed no need to call them away. It was because she was looking in their direction, however, that as she passed she looked beyond them, to where the solitary tree stood rooted in the baked earth, sheltering its little mat of grass.

There was a man in a yellow robe sitting cross-legged in the shade there, dappled with the sunlight filtering through the leaves over him. She saw the coils of wooden beads and coloured cords round his neck, the tangle of black hair, and the ash-smeared forehead with the cult mark of Siva. He was motionless, his body facing the street, but his head turned towards her father's house.

For one instant she had checked at sight of him; and though she resumed her purposeful walk at once, she could not be sure that he had not noticed and understood. She went on into the house, and poured fresh coffee; and then, without a word to anyone, and hardly missed among so many, she darted out again, down the steps and straight across towards the tree. For he could not be a coincidence, and she knew he was no illusion. She had no idea what she was going to say to him, or how he would answer her; but she must confront him, challenge him, and at least get a close look at him, face to face, so that in future she would be able to identify him wherever they met, and through whatever disguise he might put on. Here on the public street, among so many people, what could happen to her?

The grass-plot under the tree was empty, the scintillation of leaves quivered over the place where he had sat only a minute ago. The sadhu was gone.

She went on into the street, and searched in both directions for the flutter of saffron cloth, or a glimpse of the tangled, oily black hair; but he had vanished utterly.

She walked back slowly to the house. Now, she thought, I know that it was Purushottam they wanted, and not Patti, and having failed, they will try again. However he did it, this spy, he has found us. He is not wasting his time watching Lakshman from a distance at Malaikuppam; he is here, hard on our heels. And now, what are we to do?

He knows that I've seen him, this man. He went away because he didn't want me to see him more closely. So he knows we're warned. Would it be best to stay here, in a town, surrounded by people, where nothing can happen without instant detection, where action would be suicide? But no, we've seen already that they will contemplate suicide without a qualm, if they must. Death does not frighten them, not even their own. No, hundreds of innocent people passing by would be no protection, they would still toss a bomb in at the door and kill as many as need be, just to kill one....

A private part of her mind said, and she heard it and did not try to pretend deafness: '... *that one!*'

She had a family, parents, all those younger brothers and sisters and nephews and nieces....

No, she thought, we must go. Get out of here as soon as we can. The departure of the Land-Rover will be sign enough. If we can whip it away unobserved, now, while he is keeping out of my way for his own ends, I can guide it by a roundabout route, and not pass where we should pass on the direct road to the Cape. We may be able to lose them completely, and yet the fact that the Land-Rover is gone should leave my family undisturbed. All will be quiet here. The visitors gone – any neighbour will tell them. But not where! I must warn my father not to tell anyone where we are going.

All along, of course, it had been 'we'. She knew that she had never meant to remain here, and let him go on without her, still under that shadow. Not even before she had sighted the pursuit, much less now. Not until the threat had passed, once for all, would she part company with Purushottam.

She went back into the house, which was full of voices, and made her own quiet voice cut through them all, clapping her hands under her chin with a bright, apologetic smile. Purushottam had been trying for half an hour to raise his courage, and find the right words in which to request that she might be allowed to travel on to the Cape with them, and even in this liberating atmosphere he had found it a hard thing to do. Yet if he did not make some move now to continue the acquaintance, how could he hope to revive it later through the good offices of his one surviving aunt, who in any case would think the match most ill-advised? But Priya simply raised the pitch of her soft voice a couple of tones, and said deprecatingly: 'I am so sorry, but it is quite time that we should think of leaving now. Please forgive us!' and everything was resolved.

Ten

Cape Comorin: Friday Afternoon

On the last eight miles to Cape Comorin the Western Ghats had been left behind at last, the country opened level and green with paddy-fields and palms, broken only, here and there, by small, astonishingly abrupt, mole-hill-shaped mountains that erupted out of nowhere like the remains of old volcanic activity. Most of their area was bare, bluish rock; only in the scanty folds of their lowest slopes did trees and bushes cling.

'You didn't tell us,' said Parushottam, in the back of the Land-Rover with Priya, 'that you were a Christian.'

She did not take her eyes from the road unrolling dustily behind them; but she smiled. 'I'm not sure that I am. Not sure *what* I am. I think I am religious, but I am not very partisan. But I was brought up as a Christian, and I have never seen any point in changing, when calling myself something else will not really be any more appropriate to what I believe. I expect I don't think very logically about these things, but categories are so limiting, and so confusing.'

Still she watched their wake; she had been watching it ever since she had guided them out of the town by bewildering lanes and alleys, and round by cart-tracks to reach this southern highway at last. But there was no vehicle in sight behind them.

'Why are you watching the-road so carefully?' he asked.

'To make sure that we're not followed.'

His mind had been too full of other thoughts to have any room for the consideration of his own safety. He had forgotten, temporarily, that it had ever been threatened. 'We shan't be followed now? Why should we?'

'I hope not,' she said. 'But there's no harm in keeping our eyes open.'

The tall gopuram of a temple showed ahead, rearing out of the palms. A large grove of trees surrounded it, but the tapering, gilded tower stood out far above the fronds of their crests, covered with carvings and alive with colours. In five minutes more they reached the gates, and the broad, ceremonial path that led into its courts. There were several cars standing before the entrance, and at sight of the rearmost of them Dominic laughed, and slapped a hand lightly on the wheel.

'This is where we came in! What did we say? Provincial France has caught up with us again.'

There was no mistaking that old, sky-blue Ford, with the scratches of some ancient skirmish ripped across one door, and dabs of red retouching on the rear wing. The Bessancourts must be inside the temple enclosure with their box camera, doggedly making up the record of their travels. A tall, rangy young man in khaki shirt and shorts and a white headcloth sat on his heels, leaning back comfortably against the enclosure wall, his arms embracing his legs and his head pillowed on his knees, contentedly asleep, though they could only assume that his job was to guard the parked cars and discarded shoes.

'Shall we stop? Do you want to have a look at the temple?' asked Dominic, slowing down.

'No, let's go on,' said Larry. 'If everybody's going to be making for this hotel at the Cape, maybe we'd better get there ahead of the rest. Not much doubt we'll be seeing the Bessancourts this evening, is there?'

They could smell the sea, and trace the direction of the wind by the slant of the trees, before they came within sight of village, temple or cape. There were roofs of buildings ahead, more palmyra palms, and then a crossroads where a battered bus had just turned, clearly having reached its terminus. A few houses, small and modest, and a stall selling fruit and drinks, the cheerful stall-holder brandishing a machete to behead the coconuts, and slice a way through to the three pockets of sweet juice in the palmyra fruits for his customers. And that was all.

'Here we must turn to the right,' said Priya. 'Look, that big house – that is the hotel.'

A lane brought them to its gates, and to a parking-ground within. The house was quite un-Indian; it might have been more at home in any expensive Victorian suburb of any northern commercial town in England, and indeed it had once been a British Residency; but it had broad, grassy surroundings, and a few windswept flower-beds, and it looked solid, spacious and comfortable.

'The first chance I have had,' said Purushottam buoyantly, 'to be a proper courier for you.' And he led the way inside to book rooms for them all. They followed more slowly, and in the dimmer light within looked round them among the panelling and potted palms, glimpsing through open doors and rear windows a sudden dazzling vista of sand, flowing in undulating dunes along the edge of a half-buried road; and beyond that the glitter of water. The Indian Ocean, which had seemed still far away from them, was almost lipping at their back doorstep.

Their rooms were on the first floor. As usual they were all double rooms, but because of Priya's presence they needed three, so that one of the men was also privileged to enjoy a room to himself. 'You take that one,' Dominic said, and took Larry's bag from the room-boy and dumped it within.

'Suits me,' Larry agreed accommodatingly, and followed his belongings.

Purushottam caught Dominic's eye, and smiled. 'You feel responsible for me?'

'No sense in taking any unnecessary chances, you'd better share with one of us. Doesn't matter which.' But it did. He was the one who would feel answerable to the Swami for

Purushottam's safety, and that mattered a great deal.

Priya's room and Larry's were neighbours, and faced east. The third room was approached by a small side-corridor of its own, and faced south. All three of them opened on a long balcony with railings of ornamental ironwork, supported on painted iron pillars from below. Purushottam tossed his bag on the left-hand bed, and unzipped it in search of a clean shirt. For verisimilitude he had brought away the bag which belonged to Lakshman, but he had put in his own toilet articles and pyjamas and a change of clothes. After the dusty journey he wanted a shower.

He was still revolving under the cool water when he heard, distantly through this splashing music, the shrill, peremptory shriek of a woman's voice, and then Dominic's resigned groan of: 'Oh, *no*!' from the balcony. In pure curiosity Purushottam emerged glistening and golden from the bathroom, trailing his towel over one shoulder and leaving moist footprints behind him.

'Why: Oh, *no*! – and so fervently? What was it?'

Dominic drew back a little from the railing, and pointed down into the garden.

The Manis, in all their glory, were just returning from a leisurely stroll along the coastal road from the village; Gopal Krishna in immaculate beige linen and immense sunglasses, with his expensive camera round his neck, Sudha in a lilac and blue sari woven in subtle stripes that changed shade with the light, her wrists laden with portable treasure of good bracelets, and her pale golden face plaintive with vexation. Sushil Dastur, harried as ever, trotted at her elbow bearing her bag, folding canvas chair, cushion and book. And what had occasioned the shriek of reproof was that he had let fall her bookmark, and lost her place in the book. Profuse and voluble in apology and reassurance, he was already feverishly hunting for it again, at the peril of dropping her cushion at any moment.

'*That* is what it was – the lady. You haven't encountered

the Manis yet, but you will, the minute they set eyes on us. One of those cars outside must be theirs, but I never thought. All those black hire jobs look alike. And the devil of it is that they know Lakshman. In any case, they'll have read about Patti.' The mention of her name was like a stab, all the more because it was entirely possible, for brief periods, and on the tide of such crazy pleasure as they had experienced at Nagarcoil, to forget all about her. The reminder was still a crude shock when it came; and reality was treading on their heels even here.

'Do they matter?' Purushottam asked, watching the three figures advance towards the hotel.

'Do we know what matters? They were at Thekady. They'd seen us a couple of times before that. For that matter, the French people are surely on their way, too. The car we passed at the temple. A pity! As we were a couple of days behind schedule, I thought they might all have turned back northwards by now. Not that the Manis ever actually acknowledged Lakshman's existence,' he added scornfully. 'I don't believe they ever addressed a word to him. But the Bessancourts did. And in any case none of them can help noticing, at close quarters, that you're *not* Lakshman, whether they expect you to be introduced or not. Now how are we going to account for you?'

Purushottam wrapped the towel round him, massaged his slender body pleasurably and considered. 'Lakshman had to leave you, and I'm your new guide. My name's Narayanan. Why not? Supposing there is anyone here who already knows of me – the chap you're worrying about – then he knows my name. And for any others, Narayanan is a perfectly good name, common enough, you meet a few of us everywhere. It will do for a guide as well as for anyone else. Who knows, they might even take me for a plainclothes policeman detailed off to escort you!'

'Good advice,' agreed Dominic, after a moment's reflection. 'Why complicate things unnecessarily? Hurry up and get dressed, and we'll go and brief the others.'

They had need of a united front; for the moment they appeared in the lounge, with its range of large windows giving on the coast road and the dunes, Sudha Mani rose with a small, melodious shriek of recognition and sympathy from her tea-tray, and bore down upon them in a gust of perfumed air, her sari fluttering.

'Oh, Miss Madhavan – Mr Preisinger – Mr Felse—Oh, we have been so anxious about you all! It was all in the papers – such a dreadful thing, that poor young lady! Ah, how we felt for her, and for her unhappy parents, so far away! Oh, how little we realised, when we said good-bye in Thekady, that in so short a time —' Her breath gave out; she held her swelling bosom, and heaved great sighs.

'My wife,' intoned Gopal Krishna, rolling ponderously up to her support, 'is so hypersensitive. Your bad news – such a shock to hear ...'

'Yes, it is a wretched business,' Larry agreed rather forbiddingly.

'But why, I ask myself, should anyone wish to hurt a young English lady like Miss Galloway?' Gopal Krishna blinked behind his dark glasses, and shook his head heavily. 'The police have a theory? They did not detain you, I am so glad of that.'

'No, they didn't want us to stay put. Though of course we're in constant touch,' Dominic said. No harm to plant the idea that wherever they went the police might well have a shadow not far behind. 'As far as we could gather, they think that Miss Galloway may have seen something incriminating at Thekady, perhaps without even realising it, and someone wanted her silenced. But of course we may be wrong – it's just an impression. They haven't found it necessary to interfere with your movements, I hope?'

Sudha raised her fine black brows, a little disposed to be affronted by the suggestion, but her husband flowed on complacently enough: 'Oh, no, indeed no, we have not been troubled at all. But for such distressing happenings, it could have been a most pleasant trip. We spent two nights at Tirunelveli, and went out to the coast there to see the Subrahmanya temple at Tiruchendur, and the cave sculptures. We arrived here for lunch today. You are also staying overnight? That will be very nice, we shall see more of you.'

They withdrew, smiling their goodwill and shaking their heads over all that had proved regrettable and spoiled a perfect trip, and went back to their tea. Neither of them had given more than a faintly curious glance at Purushottam, who hovered in the background with a very fair imitation of Lakshman's ambiguous manner.

'Let's get out of here and have a look for the Cape we've heard so much about,' said Larry restively, and led the way out, straight through the lounge to an open door, and out into a narrow garden, a levelled waste-land of grass half silted over with the encroaching edges of the dunes. It was like Cornwall in many ways, the furtive wavelets of sand creeping towards the house, the sparse plantations of tamarisks, the smell of the sea.

A light, insinuating hand plucked gently at Dominic's arm as he passed through the doorway, last of the four. He looked down into the timid, apologetic dark eyes of Sushil Dastur.

'Mr Felse, I wanted only to say . . . I read in the papers yesterday, about Miss Galloway.' He shrank a little, drawing his large, bony head into his hunched shoulders. 'It is not for me – I am only a retainer . . . But I am so very sorry!'

Startled by the very simplicity of this direct approach, Dominic looked at him as if for the first time. The Manis made it difficult to view Sushil Dastur as anything but an adjunct of their passing, a kind of comic postscript. And the man himself made it no easier to see him clearly, since he saw himself in much the same manner, and would, in a sense, have preferred to be invisible. It was an act of courage and decision on his part to speak for himself. And even now he had in his other hand a silk scarf belonging to Sudha, and before he could break away she gave tongue in quest of it; 'Sushil Dastur, quickly! There is a draught here!'

'Thank you,' said Dominic hurriedly, and briefly touched the arresting hand with his own. 'We appreciate that very much. You're very kind.'

Sushil Dastur fled. And Dominic followed the others out into the seaward garden. It was from the right, from the west, that the sand was advancing, marching so softly, so insidiously, that for long months a broom might hold it at bay, and then suddenly one morning the broom would have to be exchanged for a spade. To the left the garden opened into an untroubled expanse of grass, and a few clumps of shrubs and trees. The drive wound round the building to this frontage, braving the rim of the dunes, and here, too, a few cars had found parking space, though that at the landward side of the hotel was higher by several feet, and quite free of sand. And there among the parked cars was the sky-blue Ford with the scratched door; and just hoisting out the bags and locking the boot again was the rangy young man in khaki shorts and bush shirt, who had been sleeping placidly under the temple wall on the road from Nagarcoil.

He lifted his head at the sound of their voices, staring for a moment in tension between delight and disbelief, and then his face split open in a broad and bountiful smile, and he dropped the Bessancourts' bags on the ground, and came gladly salaaming over the gravel pathway to meet them.

'Sahib ... sahib! So I find you here also! You know me? You remember me? Romesh Iyar, boat-boy?'

'Romesh!' It was impossible not to be warmed by the reflection of his pleasure. Larry halted willingly. 'We never expected to see you here, you're way off your beat. I thought you had a job waiting on the railway at Tenkasi. What are you doing here?'

'Sahib, I stay in Tenkasi three days, work sometimes, but no regular job. My brother very poor man, I not stay there to live on him. Third day police say can go now, not report any more. In Tenkasi is not good, no jobs there. So I go try in Trivandrum, but there also I got no luck. Everywhere many men without jobs.'

'You'd have done better,' Dominic suggested ruefully, 'to stay in Thekady, where you had a job.'

The turbaned head shook violently. Anything rather than that. 'No, sahib, no stay there. No go there again. That was bad place, bad luck, must get away from that place.'

'But what will you do, then? Are you working for the Bessancourts now?' Self-contained and self-sufficient, those two elderly, invincible people seemed the last pair in the world to need or want a servant.

'I very lucky, sahib. Someone tell me, good jobs going in Dindigul, in tobacco factories, so I want go there, but it is long way, cost too much money. But then I meet Bessancourt Sahib and lady, and they remember Romesh. They say they go from here to Pondicherry. Best road to Pondicherry is through Dindigul. So I ask, please take me like servant, you not pay me anything, only food and let me ride with you, and I do for you everything. They very kind, tell me yes, can come.'

'Fine! And you think there really will be a job for you there?' asked Larry.

'Oh, yes, sahib, very good jobs in tobacco factories. I am good worker, can do all.'

'You drive a car, too?' Not that the Bessancourts seemed to need a relief driver, but there was little else for a travelling servant to do for them, they were so used to being self-supporting.

'Oh, yes, sahib, I drive anything with wheels, very good driver.' He went and picked up the discarded bags from where he had dropped them. 'Must go now, Bessancourt Sahib waiting for luggage. You stay here tonight, sahib?'

'Yes.' Dominic thought, as perhaps they were all thinking, it's Thekady all over again, but without Patti. The same cast, even a rather similar Victorian hotel, the same parked cars, the same – though very different – tourist spectacle long since formalised by strict custom. Here you don't go out to watch elephants from a boat; but the rules are no less firmly laid down. You go out in the evening towards the west, to watch the sun go down in the Arabian Sea, and in the morning you get up early and go out towards the east, and watch it come up again out of the Bay of Bengal, far away beyond invisible Ceylon.

Romesh Iyar had been an employee at Thekady for a matter of months, he remembered; and suddenly he asked on impulse: 'Romesh, all the time you were at the lake, did you ever see a sadhu begging by the Siva shrine, the one near the forestry bungalow? Wearing this cult sign?' He drew it with a stick in the gravel. Romesh had put down the bags again, and was gazing down at the scratched drawing with a face suddenly tight and wary. He took some moments for thought, though they could not escape the feeling that he had known the answer from the beginning. Finally he looked up into Dominic's face, and he was no longer smiling.

'Yes, sahib – once I see such a man. That is strange – it was that same time, same weekend when *that thing* happen. Day before you come to my boat, I go down to village with truck to bring flour, in afternoon I go. I see this sadhu then, sitting by lingam. I remember it because never before I see anyone sitting there. This once only I see him.' His face was clouded, even uneasy; something more was stirring in the back of his mind. 'Sahib, why you ask me this?'

'We saw him, too,' said Dominic, 'that same day. We wondered if perhaps he was often there.'

'No, never before I see him. Only that once. But, sahib –

there is something else, now you have spoken of this man. Just such a man I see also today.'

'Today?' said Dominic sharply. 'Where?'

'Sahib, in Nagarcoil. Bessancourt Sahib stop there for midday meal, and I go look at the town. In Krishnancoil district I see this sadhu, sitting under a tree, in Jambukeshwar Lane. This same mark he had. Sahib, was this the same man? Was it he ... ' His voice foundered. The whites began to show in a widening band all round the pupils of his eyes. 'But, sahib, this was *a holy man....*'

'I shouldn't worry,' Dominic reassured him quickly. 'The police wanted to check on everyone who was in the area, that's all. Why should you be anxious about it now? You're with the Bessancourts, and in a day or so you'll be heading for Dindigul with them. You'll get your job, and never hear any more about this.'

'Yes,' said Romesh, but abstractedly, and as he picked up the bags for the third time his face was still taut and alert with something that did not quite amount to fear – wariness, uncertainty, disquiet. He would be glad when the sky-blue Ford headed north-east again. 'I go now, sahib, must go, got work to do.'

He set off round the corner of the house, and they stood looking after him until he vanished.

'You don't suppose,' Larry said tentatively, 'that he was making up today's sadhu, just to oblige?'

'No,' said Priya quietly, 'he is speaking the truth. The man was there. I know, because I saw him, too. Perhaps you did not notice – Jambukeshwar Lane is the name of the road where we live.'

She told them the whole story. 'If the Bessancourts were at lunch, that would be about the right time. I think Romesh must have passed by and seen him before I noticed him. When I went out again, he was gone. I think he knew I had seen him, and he did not wish to be seen at closer quarters. So I thought the best thing to do was to get you away from there at once, while he was keeping out of sight for his own sake. And that is what I did.'

'But why,' demanded Purushottam, aghast, '*why* did you say nothing? If I'd known we were being followed – if I'd known they were watching us – I'd never have brought you with us into this danger.'

She looked at him with a pale but radiant smile, and said: 'But that *is* why. Now I am here, and there is nothing you can do about it. It was not only that I wanted to come with you, it was partly because there was no time for explanations, and I did not want to alarm my family. Also I did want to get you out of Nagarcoil by a roundabout way, in the hope of losing our shadow. And we may have done so, you know – I hope so. I feel sure no vehicle actually followed us. It seemes that they know quite well who you are. But if they now know *where* you are, it's because they knew in advance where we were going, or at least were able to guess. Or because once again they have simply found us, as *he* found us in Nagarcoil. A Land-Rover is not so anonymous as one of those black hire-cars and taxis.'

Purushottam said, with eyes for no one but Priya, and in a hurt, reproachful voice, like a baffled child: 'You shouldn't have done this to me. Of all things in the world I wanted you safe.'

'Of all things in the world,' said Priya, almost crossly. 'I want you alive.'

It struck Dominic as being one of the oddest, as well as one of the briefest, love-scenes of all time, but it was exceedingly illuminating. Even Larry, whose perceptions were inordinately obtuse where women were concerned, looked astonished and enlightened. The retrospect of Nagarcoil acquired undreamed-of implications. That fantastic set-up knocked on the head all considerations of caste, and even of poverty and wealth. On the one hand this girl so extravagantly rich in relatives and so poor in terms of money, and on the other this lonely, aristocratic, voluntary exile from caste and class, with his head full of exalted ideas and his life empty of kin. An excellent arrangement, Dominic thought, the pooling of equal but different resources. I wouldn't mind betting the Swami saw this coming. For a life-long non-swimmer he is certainly pretty good at forecasting the tides.

'No point in arguing, anyhow,' he said reasonably, standing-in for his distant mentor, 'she's here now. Look, you go on out to the shore, and I'll join you in a few minutes. I've just remembered something I'd better do now, while I think of it.'

What he had remembered – though he had never actually forgotten it, or detached his mind from it – was that he had promised to telephone the Swami whenever anything occurred that might be relevant to the matter in hand. And a Saivite sadhu seated in contemplation outside the little house in Jambukeshwar Lane seemed, in the light of past experience, alarmingly relevant.

'I see,' said the distant, meticulous voice, with evident concern, 'that I have miscalculated. I was afraid of it. Nothing has happened here. Lakshman is exemplary and immune – and I must say that I now feel every confidence in him – and no suspicious characters have been seen within a radius of miles. I am afraid no one is interested in us. The hunt has not been side-tracked. You understand what this means? Someone knew about that change of identities.'

There seemed no other explanation. From Koilpatti down to Nagarcoil they had seemed to have the road almost to themselves. If they had been followed – and they must have been – it had been at a most discreet distance. The pursuer had not had to depend on keeping his quarry in sight. And why set out to shadow the Land-Rover at all, unless someone had watched the embarkation, and observed and understood the change in the cast?

'It is a possibility,' admitted the Swami, 'that someone

already knew Purushottam by sight, but it cannot be put higher than a possibility. Much more probable is that someone was watching *who knew Lakshman.* And now you tell me that there are no less than six people there who know Lakshman quite well, from the events at Thekady.'

'Seven,' said Dominic, reluctantly. 'There's Larry. I don't seriously believe he's anything but what he seems, but I daren't take it for granted. And if one of us was involved, there wouldn't have to be any watcher to find out the score, would there?'

The Swami blandly ignored the omission of Priya, even though the blanket phrase 'one of us' could have been interpreted as including her. He pointed out practically: 'But there *was* a watcher. At Nagarcoil, if not at Malaikuppam, he was seen. By two quite independent witnesses, whose evidence is mutually corroborative. However, I agree with you, we must lose sight of no one, of no possibility.'

'You do take this seriously, then?' He was dismayed but not surprised; he had known in his own heart that it must be taken seriously.

'I take it very seriously indeed. And since it is known to all these people that Purushottam is in the hotel, that is clearly the most dangerous place, and what I feel we must do is get him out of it as much as possible. Forgive me,' said the Swami with his habitual subtlety and courtesy, 'if I say "we", for of course in every case you will do as you see fit, and I have complete confidence that you will do rightly. But since it was I who sent you there into danger, in the belief that I was sending you out of it, I must take my share of the responsibility for your situation.'

'Give me your advice,' said Dominic. 'I need it.'

'It will be best if you behave exactly as visitors to Cape Comorin are supposed to behave, and take advantage of the possibilities that offers. It is nearly time now for the evening ritual. Go out loudly and noticeably in a party to the sand dunes to watch the sunset. In dispersed groups everyone will be doing the same. Out there you will soon find more company, the women and boys who sell shell necklaces and other souvenirs. It will be quite cheap to add them to your party – a little conversation, a few strings of shells, and they will gladly go with you for the evening, and hope to make a few more sales on the dunes. Surround Purushottam on all sides – go to the village and the temple afterwards if it is still too early to disperse for the night. No one will attempt the assassination of someone enclosed in a large, mobile group visible for miles around. And I do not think the enemy will be found among the humble people encountered there on the spot, the poorest of the poor who make shell necklaces to sell to tourists. In all their lives few of them travel more than twenty miles from home, or are acquainted with news from much farther afield than that. Also I do not think it will be advisable to eat at the hotel. At the temple and in the village there will be booths. Where there are pilgrims there are always people to supply their needs. And when you come back to the hotel – how are your rooms situated?'

Dominic told him.

'Good, that may simplify things. Then say good night to the others, lock your door, disarrange your beds as though you have slept in them, and leave by the balcony, taking the key with you. It should be a warm, gentle night, you can safely spend it out in the sands or in the village. Do not come back until the hotel begins to stir, then rouse your friends and go out to see the sun rise. And everything with care!'

'And not a word to Larry? – or even to Priya?'

'The innocent are safer knowing as little as possible,' said the Swami very seriously, after prolonged consideration. 'From tomorrow it may be necessary to improvise afresh, but let us first take care of tonight.'

'It seems crazy,' Dominic said in helpless protest, 'that four of us here should be virtually under siege from one miserable individual. Aren't we attaching too much importance to this threat?'

'The man without scruples,' said the Swami sadly, 'to whom every life but his own is expendable, always starts with an advantage worth a whole army over the man who regards life as holy. And the man who creeps in secret is more dangerous than armies. Never be ashamed of taking precautions against snakes. Though indeed,' he added remorsefully, 'not all snakes are vicious or treacherous, they want only to defend themselves. Men who should walk upright, but creep in the grass with poison like snakes, have no such justification.'

'And tomorrow?' Dominic asked. 'Do we pay our score and get out of here?'

The distant voice, after due thought, said gently and finally: 'Cape Comorin is the end of the world, where is there to go beyond? In the end one battlefield is as good as another.'

Dominic waited, but there was nothing more. And after a moment he heard the soft click of the distant receiver being replaced in its cradle.

Eleven

Cape Comorin: Friday Evening

Beyond the garden, all grass and sand, they stepped out on to a metalled road. To the left it wound away along the coast, growing more confident and freer of sand with every yard gained, to the village and the temple; but to the right, to westward, it struggled feebly along for only a few hundred yards, increasingly trammelled with sand, before the dunes swept over it, and rose in undulating waves of yellow and dun and grey to the skyline, unbroken to the very edge of the rocks. In that direction the coastline also rose, jutting in low but jagged cliffs; but in the sector where they stood the road was not very far above the level of beach and sea. They crossed it, and advanced into a zone of broken gunmetal rocks that slashed out into the ocean in oblique strata, knife-edge beyond knife-edge, laced with the froth of surf, and ripping every incoming wave to angry shreds. And behind this boiling filigree of black rocks and reefs and white foam, the Indian Ocean opened, sun-drenched and cobalt blue, surging away due south without a break to the Antarctic.

Because of the stormy contention of the rocks against the incoming tide they had the impression that there was a fine gale blowing, but in fact it was no more than a fresh breeze that fluttered their hair, and the air was warm and clear. They scrambled out to the edge of the rocks, and looked down upon a narrow beach of smooth sand, up which the waves hissed and withdrew in steady rhythm; and to their left, perhaps half a mile away beyond an arc of troubled water, they saw the cape itself at last, the final promontory of rocks jutting far into the sea, with tidal foam washing round its feet.

Inland from it the roofs of the village began, and the temple of Kumari, the virgin aspect of Parvati, who gives Cape Comorin its name. And firmly planted on the outer-most platform of rock, its *shikhara* tapering into the air to provide the vertical accent this largely horizontal and oblique land-and-seascape needed, stood the modern white memorial built on the spot where Mahatma Gandhi's ashes rested before they were committed to the Indian Ocean. All smooth white, touched with blue, rooted solidly into the dark rocks, with the cobalt sea beyond, and a scud of white cloud overhead.

'It's odd,' said Priya, 'but seen from here it fits in so well. And when you see it close to it's rather dreadful, like blue and white plastic.'

They turned westwards, following the road until it succumbed to the encroachments of the sand, and then began to climb up into the dunes. And presently there were small naked feet pattering alongside, and two little boys who had appeared out of nowhere were uttering soft blandishments in Malayalam and English, and holding out for their inspection long strings of pierced shells, some inch-long and oval-smooth in matt brown and white, some smaller and slimmer, textured liked fine hoar-frost in several shades from white to fawn. The Swami had known this coast. Probably these bead-sellers were never far from the hotel, waiting for a well-disposed tourist to emerge on the evening pilgrimage. A young woman, wearing a faded red sari without a blouse, added herself to the group, proffering her own merchandise. The woman spoke a few words of English, one of the boys rather more, and Purushottam, at his most serene and sociable, spoke Malayalam with the other one. At the cost of a few *naye paise* they acquired three satisfied business contacts, who accompanied them cheerfully as they walked on up the heaving slope of the dunes. Soon other visitors would be making their way up here to watch the sun go down, and this was as good a spot for sales as any.

They reached the crest, and emerged upon an undulating plateau of fine sand, dappled only, here and there, by low clumps of tamarisks and wisps of dry grass in the slightly sheltered places, and little stars of sea plants. Here the coast rose in a jagged series of low cliffs embracing, with long, steely arms and granite talons, deeply indented coves into which the waves came seething at high speed, over sands fantastically coloured in shades of dark blackberry reds, and angry purples, and rusty black. These shades seemed to be laid down by the tides in a series of overlapping scallops, and in places the dark, sultry colours were varied by planes of yellow and grey-green. The necklace boys, amused by Larry's surprise and interest, shrugged their shoulders over this phenomenon; everyone knew that the sands at the Cape, and further up this western coast in Kerala, too, were coloured like this.

'It's ilmenite and monazite mostly,' said Purushottam. 'Quite valuable deposits. They get most of the world's thorium supply out of monazite sand. It occurs in this same form in other places, too.'

They slithered down a narrow, rocky path, and picked up handfuls of the copper-beech-red and crow-black sand, clean and fine and glittering, cool in the palm of the hand. For a while they walked along the beach, but the coastline was too deeply indented, and rocks and tide drove them up to the dunes again. Fold upon fold of sand, rolling in smooth curves from the broken coast more than a mile inland, to where the distant and scattered crests of trees showed like stains of green moss. The Swami had known what he was talking about. No one in his senses would dare to attempt to get within striking distance of a prospective victim here at this hour, where there was no cover at all, and no hope of withdrawal unseen.

There was only one thing to break the monotony, a squat little hut of timber and matting and thatch, perched on the neck of a long, narrow peninsula of rocks, tilted in knife-edged, striated layers. There was a small cove beneath it, the alluvial sand patterning it in dull green and sultry crimson. They crossed the neck of the peninsula behind the hut – it was only a few yards – and looked down into another bay, somewhat larger than the first and much more sheltered by the enfolding arm of rock; and here there were two fishing boats beached above the tide, and covered over with little gabled roofs of coconut fibre matting, and a net lay draped to dry in long serpentines across the sand, which here was clear and golden. The hut was evidently for the storage of nets and ropes and tackle, and had access by steep and difficult rock tracks to both little bays. It turned its back upon the weather and the sea, crouched into the last sheltering rise to the cliff-edge, and opened its narrow doorway and mat-screened window towards the land, scanning the miles of dunes with one blank dark eye beneath a coconut fibre eyebrow.

They sat down in the sand, in the lee of the hut on its blind side, facing westwards over the beach and the cobalt sea. Over the yellow of the sand the deep blue was transmuted into emerald green. The deserted boat below had a high prow like a gondola, and the net was a muted sand-brown, faint as a mist against the gold.

They saw when they looked back over the dunes that the solitude was beginning to be peopled. Several family parties of Indian pilgrims and tourists had streamed out from the village, and were making their way at leisure towards the sinking sun. And there among them came the Bessancourts, Madame thrusting indomitably through the sand in her sensible sandals and her black *shalwar* and *kameez*, her husband plodding tirelessly beside her with his box camera. And the Manis, immaculate and determined as ever, with Sushil Dastur labouring behind, this time with two small folding chairs in addition to Sudha's beach-bag. The sun was going to have a very respectable audience, in spite of the fact that it was already half-obscured by towering clouds, and more were driving up to join the accumulation.

'As a matter of fact,' Priya said almost apologetically, 'it almost always is cloudy. In the morning, too. Even if the day is very fine.'

The spectacle, nevertheless, was sufficiently arresting The clouds changed and dissolved in a multiplicity of colours and shapes, and at the fieriest moment of the sunset, over that dazzling, dark sea, they ripped themselves away on either side, and let the crimson eye burn through and set fire to the miles of shadowy sand and the upturned, devout faces. For a few moments the dunes were molten. Then the great eye closed again, and the clouds banked low, touching the sea; and quite suddenly it was more than halfway to being night.

The bead-sellers had left them by then to go and tout for a few more sales among the pilgrims; but when they turned back towards the hotel and the village, one of the boys came trotting back and re-attached himself, making gay conversation with Purushottam all the way back to where the dunes dived headlong to the submerged road. Then he suddenly salaamed, and made off at a brisk trot towards the village, taking it for granted that his friends would turn aside into the hotel garden.

'Let's go on to the temple and the memorial,' Dominic suggested. 'There's plenty of time, no need to go in yet.'

It was very easy. They were ready to fall in with any plan that kept them outdoors in this mild, pleasant evening, and a part of this curious holiday scene. No one needed any persuading even when he proposed that they should forego dinner at the hotel, and eat like the pilgrims who thronged the forecourts of Kumari's temple. There were stalls selling every conceivable kind of spice, hot food, soft drinks, fruit, rice, various breads and in particular the highly-coloured and highly-sugared sweets that proliferate everywhere in India. After the dunes, the village was a revelation, crowded, busy, noisy and gay, a twilit fairground soon sparkling with little lanterns. Both village and temple stood on the levelled strata of the rocks, as near kin to ocean as to land. The sound of surf was a continuo to the sound of so many voices.

Afterwards they went, among many others, to the highly-polished blue-and-white plastic memorial, and climbed to the base of its white, lotus-bud-shaped tower to look out over the sea. A few child beggars came pestering, the first they had seen here; naturally they made their base where the foreign tourists were most likely to be found in profitable numbers. Purushottam bore with them for a while, and then gave them some small coins and ordered them crisply away, and they removed themselves without resentment, grinning.

'They do quite well here,' said Priya practically. 'Where there are pilgrims there must be some tender consciences, and the easiest way to peace of mind is to give. It is a fairly cheap way to acquire merit.'

The fairground showed no signs of closing down with nightfall. When they had walked themselves into a pleasant weariness, the village was as gay as ever; and when at last they turned back towards the hotel, the lighted stalls were still twinkling behind them like terrestrial stars.

Madame Bessancourt was installed in the foyer with her knitting, now a formidable roll of blue moss-stitch. She saw them come in from the night, and made them her invariable brisk bow over the flashing needles. Her smile was immemorial France, friendly but self-contained. The three who knew her halted to exchange the customary courtesies; Purushottam, after a quick glance, went on to the desk like a conscientious guide, and collected the keys.

'I saw in the newspapers,' she said, putting down her needles momentarily into her lap, 'about the death of your friend. I am very sorry. When Romesh told me you were here, I hoped to see you again, and at least express my sympathy. I know well there is no more one can do. The death of the young cannot be made good by anything the old may do or say. I have experienced it. But for my husband and myself, I offer you our sincere sorrow.'

There were no evasions about Madame Bessancourt. She looked them in the eyes, one by one, and her own eyes were as steady and dark as the rocks under Cape Comorin.

They told her she was very kind, and could find almost nothing else to say. To comment on the beauties of the Cape and the coast, after that direct assault, seemed meaningless. But she was not curious about their presence here, or about the new member they had acquired in place of Lakshman, or about any item of what was essentially their business. She had said her say and done her duty. After a few civil exchanges they said good night, and moved on to join Purushottam, who was waiting with the keys.

On impulse, Dominic turned back. There was never any harm in checking credentials.

'Madame – Romesh tells me you've taken him on to travel with you as far as Dindigul.'

'Yes,' she said, her needles clicking again. 'He asked us. And it is a very little thing to do for him. I only hope there will really be a job for him there, since we are not in a position to provide one. He seems a good boy.'

That was all he had had to ask, but for some reason he still lingered. 'You're going on to Pondicherry?'

'Yes. It is not so far now, we don't really need a third driver, but it satisfies him that he's doing something for his keep. Two days' drive, would you say?'

'Or three, as you feel inclined. I suppose it must be about three hundred and forty miles or so. Will you be making an early start tomorrow?'

'No, we want to have a look at the village and the temple in the morning. We have plenty of time.'

'And after Pondicherry?'

'Our tour ends with Pondicherry,' she said. Her fingers, broad and strong and brown, halted on the needles. She looked up at him with a shrewd smile. 'I think you must find it a little strange that two elderly people like my husband and myself should suddenly leave our provincial town and come here to India like this. No, no, please don't apologise, it is very natural. Sometimes I find it a little strange myself. Monsieur Bessancourt and I had a son, you see – our only child, and born rather late in our lives. He was a student of architecture. Three years ago he came out here to join the international team which is working on the first stages of Auroville. You have heard of Auroville?'

'Yes,' said Dominic. 'It's the ideal city of the future that they're hoping to build near Pondicherry. The people at the Sri Aurobindo ashram there started the idea, and I know a lot of the drive and talent is coming from France.'

'Raoul was an idealist. He believed in the future, and he wanted to have a hand in building it.' She folded her needles together with perfect composure, and began to roll the blue knitting round them. Her husband had just appeared in the doorway, returning from a last stroll before bed. 'Two days after he landed in Bombay,' said Madame, 'he was killed in a street accident.'

There was nothing he could say to her; she had herself made it impossible to offer her anything, nor did she need anything from him. She gave him a small, reassuring smile, well aware of everything that was happening within him. 'We were in any case near retirement. We sold our business, and came out here after him. And a part of the proceeds we have spent in travelling round India, where he wished to live and work. Is it very surprising that we should plan the tour to end at Pondicherry?'

'No,' he said in a low voice, 'not surprising at all. I can understand that very well.' He looked her in the eyes, and said, as she had said: 'I am very sorry.' And then, in delicate withdrawal: 'You will have a whole world of memories, when you get back to France.'

Madame Bessancourt tucked her knitting into her bag, and rose smilingly to meet her husband, who was crossing the hall.

'We are not going back to France,' she said. 'We are not young, we have not much to offer – yet still, perhaps something more than merely what remains of the price we got for the shop. When the time comes, we shall die in Auroville.'

They took Priya to her door and said good night there very quietly, for by the hush that had settled over the house they knew that most of the guests were already in bed. Larry let himself into the room next door, and Dominic and Purushottam went on, soft-footed, into their narrow side-corridor.

A dim light had been left burning at the turn. By its subdued gleam they saw, the moment they turned the corner, that the louvred outer door of their room was not closed. One leaf of it jutted into the passage, and a squat figure was leaning inside it, a hand on the door-handle, and an ear inclined against the upper panels, listening for any sound within.

Dominic came out of the haze in which Madame Bessancourt's confidences had left him, and leaped at the intruder. He made very little noise, but the rush of air alerted the listening man. He recoiled across the passage with a faint squeak of terror, turning to face the threat with shrinking shoulders and apprehensive eyes; but he did not run, for the corridor was a dead end, and there was nowhere to run to. The louvre swung back and forth, gently creaking; and they found themselves staring into the frightened and mortified face of Sushil Dastur.

Before they could utter a word he began to babble in a frantic whisper, excuse and apology tumbling over each other in their haste. 'Please, please, I beg you, Mr Felse, please don't rouse the house, please, I beg for silence. I can explain all . . . I was not trying to enter . . . I am not a thief, please believe me, I would not . . . It was a mistake, only a mistake. I thought this was Mr Preisinger's room . . . . I wished to speak with Mr Preisinger . . .'

'At this time of night?' demanded Dominic disbelievingly.

'Hush!' pleaded Sushil Dastur in a frenzy of muted terror. 'Please, please keep your voice down! If Mr Mani should hear — Oh, I am so unlucky, so ashamed! What can you think of me? I wanted only to speak with Mr Preisinger privately . . . Mr Mani must not know about it, please, I beg you, don't tell him I came here . . .'

'What did you want with Mr Preisinger that Mr Mani mustn't know about?' Dominic asked in a milder tone, baffled by so sudden a manifestation of the devious in this hitherto predictable and inoffensive person. How could you tell, when it came to the point, who was capable of involved and circuitous evil, and who was not?

'I wanted to ask him — Mr Preisinger is an American, he travels with an Indian guide, he must surely be a person of importance. I wished to ask him,' whispered Sushil Dastur abjectly, 'if he does not need a good secretary during his stay in India. I should be glad to work for him if he can employ me . . .' No wonder he was trembling at his own daring and its ignominious ending. 'Or I thought that perhaps Mr Preisinger is connected with some firm which has business interests here, and could get me a job with them if I asked him. Please, please, Mr Felse,' he begged piteously, 'don't tell Mr Mani about this . . . You understand, it would be very unpleasant for me . . . very difficult . . .'

It would indeed, Dominic thought, it would be a minor hell, especially if he really is a poor relation. They'd never let him forget it, life-long. And jobs in India are very, very hard to get, that's no lie.

'I am so unhappy . . . I have made you think ill of me,

and I so much wanted your good opinion. Please do not think badly of me, I am telling you the truth – I had no other reason for coming here, none. It was a mistake about the room, please believe me . . .'

He was nearly in tears of mortification. It all sounded plausible enough, even probable. Many a time he must have toyed desperately with the idea of putting an end to the endless hectoring and harassment to which the Manis subjected him, and looked in vain for a way of setting about it. Small blame to him if he at least attempted it when an apparently well-to-do American came his way; and small blame to him if he did his best to keep the move secret from Gopal Krishna. All quite plausible. But then a story for an occasion like this would have to be plausible. And might it not be even a little too apposite? Thought out in advance to be used in the event of discovery?

'All right,' Dominic said. 'But better not disturb Mr Preisinger tonight. Mind you, I doubt very much if he wants or needs a secretary, or has any jobs to offer, but you can ask him tomorrow if you still want to.'

'Oh, no, I could not ask him now, I am so ashamed . . . But thank you, thank you . . . And you will not say anything to Mr Mani?'

'No, we won't say a word to Mr Mani.' What else could he do but accept it at face value and let the man go? There was no possible way of proving any ill intent on his part, and nothing to be done but go on keeping a close watch on Purushottam until morning. And then? The Swami had said no word of what was to happen afterwards.

'You are most kind, Mr Felse, I am grateful . . . So unfortunate, I'm sorry . . . I'm sorry . . . Good night! . . .'

Sushil Dastur scuttled away thankfully but still miserably, his big head drawn deep into his shoulders with shame and distress. They watched him creep round the corner, and heard the soft slur of his feet on the stairs. Without a word Purushottam inserted the key into the lock of the inner door, and opened it. Nothing was said until he had locked it again carefully after them. Dominic switched on his bedside light, and they looked at each other doubtfully.

'It could be true,' said Dominic fairly. 'You haven't seen as much of them as we have.'

'In any case, even if he was up to something, he seemed to be only just trying the door. It was double-locked, I doubt if he could have got in.'

Purushottam crossed to the window, which was open on the balcony. The filigree of the wrought-iron railings stood out blackly against the phosphorescence of the sea, and the lambent sky that seemed to reflect its glow.

'Come in,' said Dominic shortly. 'Leave the window open but draw the curtains. We've got our orders for the night, and we don't want to advertise the preparations. As far as the outside world's concerned we're now peacably getting ready for bed.'

Purushottam turned back into the room obediently, though he did nothing about the curtains. 'And aren't we?'

'Not here, anyway.'

'Interesting! And when did we get our orders? And from whom?'

'From the Swami. I telephoned him this afternoon, before we went out.' He told him exactly what had been said. Purushottam stood attentive but frowning; his respect for the Swami Premanathanand was immense, but he still found it hard to credit that so much ingenuity was being spent either on hunting him or protecting him.

'Couldn't we have told the others? I don't like even the appearance of deceiving Priya.'

'As the Swami sees it, I think what you'll be doing is sparing her anxiety rather than deceiving her. He said, the less the innocent know, the safer they'll be.'

Dominic crossed to the window and attacked the curtains himself. They were opaque enough to hide all light, heavy, ancient velvet, perhaps from the days when this had been the district Residency. And they must have cost a great deal when they were new, for the room was exceedingly lofty, and the windows went right up to the ceiling. Dominic tugged at the dusty velvet, and found it weighty and obstinate, moving reluctantly on huge old wooden rings. The rail was a yard and more out of his reach. He was looking round for something to stand on, when he saw the long iron rod, with a blunted hook at one end, standing propped in the corner of the window. The answer had been provided along with the problem, many years ago. He reached up with the rod, inserting the hook among the rings, and drew them across until the curtains closed.

'All right,' said Purushottam, making up his mind. 'I agreed to come, so now I must keep the rules, I suppose. We'll need coats if we're going to sleep out. It won't be cold, exactly, but there'll be a chilly hour or two before dawn. And the beds ... that's easy!'

Dominic turned back into the room with the rod still in his hand, swinging it experimentally like a player trying the weight of an unfamiliar golf club, just as Purushottam laid hands on the covers of his bed at the pillow, and stripped them down in one sweep of his arm, sending his discarded shirt of the morning billowing on to the floor.

Something else flashed from between the disturbed sheets, and flew in a writhing, spiralling arabesque through the air between the two beds. Dominic saw a lightning convulsion of black and white, slender and glistening from burnished scales; and in an inspired movement which was part nervous reflex and part conscious recognition, he lashed out with the long iron rod in his hand. It was thin, rigid and murderous, and he hit out with all his strength. The fluid thing and the unyielding thing met in mid-air with the lightest and most agonising of sounds, and the one coiled about the other with electrifying vehemence and rapidity, sound and motion all one indistinguishable reaction. Blackness and whiteness span so close to Dominic's hand that he dropped the rod in a frantic hurry, and leaped back as it fell.

On the dull brown carpet between the beds the snake lay threshing the quicksilver coils of its body and tail in feeble rage and helpless agony, tightening and relaxing about the rod, its head making only faint, jerky motions that did not move it from where it lay crippled. Its back was broken. Not quite three feet – but coiled and shrunken it looked even less than that – of black body banded with white rings, the scales on its back noticeably enlarged. Not a very big specimen, not a very spectacular species, nothing so impressive as the cobra with its spectacled hood. *Bungarus caerulius*, the common Indian krait, one of the most venomous snakes alive.

Twelve

Cape Comorin: Friday Night to Saturday Dawn

Purushottam had remained standing frozen in ludicrous astonishment, his hand still clutching the edge of the sheet, his face bright and blank, like a page not yet written on. But the page was rapidly, almost instantly, filled; with realisation and understanding, and a quality of horror that belonged to this death of all deaths. Everyone has his own private fears; snake-bite was Purushottam's, a dread aggravated rather than otherwise by the very thought that the luckless creature that could kill in such a frightful way was without malice, not even aggressive except when hunting food, rather a shy and retiring being, anxious to avoid conflict rather than to go looking for it. He stood rigid, staring at the wriggling thing that both horrified him and stirred him to pity. It was the first time he had seriously contemplated the creature behind this creature, the force that must pay for the krait's wretched end as well as for the attempt against him. He knew quite positively, at that moment, that the krait had been brought here to kill him. It could have been there by accident, having crept of its own will into a warm place to sleep; there was no way of proving the contrary. Nevertheless, he knew.

There are, of course, he thought with curious detachment, too many kraits in India, as there are too many cobras, and too many men. Their world is over-populated, like ours.

The krait still writhed feebly. A thread-like, forked tongue flickered in and out of its open mouth between the poison fangs. Its tight coils relaxed limply, quivering.

Purushottam reached out his hand almost stealthily, and slowly closed his fingers around the extreme end of the rod.

With gingerly movements he eased it out of the flaccid coils until he could draw it free. He stood back and waited for the head to be clear of the contorted body, and then struck accurately at the neck. The carpet, old and good, absorbed the sound of the blow. The krait shuddered and jerked, twitched its tail once or twice, and was still. Over the dulling body Purushottam and Dominic looked up rather dazedly at each other.

'That'll be twenty rupees, please,' Dominic said inanely.

'I'll give you an I.O.U,' said Purushottam, and meant it. His knees gave under him weakly, and he sat down abruptly on the edge of his bed, and as hastily picked himself up again the next moment and stood away from it, shivering with distaste. 'Another kind of explosive this time,' he said grimly. 'If I'd simply undressed and gone to bed I should almost certainly have been bitten. They're not vicious, it takes quite a lot to make them bite, but having a great human oaf come plunging in on top of you when you're half asleep is a bit too much to take. And if you hadn't happened to have that thing in your hand, and lashed out with it like that, he'd have been away out of sight the instant he hit the floor, and he might have got one of us yet.' He held out the rod to Dominic. 'Here, use this to strip your sheets down, don't risk your hands... He may have brought two!'

'No need,' said Dominic, equally tense and pale, and pointed to the shirt now crumpled on the carpet, and the initialled bag at the foot of the bed. 'He knew which was yours. He knew who he wanted, all right.'

'Maybe, but don't take risks,' Purushottam insisted.

'But could it really have been planted deliberately? Would anyone use such a chancy method?' Dominic circled round the carcase warily, hooked the end of the rod in the neat covers of his own bed, and drew them down. 'In all the time I've been in India, this is the first time I've ever actually *seen* a krait, except in a zoo.'

'Plenty of people die of snake-bite in India,' said Purushottam soberly, 'who've never seen a snake – not even the one that bit them. But they're everywhere, all the same. Not as common down here as in Bengal, maybe, but there are plenty round Madurai if you look for them. Yes, it's quite a credible method of getting rid of someone you dislike. It's been used often enough before. There are people who make a study of handling these fellows. A stick with a noose, and the right sort of meal.... Some people even used to keep them and breed them, in the days when there was a tally paid for killing them, just to be able to produce a constant supply of bodies. They make a profession of snakes. Looks as if your bed's clear, though. Two kraits in one room could hardly have been passed off as accidental. Do we still get out of here?'

'Faster than ever,' said Dominic, draping his bedclothes convincingly. 'Because whoever planted this chap will be standing by, expecting one of us – me! – to rouse the house any moment. Just to make sure everything's gone according to plan, and his job's done. He may even be watching our window...' The thought jolted him. Nothing would be gained if he withdrew Purushottam from this dangerous place only to draw the danger after him. But Purushottam reassured him instantly and confidently.

'He won't! That's the last thing he'll do if he's not just a thug from outside, but somebody known around the place, staff, guide, guests, whoever you like. He'll be with somebody else now, setting up all the alibis he can, preferably with three or four others – a card party, something like that.' He was thinking, perhaps, of the voluble and intent card party they had seen going on by lantern-light in the car-park, round a head-cloth spread out on the sand, with two of the room boys, an off-duty porter, and the Manis' sleepy, cynical hired driver, slapping down the cards like gauntlets. The Manis' driver – yes. A bored professional from Madurai, where kraits are common enough. They had never really looked at that driver; usually he seemed to be asleep. Dominic remembered him as an inanimate body curled up in the back seat at Thekady, while the whole place boiled with excitement round him.

'He'll be listening for the alarm,' Purushottam said with conviction, 'but round at the front, somewhere innocent, and in company, primed to be more surprised and shocked than anyone else. But if we delay, he may get anxious and come round to see if anything's happening.'

'Switch on the light in the shower-room,' said Dominic. 'As long as that's on, and a bedside light here, he won't wonder what's gone wrong, he'll just think we take the devil of a time to get to bed. That's it! We'll leave the curtains parted just a crack, to let the light show through.'

They took the wind-jackets they had luckily brought in with them, when they might just as easily have left them in the Land-Rover, and a torch which Dominic happened to have in his night kit, and cautiously parted the curtains to slip out on to the balcony and prospect the dark garden below. Everything was still. They stood tensed, listening, and there was no sound at all except from the distant sea, a muted, plangent, regular sound that had nothing of the spasmodic motivations of man in it, only the rhythmic cadences of eternity, reassuring and terrifying, like the Swami's smile.

'Wait a minute, we'd better get rid of the krait.' Purushottam went back to hoist it carefully in the hook of the curtain rod, and carry it out to the balcony. 'Not even a big one,' he said in a whisper. 'They grow to four feet and more, this kind.' He slid the carcase through the railings, well aside from the iron pillar that held up the balcony, and let it slide dully into the thin grass below. 'All right, I've got the key. You go first.'

Dominic climbed over the railing, and let himself down to grip the pillar, and edge his way silently down to the ground. Purushottam propped the rod back in its place, and readjusted the curtain behind him so that a chink of subdued light showed through, and then followed him over. The balcony continued on round the corner, providing access to all the first-floor rooms, and at the far end on the eastern side, close to Priya's room, there was an iron stairway down into the garden; but the last thing they wanted was to run the risk of disturbing Priya. Purushottam lowered himself to the last decorative curlicues of wrought iron sprouting from the capital of the pillar, and then hung by his hands and dropped lightly into the sand below. They stood for a moment braced and listening, but the night was silent and still. The quickest way to cover was across the narrowest zone of the garden and out on to the road. They took it, moving carefully and quietly, the sand swallowing their footsteps; and once on the road, they turned towards the village.

The night was calm, mild and only moderately dark; after a brief period abroad in it they could distinguish each other's features clearly, and make out the shapes of land and sea as lucidly as by day, though through a pure veil of darkness. There was less cloud in the sky now than at the sunset, and the stars were huge and many, encrusted like jewelled inlays on a vault of ebony.

They spent the first part of the night in the village, fascinated by a life which had not ceased with darkness, but only slowed its tempo a little, and rested half its cast. There was something very comforting in moving among people who accepted them casually as a part of normality, and had no special interest in them, and certainly no design on them, except perhaps to extort the occasional coin. They even toyed with the idea of sleeping in the dormitory provided for the pilgrims, but discarded it finally in favour of a solitude. They were not the only ones sleeping outdoors that night, but in this dormitory there was room for all. They found themselves a hollow in a sheltered, sandy cove, not far from the village, high and dry above the tide-line, though the tide was well down now and still receding, and made themselves a comfortable nest there. The sand, at this higher level, felt warm to the touch, unlike the coolness of the alluvial deposits on the foreshore.

'I've slept in worse beds,' said Dominic.

Purushottam laughed rather hollowly, remembering the bed and the bed-fellow he had just escaped. Until now they had said not a word about that since leaving the hotel, but now he peered into the recent past and frowned, wondering.

'Dominic – was he really just trying the door, or just re-locking it? – Sushil Dastur? They're old, big locks, maybe child's play to a professional, after all...'

'Do I know?' Dominic had wondered the same thing. 'But then there must have been a box, a bag, something – you don't walk in with a snake dangling from your hand. A rush basket – some sort of container...'

'That's true. And he didn't have anything.'

'All the same,' said Dominic very seriously, 'no one can logically be ruled out. There are six people here who were also at Thekady. Not counting our own party. Not forgetting myself,' he said firmly. 'From where you're standing...'

'Lying,' corrected Purushottam drowsily, working his shoulders comfortably into the sand.

'— you can't afford to rule out any possibility.'

Purushottam's tranquil face gazed up into the stars, and smiled, quite unshaken. 'I'll overlook that. Just so long as you don't ask me to suspect Priya.' He lay quiet for a moment, relaxed and still. 'Dominic! Are you ... is there a girl somewhere belonging to you?'

'I'm engaged,' said Dominic. 'Tossa's still at Oxford, finishing her arts degree. After that we shall get married. We haven't made any further plans yet, but I think – I really think we may come back here together.'

'You make it sound so easy,' sighed Purushottam.

'Don't kid yourself, it's never easy. You have to work at

it, like everything else. What are you worrying about?' he said reasonably to the silent, doubtful figure beside him. 'You've got virtually no family to make difficulties, and she's got a family that could absorb half a dozen sons- and daughters-in-law, and never turn a hair.

'She has, hasn't she?' agreed Purushottam warmly, remembering and taking heart. 'Not that I'm the best bargain there ever was in the marriage market. Did you know that even an ordinary close friendship with a fellow-student in England – a girl, that is – could send a bridegroom's prospects crashing to the very bottom of the scale? And having crazy ideas about getting rid of your money, instead of making more and more, wouldn't do a man's chances any good, either. But *her* family – there ought to be enough Christian charity there, don't you think? Even for someone as odd as I am?'

'I wouldn't be surprised,' said Dominic encouragingly, 'if they're eccentric enough themselves positively to *like* oddities.'

'Good, you hearten me.' He lay still for a few minutes, his eyelids low over the dark, thoughtful eyes, his fingertips playing gently in the sand. 'So now all we have to do is get clear of this tangle. Alive.'

'That's all.'

Purushottam sighed, stretched, turned on his side and scooped a hollow for his shoulder. In a few minutes he was asleep. Dominic braced his back into the slope of the ground, worked his heels comfortably into the sand and settled down to stay awake through the night.

They worked their way back to the road opposite the hotel at the first hint of daylight, some time before the sun began to colour the eastern sky. From the garden they could see the staff already stirring, and a light in one or two of the guest-rooms, where visitors were rousing themselves in good time to go out and see the sunrise. The timing appeared to be good; even if they were seen strolling in from the road and mounting the stairs to the balcony at this hour, they would merely be written off as eccentric enough, or over-anxious enough, to have got up an hour too early for the prescribed spectacle. They looked under the balcony for the carcase of the krait, and found it where Purushottam had let it fall, its bright black and white dulled now to a dim greyness. It was a reminder of a situation which was still with them, and still unchanged, but in the first light of day it was difficult to believe in it. The bedroom was as they had left it; no sign of any further intrusion, though they tended to handle things and move about the room with wincing care, and to watch every step they took.

'Better wake the others, if they're not up already,' Dominic judged.

'I think we're leading the field this morning.'

But they were not. When they walked along the corridor it was to see the Bessancourts just descending the stairs, almost certainly going out to watch the sunrise before breakfast, prior to making their planned tour of the temple and the village afterwards. Dominic watched the two straight, square backs marching steadily away towards the outer doorway, and suddenly saw for the first time the immensity of what they had done. Even for a middle-aged English couple, taking up their roots and committing themselves and all their capital to a new and unknown life at this stage would have been a daunting step; for these twin pillars of the solidity of France it was at once lunatic and heroic. Ideal undertakings like Auroville so often foundered for want of both faith and works, and they had made no preliminary inspection on the spot – though no doubt there had been correspondence – but simply realised everything they had, and set out. Auroville was to be the end of their journey; they were committed. He thought, the chances of one dream being realised will at any rate go up several notches when those two arrive.

They knocked on Larry's door, and elicited a sleepy grunt from within, and then a clearer utterance promising compliance. In a few minutes they heard him moving about, and the splash of the shower. They tapped on Priya's door and got no answer.

'Still asleep,' said Purushottam. 'Ought we to disturb her?'

They waited a little while, listening for any sound of activity from within. Then they knocked again, but still there was no answer. Larry opened his door to them, towelling his crew-cut vigorously, and still there was no reply from Priya.

'Perhaps she's dressed and gone out already, before we came,' said Purushottam, arguing with himself. His face had grown pale, and his eyes large. 'May I go through by the balcony, and see?'

They followed at his heels, across the room and out to the balcony beside the iron stairway. Priya's window stood open, the curtains half-drawn across it, just as when they had passed it quietly on coming in. The quietness began to seem ominous, the pre-dawn light inauspicious, though it had not seemed so then.

Purushottam tapped at the glass. 'Priya? Are you awake? Priya! ...'

He knew she was not there; there was no sense of her presence, no lingering hint of her movements in the air, nothing. He opened the window wider, and went into the room.

The nearer of the two beds still bore the light imprint of her body, and was disarranged only as it would have been if she had recently risen from it in a perfectly normal way; but it was cold. The door was locked, and the key in the lock. Nothing seemed to be disturbed. But in the shower-room the film of water and the splashed drops from her overnight shower had already dried completely; the hand-basin, too, was dry, the towels were dry. The sari she had worn yesterday was draped neatly over the back of a chair in the bedroom, ready to put on again. Priya had neither washed nor dressed this morning. Of all her belongings, nothing was missing but her white night sari and her dark silk dressing-gown, and the sandals of light fawn leather she habitually wore.

'Look,' Larry said, hushed and uneasy, 'she was writing a letter last night.'

The letter, to her Punjabi room-mate in the Nurses' Home at Madras, was necessarily in English. It had reached one and a half pages, and then been tidily abandoned for the night, folded into her writing-case with the address and salutation protruding. And on top of the case was another sheet torn from her writing-pad and folded in two. 'There's a note here, addressed to someone – that's Tamil, isn't it?'

Purushottam came flashing anxiously across the room, and took it up with a soft cry of hope and relief. 'It's to me!' But even in the act of unfolding it he was shaken afresh by awful doubts, and looked again at his own name. He had never seen Priya's writing until now, in the neat, precise English of her letter; but these fiercely formed characters in Tamil gave him no sense of handling something which had come to him from her.

His hands were shaking as he began to read; they were like stone when he ended, and all the light was gone from his face, which for one moment was stunned and dead, until the dreadful certainty came.

'He's taken her – taken Priya.' He raised his eyes to their faces. 'Because the krait was a failure . . . because I was out of reach when he came to see what had gone wrong. This time he meant to make sure. You want to know what he has to say to me?'

He read, translating slowly, freely and coldly, like a voice out of a computer:

' "It is you we want, not her. Now you shall come to us,

and of your own will, if you want the girl to go free. You will come to the fisherman's hut on the dunes to take her place, *and come alone*. If I do not see you coming – *alone* – by seven o'clock, I cut her throat." '

The sheet of notepaper with its words carved deep like stabs dropped from his hand, done with. He was back on the balcony before they had wrenched themselves out of their appalled daze and realised what he was about. They started after him, Larry catching at his arm.

'The police – we must get them! They'll have to —'

'No police,' said Purushottam, biting off the word and shutting upon it lips drawn pale and thin. 'No police, no tricks, no anything. There isn't time.'

'But we've got to do something! They'll turn out all the forces they've got – they'll get her back —'

'Dead!' said Purushottam. 'You know what time it is? Well past six.'

'But the police have resources —'

'*No!* I say no police. Not a word to anyone, no hunt, nothing. If you try to be clever, Priya will simply be murdered at once. Do you doubt it?'

They did not doubt it. 'But the police are as capable as we are of moving discreetly, they have resources, they'll arrange it so that —'

'Fool!' said Purushottam without heat, his feet clattering on the iron staircase down which Priya had been dragged in the night. 'Have you forgotten how the hut lies? You could cover the whole sweep of the dunes from it. No one could approach without being seen long before. And Priya would die.'

Dominic said – it was the first thing he had found it needful to say, and it was no comfort at all, but it was the truth: 'At best she may – you know that. If she can identify him now.'

'Yes, I do know. But even such people as he *may* keep

their word – I daren't stop hoping. If we start a hunt, then she will certainly die. To give him a better chance to get away. And to kill me by another way.'

'But a boat...' said Dominic.

Halfway across the garden, Purushottam spared him one quick glance, from very far away, and the brief ghost of a smile. 'Yes. If there was time, by water one might reach them. Even that would be a risk. But there's no time. It would be past seven before you got hold of a boat.'

It was true, and they knew it; the chances of beating that deadline were practically nil, without a motor-boat, and a motor-boat, even if one were to be had, might by its sound alert the kidnapper and precipitate what they most wished to prevent. Nevertheless, Larry suddenly swerved away from the hapless procession heading for the dunes, and turned and ran like a hare, not for the hotel, but for the village. At least to try – to make some sort of attempt to defeat what outraged him. Purushottam checked, and looked after him in exasperated distress.

'He's crazy! He'll only kill her!'

'No,' said Dominic with awful certainty. 'He won't have time.'

'No – that's true. He won't have time.' Purushottam sank his face between his palms for a moment, and shook his head from side to side helplessly. 'I did this to her. She never should have known me!'

'I don't believe she'd say so,' said Dominic, 'even now.'

They were motionless there in the garden for only a moment. But even so Dominic heard, shrill and indignant on the air, wafting from one of the first-floor balconies: 'Sushil Dastur! *Sushil Dastur!*' And Gopal Krishna's booming response, equally indignant but even more incredulous: 'He is not there! No one has seen him! Where can he have got to? What is he thinking off?' Mutually complaining, voices out of another world, they faded into the interior of the hotel.

But perhaps not another world, after all! Sushil Dastur, stooping at the doorway of a room where a krait had been introduced to do the dirty work for men....

Purushottam seemed not to have heard. He lifted a pale, set face out of his hands, and turned with determination towards the road, and the rising folds of sand.

'Don't go away! Come with me. As far as you can... You see I can't do anything else. There isn't any time left. I have to go. I have to do what he says, and hope he has a sort of honour. There's nothing else I can do. One step wrong – one foot out of place – and she will be the first to die.'

'I know,' said Dominic. 'I won't leave you. Not until you give the word.'

Thirteen

Cape Comorin: Saturday Morning

Priya crouched in heavy darkness against the seaward wall of the hut, her back against the matting, the harsh coils of old fishing nets scoring her arms and shoulders. Her wrists were crossed behind her, and tethered uncomfortably tightly to a staple in one of the timbers of the wall. While her numbed fingers retained some sensitivity she could feel the grain of the wood with them, and touch the cold iron. Now that her eyes were more accustomed to the dark she could distinguish shapes and shades, the vague, formless monsters that were piles of coiled rope and cord, and stacked nets, and oars, and the heavy bamboo poles with which many of the boatmen steered their craft. But in particular nets; great coils of net, mesh within mesh. She sat upon a low mound of them, and the air she breathed was thick with the thready dust of coconut fibres, and their rank scent, and the smell of the many hauls of fish they had brought in in their time. The odour, too, of oil and joss and sweat, the irrational sweat of excitement and exultation.

She had drawn herself as far back against the wall as she could, and pulled in her feet and made herself small, to put as much distance as possible – whatever she did, it was all too little – between herself and the man. She saw him as two blurs of pallor in the darkness, one his head and one his loins. Here in the hut she could have sworn that the cotton cloths he wore were white, if she had not seen them in her own room at the hotel, and outside in the starry night, and known them for the faded peach-yellow that holy men wear. He had nothing on but those two lengths of thin cloth, and the oil with which his body was smeared. To make him hard to hold should anyone ever get to grips with him, and to enable him to withstand a long period in the water should he have to swim for it. He had his back to her now, but she knew better than to move a muscle; he could turn like a snake, and he still had the knife in his hand. He had made a horizontal slit in the matting shutter of the small window space, close to the door on the landward side, and he was watching the long expanse of the dunes through it, waiting for the light to come. Sometimes he talked to himself, low-voiced, forgetful of her. She did not exist for him except as a means to an end, she had realised that now. Sometimes he laughed, quite a sane laugh, contented, self-congratulatory, chilling her blood.

He was waiting for Purushottam. She knew that now; it was her sorrow that she had not realised it in time, and avoided the two fatal mistakes she had made. Now it was too late to redeem them; she had missed her chance.

She had started out of a dream to the awareness of someone in her room, and close to her bed, and in instant alarm for Purushottam she had opened her lips to cry out his name but never got beyond the first syllable before a hand was clamped over her mouth. That had been her first mistake, because it had told the intruder that she was indeed what he had come for, a sure and infallible bait for the man he wanted to trap. And then she had felt the cold fire of the knife against her throat, the fine prick of its tip deliberately biting under her ear, and a man's voice, muffled to a hoarse undertone, had told her to be silent or dead, as she chose. She should have taken the omen and grasped its full possibilities at once. Why had she come away with him so tamely?

But she had been half asleep and half in shock, incapable of connecting what her senses told her. A dance of fantastic details assaulted her eyes, her ears and her reason. The head that stooped over her was monstrous, swathed in saffron cotton wound twice over his face, muffling his features into a grave-mask. The hands that held the knife to her throat and covered her mouth were long and sinewy and strong. His body was naked but for the saffron loincloth, and glistened with oil. She was aware of the intent stare of his eyes through the cloth; though she could not see them, she knew that they could see well enough. The cotton was no thicker nor closer-woven than cheesecloth, it hardly hampered his vision at all, but it made him invisible.

Confused and disorientated as she was, it was no wonder that when he took away his hand, telling her flatly: 'Make one sound, and I kill you!' she lay mute and still, shrinking from the prick of the knife. No wonder that she rose from the bed at his orders, and put on her dressing-gown and sandals, and went down the iron staircase with him silently, the point of the knife pricking her onwards all the way. By then she had been aware that he was not solely dependent on the dagger. He made sure of being at the window before her, and from the place where he had propped it behind the curtain he retrieved a rifle, and slung it over his shoulder with a dexterity that told her he was well used to handling it. She had thought at first that she might be able to elude him, once in the garden, and escape in the darkness, but a rifle has a longer reach than a knife, and even in the dark, how can you be sure of evading it? And he had thought of the possibility, too, and made provision for it. She was no sooner on the ground than he had a hand twined in her hair, and dragged her back by it under the staircase, and there drew her hands behind her and knotted them fast with the girdle of her dressing-gown.

'Walk!' he ordered her, spitting the word almost soundlessly into her ear. 'Out to the road. And silently!'

And she had done it, had done everything he had ordered, his one hand always tight on the tether that bound her wrists, the other pricking her on with the ceaseless reminder of the knife. Up the undulating slope of the dunes, a moon-world in the lambent night, the smooth, dry sand sliding in and out of her sandals cool and light, like small silken hands stroking. A surrealist dream, austere and frightening. No wonder she had done everything she was told to do, and sought to keep the blade away from her throat at all costs.

But how she regretted now the slowness of her understanding! Not until they were well away from the house, from the road, from all listening ears, did she realise that she had mistaken her role and missed her once chance. She was nothing. What could this nocturnal assassin, in the saffron remnants of his old disguise as a holy man, want with her? She was accidental, simply an outsider who had blundered into a private war. Purushottam was still the quarry, must be the quarry. This man had come for Purushottam tonight. If he had taken her instead, it was because for some reason he could not reach Purushottam. She was only a second best, a second string – an alternative route to the prize.

So then, too late, she recognised her own mistakes. Her first waking thought had been for Purushottam; that must have been a gratifying confirmation of the enemy's thinking. What she should have done, as soon as the muffling hand was lifted from her mouth, was to scream and scream and arouse the entire house. She would probably have died, yes – though not certainly, since nothing was ever certain – but she could not then have been used to induce Purushottam to venture his life for hers. She should have realised when she watched the invader fold the sheet he had torn from her writing pad, and score that savage superscription across it, and laugh silently, one eye always trained upon her as she fumbled stiffly into her sandals, one hand always ready on the knife. If only she had understood in time she might even have achieved the capture and arrest of her killer, and made the future safe for others. She thought 'others', but she meant Purushottam. And who knows, the killer might not even have killed. Petrified by the first tearing scream, he might have thought of his own life first, and run with no thought but to save it. The trouble is that one never has time to consider the issues fairly until it is too late.

Now she was here, bait for a trap, and there was nothing she could do.

'He will get my message,' crooned the man, self-congratulatory and exuberant, watching the bare, motionless sea of the starlit dunes, and stroking the butt of his rifle lovingly. 'He will come! Shall I let him see you, before I fire? Shall I let him come all the way, to find you here dead before I kill him?'

Priya said nothing. She had not uttered a sound since he thrust her in here before him, stumbling among the nets. There was no point in speaking with him, none in pleading or reasoning; that she knew. Whatever eloquence she had was being expended inwardly, and directed towards whatever it was that she had made out of her odd, heretical heritage, something huge and approachable and not insensible to human outrage and anger; not necessarily just, but better, involved and indignant and compassionate, something that could be argued with, like Krishna enduring without offence the reproaches of Arjuna, and stooping to unravel for him the complexities of duty and compulsion and love.

'Listen, you,' thought Priya vehemently towards the anonymous power that hid itself from her but was patently there somewhere, too nearly palpable to be a figment of her imagination, 'I don't know what to call you, but since you must be everything in any case, what does it matter? You know all about us, all of us, I needn't tell you anything. *Don't let them win!* Not unless you're on the side of evil, and that's impossible. Don't let Purushottam come here tamely to be killed, as I've come. That's all that matters. If he survives, then *we have won*! There must be something one of us can do to unwind this wound-up machine, and break it. That's all I'm asking for. Then it wouldn't matter so much, dying ... after all, everybody has to, in the end.'

She had begun to be aware, while she closed her eyes upon this emphatic wrestling with God, that the images were forming in her mind in a kind of insistent but disciplined rhythm, as though the tabla had just struck into the improvisations of the sitar for the first time, halfway into a raga; the key moment when the first acceleration begins, and the first formal excitement. It took her some moments to track this drum-note down, even after she opened her eyes; it was soft and private, felt rather than heard, like the tabla, a vibration rather than a sound. She sensed it throbbing in her spine, gently insistent, and sprang into full consciousness with a shock of wonder and disbelief.

It really existed, and deliberately it was hardly a sound at all, only a very soft, steady, rhythmic pressure, barely even a tapping, against the matting wall at her back. Once she had grasped its source, she began to trace it to its exact location; it had reached the thick, woven wall right behind her, and just above the level of her bound hands. When first she had become aware of it, it must have been approaching, slowly and stealthily, from her right side, testing and waiting all the way for a response. Someone was outside the hut, feeling his way to where she was, demanding an answer from her, while she had been demanding an answer from whatever God was.

The mat wall pressed once, twice, against the small of her back. Painfully she hoisted her bound hands, grown prickly and numb from the tight cord, and thrust outwards with them, once, twice, three times, tapped with impotent fingers, scratched with her nails against the fibre.

Hard fingers pressed back against her fingers in recognition and reassurance. The rhythm of the tabla ceased. Whoever he was, he had found her.

'He will come,' whispered the man with the rifle, turning his featureless cotton face towards her for a moment. She saw light – already, even in this enclosed place, there was light of a kind – flow down his sinewy arms and long torso, and die into the pallor of the sadhu's cloth twisted round his loins. 'He will come, and this time he will be mine. You want to see him die, you, woman?'

Behind Priya's back, with aching, insinuating gentleness, the tip of a knife eased its way between the stitches that seamed the coconut-matting wall. She felt the steel touch her arm, sliding by above the wrist without grazing. She heard the first fibre of the first stitch part, and thought it a terrible and wonderful sound, like the trumpets outside the walls of a city under siege. Very carefully she shifted her position a little, sitting forward on the coils of net, and posing her body steadily between her captor and the knife.

They reached the loftiest rise of the dunes, and Purushottam's headlong march wavered as soon as the ridge-thatch of the distant hut broke the suave undulations of the sand like a clump of stiff grass. He turned and looked at Dominic, seemed to be searching hopelessly for something to say by way of good-bye, and then would have walked on without a word, after all, because there was nothing left to say. But Dominic laid an arresting hand on his arm.

'No, not yet. Look, it's only just after half past six. Take every moment you safely can.' Safely! How could they be sure that the word had any longer a meaning for any of them? How did they know, even, that Priya was still alive? Dead hostages are quiet hostages, make no attempts at escape, identify no suspects. But in so far as there was still any hope at all, they had to preserve it as long as they could.

'He must see me coming before the deadline,' said Purushottam, in the level, low voice that had hardly varied its tone since they had found the note. 'Before seven, not at seven.'

'He'll see you the minute you go over that crest. Forty yards. Even if you go at ten to seven, you'll be nearly half-way to him by the hour. Wait till then.'

He shook his head, but he stayed. 'Does it matter?'

'Yes, it matters. The one moment we throw away may be the one that makes the difference. At least give it a chance.'

'You expect a miracle?' said Purushottam, with the most painful of smiles. 'I've been thinking – he must have a gun, don't you think so? I think a rifle. Because he's set me up as a target he can hardly miss, even at long range. The one thing moving in all this space, and no cover anywhere. Not that I'm looking for cover. And the sea right there at his back – that's the way he means to get away.'

If he's a poor enough shot to want me at short range before he can be sure of killing me, he thought, unable to break the habit of hope, I might be able to rush him yet. He wouldn't be able to take his eye off me then to turn on Priya, and inside a hut that size a rifle will be an unwieldy weapon. If I could reach him, hit or not hit, I might at least be able to give her the chance to get away.

The sun was already well above the horizon behind them, climbing with amazing speed. The dunes put on colour, and became a rippling sea of lights and shadows.

Dominic shook the arm he held. 'Give me until ten to seven. Promise!'

'What are you going to do?' he asked it indifferently, for he knew there was nothing his friend could do to help him. They were all bound hand and foot; for at the least wrong move, Priya would pay.

'Try and work round by the shore, if I can. I give you my word I'll keep out of sight.'

'Impossible. You've seen how indented the coast is. It would take you hours.'

It was true; he was only reaching out for something he could at least seem to be doing, to avoid the one thing he could not bear, having to stand here and watch Purushottam walk out to his death without raising a hand to help him. No Sidney Cartons here, even supposing one could be that sort of hero; whoever was in that hut knew very well the appearance of the young man for whom he was waiting. Nobody else would do; and the mere sight of another person approaching would mean the end of Priya. No, there was nothing at all left for him but to watch.

'Even if you swam every bay and climbed over every headland,' Purushottam said gently, 'you couldn't possibly get near by seven o'clock. You don't know these seas. It would be suicide to try it.'

Their eyes met, and improbable as it seemed, they both smiled pallidly. 'Coming from you at this moment,' said Dominic, 'that's good.'

'If Priya dies,' said Purushottam simply, 'I don't want to survive. But I shouldn't like to have to apologise to – what was her name? Tossa? – for you. No, don't go. Stay with me.'

Dominic stayed. A quarter to seven.

'If only we'd taken her with us ...'

'No, don't! What's the use? We do the best we can.'

Twelve minutes to seven. 'I'm going now,' said Purushottam. 'Remember me to the Swami, and don't let him start saying: "If only ...", either. I've got no complaints.'

He didn't wait for any reply, and he didn't look back. He walked over the crest of the dunes, set his course towards the distant dark speck of the hut, and marched straight towards it across the empty yellow expanse of sand.

A hand came through the growing slit in the fibre wall, and fingers felt their way carefully and blindly over Priya's swollen wrists, and singled out the spot where the cords crossed. The knife followed the guiding fingers, grazed her wrist lightly, and found the cords.

How long he had been working out there she had no means of reckoning, but it felt like an age. Even the parting of a thread seemed to produce a loud, commanding sound, the knife had to work with infinite quietness and delicacy, slowly, very slowly. She knew that it was growing light, she knew the sun was up, by the shafts of brightness that entered at the rifle-slit and through the chinks of the door. The man with the gun leaned devotedly at his spyhole, the barrel of the rifle thrust out towards the dawn; and he was humming to himself sometimes, and laughing gently, sure of his triumph.

Her numbed hands lurched apart suddenly as the cords parted, and she gripped her fingers together to hold her position, afraid even of the rustle of her own clothing. Pain seeped slowly back into her wrists, a live pain; she was no longer quite so helpless. She held her place, covering her ally from sight; and with her reviving fingers she felt carefully at the slit in the matting wall behind her back. It ran upward from ground level – which was nearly at her waist, for the dune rose to the cliff's edge behind the hut – almost to the top of her head. To take it higher was more dangerous, though blessedly this was the dark side of the hut, no sun here to shine through the crack. Priya raised herself a little on the pile of coiled nets, to cover a few more inches of the wall. The gap was not yet quite long enough to allow her to slip out quietly and adroitly. The hand from outside took a moment to press her hand, warmly and quickly, before it went on with its work.

A long tremor of fulfilment and delight passed through the braced back turned towards her from the window, and a low, chuckling cry marked the moment when Purushottam came into sight. The hands that held the rifle calmed and grew still and competent upon the barrel and trigger. His whole body became a concentration of duty and efficiency. Even when he addressed her now, he could not turn away his eyes from that solitary figure to look at the bait that was bringing it into his sights. She had served her turn; she was of no importance, first or last.

'He is coming! So quickly he is coming, he is in a hurry! Now I could drop him ... no, not yet, let him come nearer ...'

It had become a race. The knife sawed away with feverish haste, ripping the slit in the matting higher. Purushottam walked rapidly, some corner of his mind still pondering the possibility – if it was a possibility – of getting just within range and then charging in like a madman, in an attempt to get to grips with his enemy. At least that would leave him no time to turn on Priya – if Priya still lived.... Fatally, he let this half-hysterical hope in speed infect his pace as he approached. He was winning his race, and to win it was to lose it. There was no time left at all. The swathed head leaned lovingly to the rifle-stock, the long, muscular hand tightened its finger on the trigger and began to squeeze, slowly, slowly....

Two more minutes, and the hands of the rescuer would have been helping Priya out silently and swiftly through the matting. But there was not even one minute left, and no means of buying one.

Dominic had stood motionless all this time where Purushottam had left him, because there was nothing else for him to do; and even to stir from the spot, unless it was to follow, which he must not do, seemed like a kind of betrayal. But tension drew him, almost against his will, up the last few yards of the slope. He raised himself just far enough to see over the plain of sand, and could not turn his eyes away. He watched the lonely figure advancing upon the distant hut, more like an attacking army than a reluctant victim, very erect, moving in an unswerving and unrelenting line – a little more, thought Dominic helplessly, and he'd be running. And already so near! He felt the hairs in his neck rising with apprehension. The shot must come any moment....

Another figure emerged suddenly from behind the hut, a diminutive, fleshless figure in yellow robes that clung to his body wetly and glistened as he moved. He walked as rapidly as Purushottam, and on a converging course. Round the corner of the hut he came, and at a distance of a few feet from the shutter he stepped deliberately into the path between the levelled rifle and its target, blotting out Purushottam from view. There was nothing in the sights of the rifle now but his bony golden body and the saffron folds of his robe.

The Swami Premanathanand, to whom violence was impossible, was fighting this last engagement in his own way and with his own unique weapon, a finite body interposed at the last moment between death and its victim.

Fourteen

Cape Comorin: Saturday Morning, Continued

For the man peering through the sights of the rifle, the world dissolved suddenly into a blur of saffron cloth only a few feet away from the barrel of the gun. The lonely, advancing figure at whose heart he had been aiming had vanished in yellow light at the very moment when his trigger finger was tightening to squeeze gently home and put an end to it. The marksman uttered a curious, wailing cry of alarm and dread, and there was one instant when everything hung in the balance, when the finger almost completed its pressure and emptied the first round into that saffron cloud. It was superstitious shock that turned his hands feeble; the barrel of the gun lurched, and was lowered. He raised his cheek from the stock, to gaze with his own eyes, instead of with the automatic eye of the gun. And the cloud that blotted out the world condensed into the apparition – for what else could it be, here where he had deliberately created an empty solitude all round him? – of an elderly, venerable, composed personage in a yellow robe and a brown woollen shawl, standing perfectly still before him, almost within touch, though he saw it only through the slit he had made for firing.

Whether this was a god, a demon or a man, he had to stare it in the face and find a way past it, and instantly, or everything was lost. It stood so still that he dreaded it might not be human, after all. What man would take his stand there and wait, saying not a word? Ah, but the interloper was looking only at a blank wall! Did he even know that there was an armed man within? He could not know. No one who knew that would dare!

The man with the rifle flung out a long left arm, and swept aside the shutter of fibre matting, gleefully expecting an ordinary man's predictable reactions of fright and retreat when suddenly confronted at short range with a loaded gun. The image remained undisturbed, serene and immovable, its mild eyes observing everything without alarm.

At the back of the hut Priya started up out of her nest of ropes and nets, stunned by the sudden burst of light from the window, and half-crazed with terror and exhaustion. Beyond her captor's shoulder she caught one glimpse of the Swami's composed, half-smiling face, but she could not believe in what she was seeing. A hand reached through the mat wall, plucking urgently and insistently at her arm.

'Come, come, please come ...!'

'Get out of my way!' screamed the swathed head in its shroud of saffron cloth, choking with rage and hatred. 'Stand out of my way, or I'll kill you!'

The Swami, so impotent, so feeble a presence, merely moved a step or two nearer to the window-opening, to ensure that whatever was behind him should remain invisible. He did not say: 'Kill me, then!', but he did not move aside. Some way behind him he heard Purushottam's wildly running feet sliding and labouring in the sand. He could not hear Dominic, though Dominic was running, too, at his fastest, and straight for this spot. The Swami folded his hands before him, just out of reach from within the window, but so near that he eclipsed the world and covered his friends from harm.

'Come, quickly, come ...' begged the voice outside the rear wall, and the timid, agitated hand tugged at Priya's wrist. She yielded to the pressure, drawn back towards the wall that gaped to let her through. And suddenly, above the Swami's golden shoulder, she saw Purushottam, running, stumbling, wild with anguish and hope; and then she could not move.

'Get out of my way!' howled the muffled head, almost inarticulate with fury. 'Now, or I will kill this girl!' He had remembered in time that he had at his disposal this more powerful persuasion, and at the recollection he swung upon her, levelling the rifle from his hip at point-blank range.

What he saw brought another thin shriek of rage out of him, for the wall at her back gaped, and a hand was holding it wide for her and urging her through the gap. He took one long, deliberate pace towards her, the rifle steadying with deadly intent on her breast. And Priya, tearing herself loose from the hand that held her for one inspired and desperate instant, scopped up in her arms the topmost coils of the pile of nets, and hurled them in his face.

She saw the closely-wound meshes open like a fantastic flower in mid-air, filling the lances of sunlight with dancing dust, and her nostrils with particles of fibre like musty pollen. Rifle and man lost their clarity of line, disintegrating into a tangled jigsaw-puzzle, as the flying lengths of net descended over both, and were carried by their weighted edges round elbows and hands, and the barrel and stock of the gun. The impact drove the man's body backwards, off-balance, and the shot went into the beaten earth at the foot of the wall, spattering Priya's feet with flecks of soil.

She turned, blindly and desperately, and clawed her way through the torn matting, the cut edges rasping her arms and her cheek. Hands reached out eagerly to help her, daylight flowed over her, clean sand filtered into her sandals. Her rescuer folded an arm protectively about her and hurried her away, across the narrow neck of land and into the first rocky defile of the path that led down into the second cove. In that maze of rocks they could hope to find safe cover even from a rifle.

The Swami stirred slowly, like a man coming out of a trance, and for once his face wore a look of immense surprise, though there was no one to witness the phenomenon. He was undoubtedly alive, and that was matter for profound surprise. He looked round, blinking at the sun. Purushottam was toiling through the last undulations of sand towards the hut, and some way behind him Dominic followed.

The Swami took the necessary three steps to the door of the hut, and pushed it open, letting in the sunlight over the heaving, trammelled form on the floor. The man had almost freed himself, slashing furiously at the folds of net with the knife he had kept in his loincloth. As the door flew open he dragged himself clear, snatched up the rifle as he rose, and charged head-down for the doorway and freedom. He had heard the pursuers drawing nearer; perhaps he thought they were more and better-armed than they were. This game, in any event, was already lost, for his hostage was gone, and if he stayed to fight he might be captured, and must be identified. He chose to run. And the Swami, to whom violence was impossible, stood courteously out of his path and gave him free passage.

It was the rifle that cheated him. A filament of the net had trapped the bolt, and as he rose and flung himself forward, grasping the stock, the net followed like a snake as far as the doorway, uncoiling until its weight became too great to be towed any further, and there ripped the rifle out of his hand. He checked for a fraction of a second, and then abandoned it and ran on, headlong for his life. He made for the nearer and smaller cove, plunged down the first steep drop into the stones of the pathway, and continued in a series of strong, passionate deer-leaps halfway down to the beach.

Not until then had he raised his head or paused even for an instant to look beyond the next step. But there he did pause, and glanced down towards the sea, and uttered a sudden enraged and desolate cry. He looked from headland to headland, but the cove was empty, sunlit and serene. He turnd wildly to look back, and Purushottam was already at the Swami's side, and Dominic not a hundred yards behind. There was no going back. He turned to the ocean again, and ran, plunged, glissaded onwards, across the yellow sand above the tide, into the fringes of the black sand now almost hidden, through the shallows that flashed at his heels as he ran, and still outwards until the surge lifted him from his feet, and he swam strongly and valiantly out to sea.

'I am afraid he was looking for his boat,' the Swami said in gentle, almost regretful explanation. 'That was where he left it, you see. We moved it in the night.'

'It is all right now, Miss Madhavan,' said an anxious, coaxing voice in Priya's ear, and the hand that held hers, and had been urging her along among the rocks, now checked her stumbling walk and quieted her into stillness. 'Quite all right now, we need not run any more. He has gone. Look, there are your friends, there on the headland. All quite safe. Everything is all right now.'

Her eyes had been open all the while, but so dazzled by daylight and blanketed by terror and tiredness that she had not truly seen even the stones among which her sandalled feet slipped and bruised themselves. Now she raised her head, and for the first time looked up, her vision and her mind clearing, into the roused, solicitous, almost unrecognisable face of Sushil Dastur.

There was no point in pursuit, no hope of overtaking him. They stood watching in helpless fascination as the swimmer sheered his way towards the headland between the coves, apparently bent on rounding it and reaching some point up-coast where he could come ashore unseen, and vanish once again into the landscape or the seascape of the south.

'He might get to one of the fishing boats,' said Dominic, looking down into the larger cove, where they lay high and dry in the sand under their thatched covers.

'He won't try,' Purushottam said, still panting from that frantic race. 'He couldn't possibly get one of those into the water alone.'

'I fear,' said the Swami apologetically, 'that he may succeed in reaching his own.' He pointed into the lee of the headland, where they could just see the high prow of a smaller boat, almost hidden under the jutting rocks where Priya stood with Sushil Dastur, and by its slight, rhythmic motion riding to anchor. 'I could not beach it alone, either, I had to leave it afloat. Though of course,' he added reasonably, 'it may not be his own, it may very well be stolen.'

'Where is he now?' The swimmer was out of sight, concealed by the rocks. When he appeared again, it was off the point, in quieter water, and well clear of the saw-edged reefs.

'He's seen the boat,' cried Purushottam. 'He's coming in for it!' He turned to run across the narrow, grassy crest of the headland, with the intention of setting off down the path and reaching the shore first, but he halted before he had gone many yards, and Dominic checked with him. 'Not a chance! He'll be there long before we shall.'

Sushil Dastur had also marked the fugitive's change of course. He looked down into the blue, bright water beneath him, and saw the long, vigorous strokes carrying the swimmer steadily nearer; he saw a long arm stretched up to get a hold on the gunwale, and a brown shoulder heaving up out of the water. He had discarded the wrapping from round his head, or the surf had taken it, and streaming black hair half-covered his face. His hands gripped strongly; he rested for a moment, and then heaved himself steadily up to climb aboard.

It was too much for Sushil Dastur. He saw the enemy

escaping, after all the evil he had done, after all they had risked in this one night to render him ineffective for ever. His sense of justice was outraged. He stooped to prise loose and hoist in his arms the largest stone he could lift, and hurled it down at the boat below. It seemed an endless while falling, before they saw it strike near the stern in a flurry of splinters and spray, causing the boat to plunge wildly and ship water; but it was a glancing blow, and the stone rebounded into the sea, though it took a length of shattered planking with it. The swimmer had clung tenaciously to his hold through the shock, and as soon as the boat righted, he hauled himself dripping over the side.

Silently they watched as he stooped to slash the riding line free, and leaned with all his weight on the heavy bamboo pole, thrusting off into deeper water. Slow though his progress upcoast might be, it would serve to get him out of sight, and ashore in some safer place, before they could do anything to prevent.

Sushil Dastur came clambering back to the headland, leading Priya with anxious solicitude. She came to Purushottam's side, and took her place there, but without a word as yet, her face drained and exhausted; and Purushottam, without a word, took her hand and held it. They watched the wake of the little boat stagger its way out to sea, and dwindle drunkenly up-coast; and already it seemed to them that it was settling a little in the water, and listing to one side like a limping man.

'I do not think,' said the Swami, between reassurance and concern, 'that he will get very far.'

The wreckage of the foundered boat did not begin to drift ashore for several days, and then most of it made its way to the Keralese beaches further to the north-west. But the boatman was brought in by the next tide, less than a mile up-coast.

The police took Dominic and Purushottam out by jeep to

identify the body. Alone upon a brilliant expanse of dark crimson and jet-black sands, like an imperial pall, stripped of his last length of saffron cloth and naked as the day he was born, lay the muscular body and once agreeable and obliging face of Romesh Iyar, the boat-boy of Thekady.

Fifteen

Cape Comorin: Saturday Evening

They sat in one of the small, seaward lounges of the hotel that evening, after Priya had slept through most of the day, after the Manis had departed, stunned and incredulous, without Sushil Dastur, and the Bessancourts, grieved but unshaken, without Romesh Iyar, and after Larry had cruised his way in a local boat fruitlessly but gallantly up the coast and down again, only to hear that everything had happened without him, and that everything was over.

The hotel was very quiet, most of its guests out on the dunes or in the village, enjoying the cool of the evening after sundown. The police had completed their notes and interrogations, and departed, taking with them Romesh Iyar's rifle, stolen during the night from the belongings of one of the room-boys on duty, but strongly suspect of being the same one originally stolen from the baggage of a well-to-do guest more than a year previously. At Malaikuppam, tomorrow, Inspector Raju would be waiting to close his file on the case. Even the sad, repulsive carcase of the krait had been removed from under the balcony. The traces were being softly sponged away out of half a dozen lives, but only to make way for something new, which in its turn had arisen out of the old.

So they sat in the hotel lounge, Priya, the Swami, Purushottam, Larry, Dominic and Sushil Dastur, and told one another whatever remained to be told.

'After I had spoken with you,' said the Swami, 'I knew that I must come. The miscalculation that sent you here was mine. There at Malaikuppam it was already clear that no one was interested in us, and even more clear that Lakshman Ray is a very honest, estimable, though perhaps rather stiff-necked young man. He will accept any challenge if he thinks a reflection has been made upon him. And indeed I did, for a while, entertain the thought that he might be the person for whom we were looking, since it had to be someone, and apparently someone closely connected with your party. Lakshman is showing a marked interest in our programme for Malaikuppam, by the way. I hope you don't mind, Purushottam, that I discussed it with him? He is an intelligent boy. I think we must see that he completes his university course, he may be very useful in the future. Now where was I? Oh, yes! I thought I should join you here at once. So I took my hired car – if you had approached from the lane instead of the garden you would have seen and recognised it – and drove down here at once. Lakshman is in charge in Malaikuppam, should there be anything needing attention. I arrived here somewhat after midnight – no, later, it must have been nearly one o'clock – parked my car, and walked a little way towards the road and the dunes, in case I might be able to find you somewhere. So it happened that I was the first person to encounter Sushil Dastur. But Sushil will tell you.'

Sushil Dastur, in some celebratory exuberance, had put on his *achkan* tonight, and sat cross-legged, Indian to the backbone, in the cushioned settee along the wall. There was a hectic flush still perceptible on his prominent cheekbones, and a spark of excitement in his dark, vulnerable, once-apprehensive eyes. Sushil Dastur had lived through a night which transformed his life, a night he would never forget.

'You see, Mr Felse, Mr Narayanan, after I left you I was so upset, so ashamed, I could not possibly go to bed and sleep. I could not think how to make things right, and I was so restless, I went out to walk a little. I was among the trees at the edge of the garden, when I saw this man going out to the road, driving Miss Madhavan before him.... It was terrible! He held her by a cord tied to her wrists, and he had a knife in his hand. You understand, I was afraid to call for help or make any sound, for fear he should kill her. So I followed them. It was the only thing I could think of to do . . .'

Sushil Dastur, who had been haunted and hounded all his life by his inadequacy and want of success in trivial things, had astonished himself, when this genuine enormity confronted him, by being moved to immense indignation instead of fear, and boldness instead of caution. He had still not recovered from the shock.

'It was the right thing,' said Purushottam warmly. He had Priya close by his side, constantly and anxiously cherished with glances and attentions. Apart from that they did not touch each other, or anticipate by a word what they both knew to be inevitable and right. There are ways of doing these things, and theirs were Indian ways.

'If I followed, I thought, at least I should know where he had hidden her, and then I could bring help. Even in the darkness I had to take great care not to be seen or heard, but I saw him take her into the hut, and then I hurried back to get help.'

'And I was the first man he met,' said the Swami, 'and he was so good as to trust me at once with this story. I urged extreme caution, for Miss Madhavan's sake, for if we had raised a general alarm she would surely have been killed. But I had hopes that otherwise this criminal's interest was not in Priya herself, but rather in her value as a lure for Purushottam, in which case she might be safe for a while, provided there was no open hue and cry. That was why we examined her room and yours, Purushottam, and found the message which was left for you. You will forgive me if I left you no further message as to what we were about, but I had hopes that perhaps you need not know until all was over, if our efforts were rewarded. We knew now how much time we had, some hours of it blessedly in darkness still, and therefore we set out at once to act by stealth, trusting to bring her back, somehow, perhaps before you ever returned to the hotel. But the note we left where it was. We had no right to take from you, in the worst event, the choice that was there offered you.'

He looked from Priya to Purushottam, and his eyes were clear and calm, Those two knew more about each other, now, than most couples know who contemplate marriage, and had more reason to be confident and glad.

'We looked in my car's tool kit for whatever might be useful. I do not know why it should include so fine a knife, but we were very glad of it. We went mainly by the shore, climbing to the edge of the dunes when we had to, swimming when we were forced to. In the end the time we had was barely enough. In the first cove there we found a boat waiting. Obviously it was there to ensure his retreat after the shooting. So I went aboard, and poled it round the headland into the other bay, while Sushil Dastur climbed up to the rear of the hut with our knife, and began tapping his way along the walls to try to find out where Priya was, and make sure that she was alive and conscious, to be able to give us what help she could. And he found her, as she has told you, and she did help us, very substantially. When I had anchored the boat in the other bay, I climbed up from there to join him, and we began to cut our way through the wall to her. Though indeed Sushil Dastur was much more expert than I, and much more silent, and he did most of the work. And the rest you know.'

Yes, the rest they knew. Only the very simple part had been left for him to do at the end, when there was no other way of delaying Purushottam's execution by the two or three minutes necessary to complete the delivery of Priya. Without a weapon – and without the slightest intention of using one even if he had had one – to step in between the hunter and the hunted. That was all. Anyone could do that.

'How strange!' said Priya wonderingly. 'At Thekady we liked him, all of us. And yet he wore such a false face. Not just the crime itself, but all that manipulation of the other boat-boy – for it must have been Romesh who not only put those Maoist papers among Ajit Ghose's possessions, but also put it into his mind that Bakhle would be a profitable client and tip him well, so that he would want to exchange duties for the day. Perhaps he even suggested it, though he got Ajit to do the asking. It was all his evidence that turned the charge against the other boy. And I think – it is a terrible thing to say about any man, but truly I believe it of him – that he designed events so that we, in his boat, should be the ones to find the bodies. Because he *wanted* to be there. Because it gave him satisfaction to have contrived everything so cleverly, and to see his plans succeed.'

'It is a seductive delight,' said the Swami, for him almost sententiously, 'to excel at anything.'

'But a poor person like Ajit Ghose – as poor as himself – how was he the enemy? And to take not only his life, but even his good name!'

'Now at least he will get that back again,' said Purushottam. 'Everyone knows now that he was quite innocent, that it was Iyar who did everything.'

Dominic looked fixedly at the Swami, but the Swami sat silent, his face composed and tranquil.

'And it seems that he himself was this sadhu we've heard so much about, and I've never seen,' said Larry. 'The one at Nagarcoil and at Thekady. In both places he claimed to have seen that sadhu himself, as soon as he was asked about him – and in the right spot, too. I suppose he threw in the sighting at Nagarcoil because he knew Priya had seen him casing the house.'

'And as it turns out,' said Dominic, 'it was only in Nagarcoil he managed to get himself taken on by the Bessancourts. He gave the impression that that had happened earlier, in Trivandrum, but actually he never was in Trivandrum, he was following us. He only happened on the Bessancourts after he'd been checking up on us at Priya's house. Being with them made it possible for him to get to close quarters with us here.'

'But I confess I have not quite understood,' said Sushil Dastur humbly, 'the significance of this pose as a sadhu. I hope I am not being obtuse,' he said sadly, with a remote echo of his old uncertainty. It was important that he should not be obtuse. Purushottam had invited him back to Malaikuppam, in the passion of his gratitude, and offered him employment there, and the fear of being inadequate is not so easy to shake off in a moment.

'I have pondered on the same matter myself,' said the Swami considerately. 'I think he was there by the lingam at Thekady by arrangement, to receive from someone – someone possibly quite unimportant, and unaware of his role – the bomb which was planted in Mr Bakhle's boat. You will remember that he was seen there for only a short time, and that everyone testified to the fact that it was most unusual for any such person to find it worthwhile patronising that spot. It would have been unwise to have the messenger come and ask for him at the lake. Yet this place was within easy reach, and simple to find. And it is not so hard to become a sadhu in two minutes. A length of cloth, a handful of dust or ash, a touch of red or yellow paint, an oily hand passed through the hair – these are all you need. Having this small equipment with him, he used it whenever he had need to be other than his apparent self. The kit costs very little, also an advantage. Holiness is not an essential – though many may indeed be holy.'

Priya put out a hand with a sudden gesture of protest and pain, and Purushottam reached out rather shyly and took it in his, flushing and burning at the touch.

'Then is that what happened to Patti? I think and think of her – and they will come, her parents, and what are we to tell them? It was Patti who gave alms to the sadhu by the lingam. Only she saw him closely, no one else looked him in the face as she did. Surely she knew, or felt she knew, that face again, even seen so differently? In the dusk there, when we found the boat – the same hour of dusk, the same light – she suspected then. And that's why she died!'

There was a moment of silence, while the Swami gazed back at her with great gentleness and profound respect.

'It was surely by reason of her recognition or non-recognition of that face that she died. For surely *he* thought that she knew him. She was a victim of forces she could not possibly understand.'

'Patti is the thing I find hardest to forgive,' said Priya.

'I, too,' said the Swami, 'hardest of all.' He cast down his eyes, regarding with calm abstraction the cupped palms of his hands. In the half-lit room, cross-legged with soles upturned in the cushions of the couch against the wall, he looked more than ever like an antique bronze. He said mysteriously, and apparently as much to himself as to them: 'The Lord said: "He who at his last hour, when he casts off the body, goes hence remembering me, goes assuredly into my being."'

Epilogue

Malaikuppam

The police came and went at Malaikuppam, took statement after statement, congratulated the household and one another, even condescended to fill in a detail or two which had emerged later, such as Romesh Iyar's mode of transport on that last chase. It seemed that a motor-cycle had been stolen, and later found abandoned at Nagarcoil, where he had rediscovered the Bessancourts through happening on their car, and had managed to get himself added to their party. And having completed all inquiries to their own satisfaction, Inspector Tilak and Inspector Raju closed the case, and departed. The terrorist was dead, the file completed, and this particular danger, at least, over for good.

The Galloways came and departed, also. During the three days that they stayed, every other person in the house walked delicately, tuned only to their needs and wishes. They were the essence of what Patti had once called suburban Cheltenham, unobtrusively well-bred, well-dressed and unadventurous. But they had also the advantages of their kind, reticence, consideration, honesty and fortitude, and the kind of durability which outlives empire. They would probably never do anything very big, very important, or very imaginative, but equally they were unlikely ever to do anything very mean, very cruel or crassly unimaginative. Their grief was contained but profound; they were not the kind to embarrass anyone with too intimate an insight into their troubles. Priya, who still had a week of leave, stayed and devoted herself to them until they left for the airport at Madurai, with Patti's ashes, en route for Bombay and home. And when they were driven away, Larry, who had also felt impelled to stay and see the affair out to its close, gazed after the departing car with a thoughtful frown, and said:

'The more I see of the New Left, the more I begin to value middle-class virtues.' To add the next moment, in case anyone had got the wrong idea: 'Virtues, I said. I know they've got their vices, too.'

He and Lakshman were the next to leave, heading westward over the Ghats to Trivandrum and up-coast to Cochin; but when their tour ended, Lakshman was to return to his college with a grant guaranteed by the Mission, and Larry, too, had asked, noncommittally enough, to be informed if ever the work of restoring the old irrigation tanks should be seriously contemplated. They would both be back; at least to visit and remember, quite probably to stay.

Then Purushottam drove Priya home to Nagarcoil, to spend her last few days of leave with her family; not to broach the idea of marriage yet – that would be a job for someone else in the first instance – but surely to keep a sharp eye open for the quality of his own welcome, in the light of all that had happened. He came back cautiously elated; very thoughtful, but with a happy, hopeful thoughtfulness that looked forward, not back. And as for Sushil Dastur, turned loose on all the papers that had been salvaged from the office, dealing with abstract things like figures, which obeyed and never nagged him, he had never been so happy in his life.

And the next day Dominic drove the Swami to Madurai in the hired car, on their way back to Madras.

The whole household waved them away from the gates. As soon as they lost sight of the wall, and were threading the dusty centre of the village, the Swami sat back with a sigh in the front passenger seat, and turned his face to the future; but not yet his thoughts, not completely, for in a few moments he said, summing up: 'Well, it is over. Not, perhaps, without loss, but I think as economically as possible.'

'Except,' said Dominic, accelerating as they drew clear of the last fringe of the village, 'that justice has not been done. And you know it.'

The Swami gazed ahead, along the reddish-yellow, rutted ribbon of road, and pondered that without haste.

'In what particular?' he asked at length.

'Granted it was Romesh Iyar who planted the bomb in Bakhle's boat at Thekady, and set up the other boat-boy to take the rap, granted it was Romesh who hunted us to the Cape when he found Purushottam and Lakshman had changed places, and did everything that was done there – planting the krait, kidnapping Priya as bait, and setting the trap to shoot Purushottam – all that, yes. But not the second bomb, the one in the office. He had nothing to do with that. He couldn't have had. He was at Tenkasi, and the police were getting regular reports from him. He was there doing casual work around the junction until he was told on Thursday evening that he could go where he liked, and needn't report any more. He was fifty miles from Malaikuppam when that bomb was planted. And you know it. And so does Inspector Raju!'

'There is this matter of the stolen motor-cycle. Fifty miles is not a great distance,' said the Swami experimentally.

'Yes, I noticed that Inspector Raju mentioned that the motor-bike was found at Nagarcoil, abandoned after Romesh hit on the idea of attaching himself to the Bessancourts. But he never said where or when it was reported missing.' Dominic smiled along his shoulder, with affection, and even a little rueful amusement. 'Oh, no, I wasn't stupid enough to ask Inspector Raju, he might not have told me this time. But I did ask Sergeant Gokhale. Everyone got the desired impression that it was stolen in Tenkasi, at some unspecified time, and that he used it to commute up here by night. But actually it vanished right here in Koilpatti during Thursday night. After the police had told Romesh he needn't report any more. After Patti's death was in the papers. He didn't leave Tenkasi until then, and he left by train. He pinched the motor-bike to get up to Malaikuppam from the station, and he kept it to follow us south when he saw us set off next morning without Lakshman – and with Purushottam.'

'The others,' said the Swami reasonably, having absorbed all this without apparent discomfiture, 'have not questioned the police conclusions.'

'The others don't happen to have that bit of information I got from Inspector Raju, as he was leaving on Thursday evening. I was asking about all the others, Romesh was only mentioned among the rest. But that's how I know he was still waiting in Tenkasi when Patti was killed in Malaikuppam.'

The Swami denied nothing of all this. He contemplated the road ahead, and looked a little tired, but not at all discomposed. 'And why have you said no word of this in front of everyone?'

'I suppose,' said Dominic gently, 'my reasons must be much the same as yours. I said justice hadn't been done – I didn't say I necessarily wanted it done.'

'And how long,' asked the Swami, after another considering silence, 'have you known?'

'Not long. Not even after we went to identify Romesh Iyar's body. I only began to understand,' he said, 'when you evaded Priya's question about how and why Patti died. It was because of her recognition *or non-recognition* of the sadhu's face, you said, that Patti died. So it was. It was because she *didn't* recognise him again in Romesh, not because she did. If she'd known him when she met him again, she might have been alive today. Not,' he added honestly, 'that it would necessarily have been much better for her.

But it was after you said that, that I began to put things together, and to remember everything that seemed insignificant at the time, and yet made absolute sense once I had the clue. Such as, for instance, that if only we'd taken the girls with us when we went to look over the estate and the old irrigation channels, again, Patti might have been alive today.'

They were out on the main road, turning left towards Koilpatti.

'As Purushottam said, at a moment when his every word merited attention,' the Swami remarked, 'we should not and must not turn to saying: "If only..." We do what we must, what seems right to us at the time, and none of us can do more.' He added with reserve, but with respect and resignation, too: 'Tell me, then, since you know so much —'

'Only because, in the first place, you told me! To see you confronted with the absolute necessity for telling a lie, and still managing not to tell one, is a revelation.'

'I see that you begin to know me too well, and to be as irreverent as a real son, my son,' lamented the Swami, with a sigh and a smile of detached affection. 'Tell me, then, if Romesh Iyar did not put the bomb in Purushottam's office – who did?'

'Patti did,' said Dominic. 'Of course!'

'Go on,' said the Swami, his face neither consenting nor denying.

'She came from England, already in rebellion against everything that represented her parents and the establishment. She came innocent, romantic, idealistic, silly if you like, a sucker for left-wing causes, and kidded into hoping to find the wonderful, easy, metaphysical way here in India. And India kicked her in the teeth, the way it does – in the belly, too, sometimes – showing her, as it shows to all silly idealists, its most deprived and venomous and ugly and venal side. She was absolutely ripe to be a fall guy. The obvious ills of India made her a sitting target for the Naxalite contacts I don't doubt she made in Calcutta – through the most vocal and articulate section of her society. It isn't any chore to sell the slogan of: "Death to the landlords!" to a girl like that, who'd never even seen anyone kick a kitten until she came here. To her violence was all abstract, until she had to see it with her own eyes, all the blood and mess that you can imagine away as long as it's still only in the mind. I don't know who got hold of her, there among the Bengali teachers and students, but someone did. And when she came on leave south, they got her to bring the two bombs from Calcutta. She had her orders about handing them over, and she knew the names of the parties for whom they were intended...'

'You are sure of that?' asked the Swami, pricking up his ears.

'Quite sure. In the boat she got the shock of her life when Romesh mentioned the name of Mahendralal Bakhle. Seeing him hadn't meant a thing to her, she hadn't known what he looked like; but she knew the name, all right. She passed it off by saying she'd read about his labour riots in the papers, but from then on she was dead quiet that day. Until then, I think, she'd sort of felt that she'd washed her hands of the first bomb, and nothing would really happen, nothing she would ever have to know about – and suddenly there was the man who was condemned to death, on the same lake with her, and she knew it was real. And again later, when we had to tell Inspector Raju where we could be contacted, and we said we were going to Purushottam Narayanan's house at Malaikuppam, she at once changed her plans and asked if she and Priya could travel with us. Oh, yes, Patti knew who the victims were. But the rest – her contact here – everything to do with the Naxalite organisation itself – no, they took good care she should know as little as possible about all that.'

'So the deliveries of those two bombs she carried, you

think, were clearly laid down for her, in such a way as to prevent her from identifying the receiver?'

'It looks that way. The first – of course you know it – was dropped into the sadhu's begging bowl by the lingam shrine, along with her few *naye paise*...'

'Yes... the face only she saw, and by twilight, behind its ash and paint, and failed to know again in Romesh Iyar.'

'And the second, I think, was to have been delivered in exactly the same way to the sadhu at Tenkasi Junction, when she and Priya de-trained there for Kuttalam. Why else should he set off for there the next day, and wait there three days? He thought she knew him, and had understood everything – or perhaps he merely thought that she would obey instructions, and use no initiative herself. Let's say, at least, that it never entered his head that she would accept the set-up at its face value, and believe absolutely that Ajit Ghose was her contact, and that he'd sacrificed his own life to fulfil his mission.'

'And therefore,' said the Swami sadly, 'that she was now orphaned – bereft of her partner, and challenged to be as selfless and as ruthless as he. That she was on her own – with a bomb, and a known victim.'

'When we found that boat it hit her like a thunderbolt,' said Dominic, sweating as he remembered the leaking hull swaying sluggishly with its wash of water and blood among the tall reeds. 'She'd never seen violence before – damn it, I don't suppose she'd ever seen death before. You contemplate it with heroic calm, yes – as long as it stays a thousand miles away from you. When you see it, smell it, touch it, that's another matter. Priya has never thought of violent injury but with compassion and the urge to jump right in and help. She's never willed it, and it doesn't frighten her. Patti *had* willed it, and then she saw it, and it was sickening. She collapsed, she was out of the reckoning all that night. And in the morning, Priya said, she was very calm, and talked of having to see Inspector Raju. Priya thought that was only because she hadn't been fit the night before, and felt a statement would be required from her. I think it was more. I think she had slept on it, then, and made up her mind to confess, and hand over the second bomb. Not because of Bakhle, so much as because she thought that her heroes, the activists, the Naxalites, had turned out to be nothing but callous murderers, to whom an innocent, incidental boat-boy was of no account, and could be wiped out like swatting a fly. In a country, my God, where the Jains won't even risk *inhaling* a fly! And she was right then. But afterwards, when she did see Inspector Raju, it was only to have it confirmed that so far from being an innocent victim, Ajit Ghose was the assassin, and a martyr for his cause, willing to die to carry out his assignment. And it was then she changed course again. She didn't confess, she didn't hand over the second bomb. On the contrary, when she heard we were to be Purushottam's guests she hitched a ride along with us. Poor Priya was shocked. One doesn't do such things, in a land where hospitality is in any case so instant, and so lavish. But Patti had risen to the occasion then, she was exalted. Ghose was dead, no longer able to take care of his second assignment. And she was confronted with his monstrous example. She was English, insubordinate, used to being allowed initiative. Romesh Iyar, who was sure she would just go ahead as planned, made off to Tenkasi to wait for her, never doubting she would come. Patti, believing she was left to hold up the world alone, and delivered from the ghastly thought that her heroes wrote off the humble as expendable – no, more than that, convinced that they regarded *themselves* as expendable – came with us to Malaikuppam dedicated to killing Purushottam.'

'You are very sure,' said the Swami, with sincere sorrow.

'Very sure. Aren't you? Who else was ever alone in Purushottam's office that day? She asked to use his typewriter to catch up with her letters, and she was in there, I suppose, an hour and a half before Priya and I went to see how she was getting on, and bring her back to the house. I don't know what she did with the bomb – taped it underneath the desk, maybe – I expect the police know. Anyhow, she left it there, set for somewhere around half past seven. You remember, we were to leave about seven, and the lawyer was to come at eight. She didn't want to kill the lawyer, she knew nothing about him. She knew nothing about Purushottam, either – I blame all of us for that, but as you say, "If only..." has no meaning. We'd talked so much in front of her about farming on a big scale, and the uselessness of a small-holding economy here – but never, until the morning we were to leave, did we mention the word co-operative in her hearing, or let her into the secret that Purushottam was not setting out to enrich himself but to give away everything he had. Without realising it, we must have confirmed her ten times over in thinking she had the right to dispatch him out of the world. But in the morning, just when we were ready to set out – I remember almost every word now – we were talking as if she wasn't there, about the welfare of the villages, about how he was aiming at transforming the district and financing the change himself... If we'd said it openly earlier – but how can you use it as a reproach against anyone that he doesn't talk a lot about his own good deeds? No, there was nothing we could have done.

'But Patti was standing there close beside us, and she heard, then, and understood. It hit her like lightning-stroke. She suddenly started rummaging in her bag, and then gasped out something about having left her diary in the office, and having to fetch it. There wasn't any diary, she wasn't the diary type, but how did we know? We barely knew her at all, even Priya. And she ran to undo what she'd done, to save Purushottam, who wasn't what she'd thought he was. It was her last change of course, it would have involved confession – everything – though I don't suppose she thought of that at all. But the bomb went off early, and killed her.

'And that's all,' he said sombrely, steering the car with care through the narrow, chaotic streets of Koilpatti, and out on the northward run to Sattur and Madurai.

'It is enough,' said the Swami. 'Do you not think so? Has she not partially answered you? Do you think that justice consists in revealing everything to everyone? I think not. Why should we discomfort those two sad people by telling them that their daughter became a dedicated terrorist, willing to kill for a cause? And do you think it would redress that balance if we also told them that afterwards she proved herself, no less, a girl with the honesty and courage to turn back just as vehemently when her eyes were opened? To undo what she had done at the cost of her own life? No, I think not. They would not be at home with either aspect. Let them continue to believe in her as in an innocent victim, too bland for either role. I believe they will be happier so. And she. . . .'

'And she?' said Dominic.

'Do not despair of Patti. Do not despair for her. She accepted the evidence that refuted her. She ran without hesitation or fear to undo what she had done, as soon as she knew it to be unjustified – even by her own lights. By mine no violence is justified. Think of it! Your departure was already some minutes delayed, it was past seven o'clock, but still she ran to prevent Purushottam's death. And having detached the bomb – for I doubt if she knew how to stop the clock mechanism once it was set – what do you suppose she meant to do with it? How dispose of it?'

Dominic watched the road, and kept his hands steady and competent on the wheel. 'I had thought of that. The office was turned away from the courtyard, with its windows on the kitchen garden. It was quite big and empty out there. I doubt if she'd thought about it at all in advance, but once there, with a bomb in her hands due to go off in about twenty minutes at the outside, I suppose her instinct would be to throw it out of the window as far as she could.'

'Yes,' said the Swami, 'so one supposes. And have you forgotten what you told me? There were three of the household children playing there in the kitchen garden. There were things Patti could not do, and that was one of them. She could not throw out the bomb where the innocents might be harmed, no, not for her own life. And then she did not know what to do. I think she was still holding it in her hands when it blew up and killed her.'

More Compelling Fiction from Headline Review

BY FIRELIGHT

A CLASSIC NOVEL FROM THE MASTER STORYTELLER

Edith Pargeter

Moving, intriguing and beautifully written, BY FIRELIGHT is a classic novel from the oeuvre of Edith Pargeter.

The untimely death of Claire Falchion's husband leaves her feeling numb, as if a phase has ended but not as if any great change has occurred. Her friend Leonora says that Claire cannot complain; she'd had everything for as long as she could expect – a career as a novelist, a husband and a child. But there is nothing within Claire except an emptiness.

She retreats to a dilapidated old schoolhouse in the tranquil village of Sunderne. But her peace is threatened by the quiet presence of her neighbour, Jonathan Kenton, with whom an acquaintance is growing, despite Claire's attempts to resist it. And the house itself seems to be unleashing strange ideas that Claire cannot explain, almost like having second sight. Even Claire's pen seems to be writing of its own accord – memories of a witch hunt in Sunderne appear on the page and the terrible scenes come alive in the countryside around her: scenes of a trial, of superstitions, of lies and pain, that end with a cruel burning.

FICTION / GENERAL 0 7472 4561 4